I0845381

Constance Santego

# Ashcroft Hollow

**Constance Santego** writes haunting tales where past lives stir, secrets linger, and love refuses to fade. Fascinated by crumbling mansions, forgotten diaries, and echoes from the beyond, she weaves gothic mysteries laced with romance and second chances.

Constance lived in an old castle tucked deep in the mist-drenched woods of British Columbia, where candlelight and creaky floorboards were a daily occurrence. When not writing, she collects antique typewriters and explores abandoned places that might still be watching.

www.constancesantego.ca

Published by
    Editor & Interior Layout: Constance Santego
    Book Layout: ©2017 BookDesignTemplates.com
    Soft Cover ISBN: 978-1-990062-87-2
    eBook ISBN: 978-1-990062-88-9

Created, published, printed and bound in the
United States of America
Maximillian Enterprises

# Also By
## Dr. Constance Santego

**NOVELS**
Illegitimate Grace

**Okanagan Trilogy:**
Beneath the Vineyards
Under the Okanagan Sun
Guardian of the Lake

**The Nine Spiritual Gifts Series:**
Journey of a Soul – (Vol 1 Michael)
Language of a Soul – (Vol 2 Gabriel)
Prophecy of a Soul – (Vol 3 Bath Kol)
Healing of a Soul – (Vol 4 Raphael)
Miracles of a Soul – (Vol 5 Hamied)
Knowledge of a Soul – (Vol 6 Raziel)
Wisdom of a Soul – (Vol 7 Uriel)
Faith of a Soul – (Vol 8 Pistis Sophia)

**NONFICTION**
The Intuitive Life, The Gift Of Prophecy, Third
Edition
Fairy Tales, Dreams And Reality… Where Are You On
Your Path? Second Edition
Your Persona… The Mask You Wear
Archangel Michael's Soul Retrieval Guide
Tesla And The Future Of Energy Medicine

Beyond Tesla: *Advancing The Science Of Energy Healing*
Tesla's Code: *Mastering Energy, Frequency, And Creative Power*
Beyond The Mind: *Harnessing The Power Of Astral Projection For Creative Awakening*
Bend, Don't Break: *Finding Your Way Back To Abundance*
Ring Therapy: *A Guide To Healing And Balance*
Ring Therapy Pocket Guide
Floraopathy™: *The Art And Science Of Vibrational Healing With Essential Oils*
Dear Older Me: *A Memoir… Of Sorts*
It's Just Like Poker: *A Spiritual Guide To Playing The Cards Life Deals You*
Signs And Meanings: *What The Feet Reveal About Health, Stress, And The Body's Story*
Dear Older Me: A Memoir…*Of Sorts*
Auricions: *Unlocking Subconscious Healing Through Quantum Medicine*
Quick Fix Acupressure Method
Type 3 Diabetes: *The Hidden Link Between Blood Sugar, Brain Health, and Healing Naturally*
Manifestation – The DREAM Method in 5 Steps

**REIKI WISDOM, SERIES:**
Angelic Lifestyle, a Vibrant Lifestyle
Angelic Lifestyle 42-Day Energy Cleanse
Reiki and the Power of The Joint Points: *Unlocking Energy Pathways for Healing* (Vol I)
*Reiki and Karmic Healing: Releasing Patterns From Past Lives* (Vol II)
Reiki and the Five Elements (Vol III)
Secrets of a Healer, Magic Of Reiki
The Reiki Master's Manual

**SECRETS OF A HEALER, SERIES:**
Magic Of Aromatherapy (Vol I)
Magic Of Reflexology (Vol II)
Magic Of The Gifts (Vol III)
Magic Of Muscle Testing (Vol IV)
Magic Of Iridology (Vol V)
Magic Of Massage (Vol VI)
Magic Of Hypnotherapy (Vol VII)
Magic Of Reiki (Vol VIII)
Magic Of Advanced Aromatherapy (Vol IX)
Magic Of Esthetics (Vol X)
The Reiki Master's Manual (Vol XI)

**ADULT COLORING JOURNALS**
SERIES-ZEN COLORING:
Quantum Energy and Mindful Living Journal (Vol 1)
Reiki Energy Journal (Vol 2)
Nine Spiritual Gifts Journal (Vol 3)
I Forgive Journal (Vol 4)

**FOR CHILDREN**
I am Big Tonight. I Don't Need the Light

**COOKBOOK**
My Favorite Recipes, with a Hint of Giggle

**BUISNESS**
How To Use Chatgpt For Authors: *From Idea To Published Book*
Scaling Beyond 6 Figures: *Strategies For Health & Wellness Professionals*
The Academypreneur's Playbook: *Turn Knowledge Into A Revenue-Generating School*

**HUMOR/GIFT BOOK**
How Do You Like Your Eggs? *Crack Into Your Personality, Yolk and All*

# *Dedicated*

To the ones who still listen
when the house creaks,
the air shifts,
and the past begins to stir.

**You know who you are.**

# Ashcroft Hollow

The past does not sleep.
It lingers beneath the floorboards,
presses through locked doors,
and breathes through the letters we were
never meant to read.
Some destinies do not begin—
they return.

—Constance Santego

# Fact:

This is a work of fiction.
But the house, the dreams, the letters that feel
too familiar,
the sense of déjà vu in places you've never
stood—
those are very real.

Though Ashcroft Hollow is imagined,
its echoes come from the places we all carry
within us:
ancestral whispers, forgotten memories,
and the question that always lingers—
**Have I been here before?**

I invite you to lose yourself in this story…
and perhaps, to remember something of your
own.

**—Constance Santego**

# Prologue

Ashcroft Hollow, 1852

They say Seraphina walked into the east wing and never came out.

Not through the front doors.

Not through the gates.

Not even in pieces.

The house was searched, of course—every room, every stairwell, every locked drawer. Her name was called until the echoes themselves grew weary, folding into the walls, whispering back long after the voices had gone silent.

Two days later, they found her diary. Not in her bedroom. Not in the study. But hidden beneath the floorboards of the ballroom—

wrapped in her wedding veil.

The final page was dated a week ahead. The last sentence was never finished.

No one speaks her name now. Not in town. Not in the family.

The ledgers are blank where she should be,
her portrait long removed from the walls.
 But the Hollow remembers.
It always remembers.
 And now—
after all these years—
it stirs.

# Chapter 1

Three weeks ago, she didn't even know she had a grandmother.

Now Vivienne Bellamy was somewhere near the northern coast of Maine, winding along Route 191 toward the fishing village of Cutler. The road had been narrowing for miles, hemmed in by spruce and fir that leaned so close they seemed to want to swallow her whole. Her GPS had gone dark nearly an hour ago, the last dot frozen somewhere outside Machias.

She hadn't seen another car since leaving the highway. The last town—if you could call it that—had been a faded cluster of buildings in Whiting: a shuttered general store with peeling white paint, a weathered lobster shack long gone to ruin, and a man sitting on the steps of an old clapboard house who watched her drive past without a word. Something in his gaze had made her grip the wheel tighter, as though he already knew where she was going and wished she wouldn't.

The air grew heavier the further she went, the forest thick with the scent of pine resin and damp earth. The coastline was somewhere beyond the trees, she knew, but she couldn't hear the ocean—only the low hum of her tires on cracked pavement. Even the birds had stopped singing.

Then, the trees broke. She crested a rise, and the land ahead seemed to drop toward the unseen sea. At the edge of the hill, nearly swallowed by tangled wild roses and salt-stained vines, stood a rusted iron gate. Its bars were twisted with age, the crest in its center dulled to a greenish blur by decades of salt air.

Vivienne's blue Honda CR-V rolled to a stop without her quite realizing it. She stared at the gate, at the shadowed gravel drive that disappeared into a stand of wind-bent spruce, and felt the odd certainty that once she passed through, something would change.

Somewhere behind the trees, far beyond the curve of the bluff, the Atlantic shifted restlessly against the rocks. The wind caught the vines on the gate, making them whisper against the rusted metal.

It almost sounded like her name.

Vivienne stared through the windshield at the wrought-iron gates, their black paint flaked like dried blood. Beyond them, the house loomed—tall, silent, and half-devoured by fog. The gravel drive was overgrown, the windows shuttered, and the air around it felt thick, like the estate had been holding its breath for decades, waiting for her to arrive. She didn't believe in ghosts. But something in her chest tightened, just the same.

"What the hell?"

Vivienne tightened her grip on the steering wheel, her knuckles whitening.

"Why didn't mom tell me about this place?"

She glanced at the passenger seat, where a large cream-colored legal envelope rested under a beam of pale light. Inside was the deed… and the key to a house she didn't know existed.

She whispered to the empty car, "She said my grandmother had died a long time ago, before I was even born. Why would she lie about that?"

Blinking away a tear, Vivienne looked at the manor again.

Ashcroft Hollow rose from the land like it had been grown rather than built—its stone walls veined with moss, its roof spiked with iron spires that reached like fingers into the mist. A cracked gargoyle crouched above the entrance, its eyes hollowed out by time. The shutters on the second floor hung crookedly, like eyelids half-closed in suspicion. Somewhere inside, something moved—or maybe it was just the wind tugging at the broken eaves.

She had seen the house in a photo, buried deep in the legal packet. But in person, it felt older, more alive. Not ruined, exactly—just… waiting.

In the rearview mirror, her own reflection stared back at her, the faint light turning her skin almost ghost-pale. Loose strands of chestnut hair clung to her cheek where the fog's damp fingers had found her. Her gray-green eyes—her mother's eyes—looked sharper than she felt, shadowed from the long drive and the years that had aged her beyond her thirty-two. The wool of her coat was worn at the collar, a favorite she couldn't bring herself to replace, and her hands, pale against the dark fabric, tightened around the steering wheel as if it were the only solid thing left.

The car's heater hummed weakly, fighting the cold that had somehow crept in with the fog. Vivienne pulled out the key from the envelope on the passenger seat. It was heavier than it looked. Ornate. Old. And slightly warm when she touched it, as if someone had just set it down.

Her fingers trembled.

She didn't believe in ghosts.

She didn't believe in haunted houses.

And yet… she wasn't sure she wanted to go inside.

# Chapter 2

Vivienne gently ran her thumb over the brass key before sliding it back into the envelope—as if putting it away might make all of this less real. The ache was deep, quiet, and sharp around the edges—like something had been carved out and never replaced—not just for the woman she never knew, but for all the truths buried with her.

She could still hear the solicitor's voice from that cold, gray office just days ago.

"They used to call it Ashcroft Hall," he had said, tapping the deed with one long finger. "But that name never stuck."

She'd asked why.

He'd only glanced toward the rain-laced window and replied,

"Because halls echo…
But hollows—they whisper."

Lost in the echo of the solicitor's words, in the grief she wasn't sure belonged to her.

BANG. BANG. BANG.

Vivienne screamed, her whole body recoiling as she slammed back into the seat. Three sharp raps against the driver's side window. Not hesitant. Not polite.

Deliberate. Violent. Close.

Her breath caught. Her fingers went numb.

For a split second, she couldn't move—couldn't even think.

Her head turned—toward the sound—her pulse roaring so loudly in her ears it nearly drowned out the fog outside.

Someone was standing right there.

Hidden by the fog.

Right outside the glass.

A man stood just inches away—his figure ghostlike in the mist. One hand rested on his hip, the other hanging loosely at his side. He didn't flinch. Didn't wave. Just stared through the glass with pale, unreadable eyes.

Vivienne's breath hitched. Her fingers scrambled for her phone, nearly knocking it off the center console. She snatched it, her thumb slipping uselessly over the screen.

The man tilted his head—calm, almost curious—and slowly motioned for her to roll down the window.

She didn't move.

Not yet.

Vivienne's fingers finally found the emergency call screen, but her eyes stayed locked on the man.

He didn't move.

Not a twitch. Not a blink.

His face, barely visible through the fog-streaked window, was all sharp angles and shadow—wet black hair clung to his forehead, and rain traced down the collar of a coat that looked a century out of place. His jaw was unshaven, his mouth unsmiling, and his eyes—those were the worst. Pale, greenish-gray, too light for comfort. Watching her like he already knew how the story ended.

He looked like someone pulled from an old photograph left too long in the attic.

Vivienne's thumb hovered over the call button.

*911. Push the button Vivienne…push the button!*

She wasn't breathing. Her lungs burned—she remembered there was no cell service as the phone slipped from her grip.

The man didn't move.

Then—slowly, like the moment itself had thickened—he lifted his hand and drew a single word on the glass with his finger.

Ashcroft.

Vivienne blinked, heart hammering, unsure if she'd really seen the word at all. The letters seemed to shimmer for half a second—and then were gone. So was he.

The space outside the window was empty. No figure. No footprints.

Only fog.

# Chapter 3

Vivienne fumbled for the phone, it had vanishing somewhere between the seat and the floor.

"No—no, no, no," she whispered, breath quickening as she patted blindly along the car mat, her fingers shaking so hard she could barely focus. Her heartbeat pounded in her throat, drowning out everything else.

She glanced back at the window.

Still empty.

No man. No word. Just fog—thick, unmoving, pressing in like walls made of smoke.

She shoved her hand farther under the seat, scraping her knuckles against the edge of something hard, cold. Her phone. She yanked it out, screen smeared, fingers slipping against the smooth glass.

Emergency call screen still open.

No cell service.

Would anyone even believe her?

He'd been standing right there.

Hadn't he?

Vivienne stared out at the space where he'd been. The fog hadn't moved. There was no sound. No footsteps. No breath but her own.

The envelope sat motionless on the passenger seat, but she could feel the key inside it—like it was watching, waiting. Like it knew something she didn't.

Her eyes drifted up the gravel drive, toward the house.

The house stood as still as before—but something had changed. The front door was open.

Just slightly. A crack.

Wide enough for her to see the blackness behind it.

Vivienne gripped the steering wheel with both hands, grounding herself. The panic hadn't left—it was coiled in her chest, tight and hot—but something else rose beside it now.

Not courage.

Not curiosity.

Recognition.

Like the house was pulling something from her.

# Chapter 4

"Vivienne, come on. This isn't you. You're not afraid of a little fog."

She gripped the steering wheel tighter, voice barely audible over the thrum of her heart. "It wasn't just the fog…"

Her gaze flicked to the window again. Still empty.

"He looked so real," she whispered. "Too real."

Silence.

Then a harder edge crept into her own voice, trying to steady the tremble.

"You're here. You have the key. What are you waiting for?"

Vivienne exhaled, jaw clenched. She reached for the envelope, retrieved the key with fingers that barely obeyed, and opened the car door.

The cold hit her instantly—wet, heavy, unnatural. It wasn't just chill. It was weight.

She walked slowly to the gate, gravel crunching beneath her boots like bones snapping in the quiet. The fog curled around her ankles and rose in slow tendrils, brushing her arms as if trying to climb.

The lock clicked open on the second try, the old metal groaning as she pushed the gate wide enough to drive through. It protested like it hadn't been moved in decades.

She slipped back into the car, shut the door fast, and gripped the wheel like it could protect her. A deep breath. A quick glance at the rearview mirror—empty.

Then she rolled forward.

The driveway narrowed, branches hanging lower now, scraping against the car like fingers trailing along the roof. Moss clung to the stone walls flanking the path, and the air grew colder the closer she got to the house.

The manor rose slowly into view again—no longer shrouded completely, but not clearer either. Its details sharpened only when she wasn't looking directly at them, like a painting you couldn't quite focus on.

The open front door was still ajar.

A light was on inside.

Faint. Flickering.

But there had been no light before, she was sure of it.

She put the car in park and sat there, unmoving.

Trying her phone again, still no service.

# Chapter 5

Vivienne stepped out of the car, the gravel crunching beneath her boots. She shut the door gently, the sound cracking through the heavy, fog-thick silence. The mist curled around her legs, denser than before—clinging, creeping, as if the air itself didn't want to let her go.

The house loomed larger at this distance—its stone facade streaked with water, moss trailing down from the corners of windows like green tears. The upper floors seemed darker than the rest, windows staring down like blind eyes. One shutter creaked softly, tapping out a rhythm she couldn't quite place.

She walked slowly, the iron key cold in her hand now, though she could've sworn it had been warm before. The envelope was tucked beneath her arm, dampening at the edges.

Her eyes stayed locked on the door. Still open, just slightly.

Ascending the stairs, she called, "Hello?" immediately regretting it. Her voice sounded thin, out of place, swallowed by the fog and stone.

No response. Not even an echo.

She stepped onto the porch—rotted boards groaning under her weight. The wood was slick, and something skittered in the far corner. A leaf, maybe. Or not.

Vivienne hesitated.

Every instinct told her to back away. That the invitation wasn't hers to accept.
But something deeper, older, whispered that it was.

She placed her hand on the doorknob, cool metal beneath trembling fingers, and pushed.

The door opened without a sound.

The moment she stepped across the threshold, something shifted. It wasn't loud or obvious—just a slight drop in pressure, like the house exhaled after holding its breath far too long.

The air inside hit her all at once—not musty or stale, like she expected from a house long abandoned. But cold. Heavy. Like something sacred had been sealed for too long and had just been disturbed.

The foyer stretched out before her—majestic, but fading. Dust coated the floor, but her first step left no footprints.

She paused, staring down.

The dust hadn't moved.

She took another step.

Still—nothing.

Vivienne's pulse thudded in her ears.

The house was waiting. But not in silence. Somewhere deep inside, behind the walls or beneath the floors, something had begun to hum.

# Chapter 6

Vivienne paused in the foyer, eyes sweeping the dim interior. The light was low, tinted gold through dust-smeared windows.

A grand staircase curved up into shadows. The chandelier above hung like a skeleton, its cobwebbed crystals dulled by time. Wallpaper peeled in long strips. She took a cautious step forward.

The hardwood floor beneath her groaned—not with age, but warning.

A whisper of movement echoed behind her. She turned.

Nothing.

Just the open door and the fog pressing against it.

She closed it, slowly, and when the latch clicked into place, the silence that followed was so complete it rang in her ears.

Vivienne took a breath, steadying herself, willing her heart to calm.

Then—
A voice. Right behind her.
"Most people knock before entering."
She gasped, spinning—and screamed.
A man stood just inside the front hall, only a few feet from where she'd been moments before. She hadn't heard a door, a step, nothing. He was just there, solid and unmoving, like he'd stepped out of the wall itself.
Dripping from the shoulders. Coat soaked. Boots caked in wet gravel.
The man from the window.
He was real.
Vivienne's breath caught in her throat.
Her body wouldn't move. Couldn't.
He didn't blink. Didn't speak again.
His eyes—those same pale, washed-out green-gray eyes—locked with hers like he was trying to find something buried inside her.
Her vision began to blur at the edges.
The key slipped from her hand and hit the floor with a dull clink.
The world tilted.
And then she was falling.
Darkness.

She woke to the scent of old books and something faintly herbal—lavender? No, something sharper, older. Like dried sage and dust.

Vivienne blinked, her vision swimming before settling on a high, coffered ceiling and a slowly turning ceiling fan. Dim light filtered in through stained glass windows that cast colored patterns across the walls. She was lying on a velvet settee, her coat still on, her boots damp.

The room was quiet. Too quiet.

She sat up too fast.

Her head throbbed.

From somewhere behind her, a low voice cut through the silence.

"You're awake."

She turned sharply toward the sound.

Callum Grey stood at the edge of the room, arms crossed, leaning casually against the dark wood frame of the doorway. His coat was gone now, revealing a worn light blue sweater and blue jeans—still damp at the hems.

He looked completely at ease, like he belonged here. Like *she* didn't.

Vivienne narrowed her eyes.

"I didn't pass out for fun," she snapped, rubbing the side of her head. "You scared the hell out of me."

Callum shrugged. "Would've scared me too if someone appeared in a house I thought was abandoned."

Vivienne froze. "Wait—who are you?"

He didn't answer.

# Chapter 7

Vivienne stood slowly, steadying herself with one hand on the arm of the couch. Her legs felt stiff, her pride worse.

Callum didn't move from the doorway. He watched her like he had all the time in the world.

"I'm going to ask this once," she said, her voice tight, "And I'd really appreciate a straight answer."

Callum raised an eyebrow.

Vivienne narrowed her eyes. "Who the hell are you, and what are you doing in my house?"

He tilted his head slightly, as if considering whether to humor her. Then he stepped into the room—slow, steady—hands tucked into the pockets of his jeans. The lamplight caught the edges of him: dark hair falling carelessly over his brow, a few days' stubble shadowing his jaw, and eyes the color of stormwater—

gray, with something deeper moving underneath. He looked to be in his mid-thirties, old enough to have lived hard years, young enough to still be dangerous. There was a rangy strength to him, the kind that didn't come from a gym but from years of work outdoors, and a stillness in the way he carried himself that made her pulse quicken for reasons she didn't care to name.

"Callum Grey."

Vivienne's eyes narrowed. "Who?"

"My grandmother lived here too," he said, glancing around the room like it held more memories than furniture.

She blinked. "Wait—you're related?"

He shook his head. "Not to you. My grandfather was your grandmother's second husband."

Vivienne crossed her arms. "Second husband?"

Callum met her gaze without flinching. "You didn't know?"

She didn't answer. The room felt colder suddenly.

He nodded toward the foyer.

"The Hollow doesn't usually let any riffraff in."

Vivienne's brow furrowed. "You talk about it like it's alive."

Callum gave a slight tilt of his head, his expression unreadable. "Some houses aren't Ashcroft Hollow."

A chill crept down her spine.

She took a slow breath, then asked, "You wrote on my car window?"

Callum didn't answer right away. He crossed the room with unhurried steps and picked up a half-burned candle from the mantle, rolling it between his fingers like he was considering how honest to be.

"Let's just say... I wanted to scare you off."

Vivienne stared at him. "You almost succeeded."

"I guess you are the reason the house creaks differently."

She gave a short, disbelieving laugh. "Are you trying to tell me the house whispered to you that I was coming?"

"Not that you were coming," Callum said with a half-smile. "But change was coming."

Vivienne's face hardened. "That's either the dumbest thing I've ever heard... or the creepiest."

Callum shrugged. "Well, you're the one who came all this way to claim a haunted house. Maybe weird runs in the family."

Vivienne stepped back like he'd slapped her. "You don't know anything about me or my family."

"More than you know," he said simply. "And the house knows even more than that."

# Chapter 8

Vivienne didn't know how to answer him. She didn't know anything about this family.

Instead, she turned on her heel and walked straight back down the hallway—past the faded portraits, the cracked sconce flickering against the paneled walls, the smell of dust and something older pressing against her skin.

She didn't run. But she didn't look back, either.

The moment the front door creaked shut behind her, she broke into a sprint across the gravel, her boots skidding as she reached the car. She yanked open the door, threw herself inside, and slammed the locks down.

Click. Click. Click.

Her breath came fast. Shaky. Her hands trembled as she reached for her phone again, the screen slick beneath her fingers. She tapped the solicitor's number.

No Service.

"No, no, no." Vivienne cursed under her breath. "This is insane. I should've stayed in Boston. I should've brought someone—anyone."

She tossed the phone onto the passenger seat and pressed her palms to her eyes.

"Okay," she muttered, trying to regulate her breathing. "Let's just think for a second. Creepy house, weird guy who shows up out of nowhere, cryptic remarks about it being alive… no phone signal. What else? Blood raining from the sky? Singing mirrors?"

A beat.

She exhaled through her nose. "Okay, Vivienne. You didn't drive all this way to hide in a car like a scared little—"

She paused, her voice softening.

"She lied to me. Mom lied to me my whole life. So what else is a lie?"

Outside, the fog pressed against the windshield like a living thing.

She sat still for a long moment, letting the silence thicken.

Then, jaw set, Vivienne unclicked the lock and opened the door.

The air outside felt colder this time. She squared her shoulders, walked slowly back toward the looming front doors, and stepped inside once more.

She scanned the dim foyer until her eyes landed on the envelope—splayed across the worn floorboards near the spot where she must have collapsed. The brass key had skittered a few inches away, catching a thin shaft of gray light filtering through the stained-glass window above the door.

It gleamed faintly. Waiting.

She stepped forward, crouched slowly, and retrieved both—the envelope creased, the key oddly warm again in her fingers.

Her grip tightened.

This time, she wouldn't tremble.

Straightening, she tucked the papers under her arm, squared her shoulders, and turned toward the shadowed hallway. She wasn't just the girl who'd fainted at the door anymore.

She was the heir.

And it was time he understood that.

She found him still standing in the library.

The scent of old paper and fireplace ash washing over her like a wave of memory she knew wasn't hers. Shelves stretched floor to ceiling, lined with leather-bound volumes that hadn't been touched in years—or touched too often. A single lamp cast a honey-gold pool of light across the worn rug, and in the middle of it stood Callum Grey, like he belonged in the house.

He didn't look at her when she re-entered.

Vivienne didn't wait to be acknowledged.

She marched forward, dropped the envelope on the low table in front of him, and crossed her arms. "Let's get something straight. The deed makes no mention of you."

Callum raised his gaze slowly, meeting hers with maddening calm. "Doesn't have to."

She narrowed her eyes. "Excuse me?"

He leaned slightly forward, "I'm not contesting ownership. The Hollow is yours. But that doesn't mean I don't belong here."

Vivienne scoffed. "On what planet do you belong in a house you weren't even mentioned in?"

"The cabin behind the orchard," he said, nodding toward the back of the house. "It was left to me. In the will. Your grandmother saw to that."

She froze. "The will? I wasn't told anything about—"

"You weren't told a lot of things."

The words hit like a slap.

Callum folded his arms across his chest. "I'm not here to take anything from you. But I'm not leaving, either. The Hollow's not just stone and ivy—it's history. And not all of it's in writing."

Vivienne clenched her jaw. "You are so arrogant."

He shrugged, eyes steady. "And you, a city slicker. You won't last a week."

Vivienne stared at him, unsettled.

"Hmm," he added, almost as an afterthought, "Not sure even a day."

Her stomach turned. "You say that like it's a threat."

"Challenge," Callum said, tilting his head.

Vivienne stared at him, fury rising—her hand tightened around the envelope again. "I don't like you."

He offered her a dry smile. "Good."

"Get out of *my* House!" she yelled.

He turned and walked out without another word, the library door groaning closed behind him.

But even with distance between them, Callum's final words lingered.

Like the whisper of something that wasn't finished speaking.

# Chapter 9

After what felt like a lifetime, Vivienne stepped back into the hallway.

The air was colder here.

She moved slowly, each step swallowed by the threadbare runner beneath her boots. The corridor stretched on before her, longer than she remembered—longer than it should've been. Shadows shifted unnaturally, curling against the wallpaper like breath held too long.

Portraits lined the walls, as before, but something was different. Their eyes.

They followed her.

It wasn't her imagination. She was sure one turned its head ever so slightly as she passed.

She picked up her pace.

Another corner. Another stretch of corridor that made no architectural sense. Where there should've been a door to the dining room, there was now only more hallway.

She stopped. "This is impossible," she whispered, voice barely audible over the creaking silence.

Had she come from the left? Or the right?

Everything looked the same. But wrong.

The lights above flickered—first one, then all. A low buzzing filled the air like a swarm of unseen insects, and for a second, she could swear the wallpaper shimmered.

Panic clawed at her throat.

"This isn't real. This house is just old. Drafty. Weird," she told herself.

She turned left.

The hallway swallowed her again, longer this time, darker. Her footsteps echoed like she was walking in a tunnel.

Then—finally—the foyer came into view, distorted through the wavy glass panels of the front doors. She almost sagged in relief.

Vivienne rushed forward and gripped the cold iron handle, yanking one of the massive doors open.

Fog.

Not just mist or morning dew—but a living, writhing wall of gray that coiled into the doorway like smoke from a dying fire.

The car was only a vague shape now, half-swallowed by the void.

Beyond that… nothing. No road. No trees. Just dense, choking fog pressing in from all sides.

She stared, heart thudding.

Something flickered deep in the gray.

A shape?

No. Just her nerves.

She checked her phone. No signal. Not even a single bar.

Even if she tried to leave, the road could spiral endlessly. She had no idea how far the next town was. And if the car broke down in this…

She let the door slam shut, the sound echoing like a gunshot through the vast house.

Her breath fogged in front of her. She could see it—inside.

The air was *that* cold now.

And yet… there was no draft.

Vivienne stood there for a long moment, her back to the door, hands still clenched at her sides.

Finally, she whispered, "Fine. One night."

The chandelier above creaked as if in answer.

She didn't look up.

With the key and deed still clutched under her arm, she turned toward the grand staircase.

It rose from the center of the house like a spine, wide and solemn. She climbed slowly, one hand trailing along the dust-coated banister.

The upper landing unfolded into another long hallway, lined with more closed doors. A draft kissed the back of her neck.

She tried the first knob. Locked.

Second.

Third.

The fourth opened with a long, reluctant creak.

Inside was a bedroom. Barely lit by the last bleed of dusk through lace-covered windows. Dust danced in the dim light. The bed was massive, old-fashioned, with carved posts and a sagging canopy.

But the sheets… were fresh. Crisp. White.

As if someone had been expecting her.

Vivienne stood in the doorway, unease trickling down her spine.

"One night," she repeated under her breath. "And in the morning, I figure out what the hell is going on."

She stepped inside and closed the door behind her with a quiet click.

The air in the room was still—too still. Heavy with the scent of lavender long faded into dust.

She reached for the light switch beside the door and flipped it once. Twice.

Nothing.

Of course.

Vivienne sighed, pulled out her phone, and flicked on the flashlight. A pale beam cut through the darkness, jittering slightly as her hand trembled. She swept it slowly across the room.

The bed dominated the space, carved dark wood rising like ribs around the mattress. The white sheets were tucked tight, the pillowcases crisp. She hadn't seen any signs of housekeeping.

So who had prepared it? Callum?

The beam drifted to the far wall—an old vanity with a cracked oval mirror. A brush still sat on its surface, its bristles tangled with strands of gray-blonde hair.

She froze.

Her light continued, revealing a tall wardrobe, its doors slightly ajar. Inside, shadows loomed—shapes of hanging clothes swaying ever so slightly, though the air was still.

Her throat tightened.

She turned back toward the bed and approached it carefully. On the nightstand, a tarnished silver frame lay facedown. She hesitated, then reached for it, flipping it over.

A photograph. Faded, black and white.

A woman stood on the front steps of the Hollow, her eyes sharp and her posture proud. Beside her stood a man—Callum. Younger, but unmistakable.

Vivienne's stomach dropped.

She wasn't sure what unsettled her more—that he was in the photo... or that he hadn't changed.

She set the frame down, a little harder than she meant to.

The flashlight dimmed suddenly—her phone battery flashing 5%. She muttered a curse and turned the beam off to save what was left.

The darkness wrapped around her instantly, thick and absolute.

With a shaky breath, she slipped out of her coat and crawled onto the bed. The mattress dipped beneath her weight with a soft sigh, like it remembered someone else.

She lay down stiffly, one hand still curled around the key beneath her pillow.

Just one night.

That's all this was.

But as she stared into the dark, she couldn't shake the feeling that the house had been waiting for her.

# Chapter 10

Morning came quietly.

No knocks. No voices. No ghostly spirals on glass.

Just a pale shaft of light slipping through the heavy curtains and warming Vivienne's face. For the first time in what felt like years, she'd slept deeply—no dreams, no tossing, no waking in the dark with a jolt of panic.

Just sleep.

She stretched slowly, wincing at the crick in her neck, and pushed herself upright. The sheets were still tucked tightly around her, undisturbed except for the shallow imprint of her body. She half-expected dust or cobwebs or some ominous sign that the Hollow had played a trick while she slept. But everything was... still.

"Not haunted," she whispered to herself, lips twitching into a skeptical smile. "No ghosts."

After splashing her face with cold water in the adjoining bathroom—where the tap groaned like it hadn't been used in years—Vivienne ran her fingers through her tangled hair and tied it into a loose knot. Her stomach growled loudly, reminding her she'd eaten nothing since the highway gas station the afternoon before.

"Coffee first. Food second. Answers third," she muttered, heading downstairs.

The kitchen was easy to find—she followed her nose to the faint, lingering scent of something old and herbal, maybe sage or thyme. But the shelves were empty, the fridge humming a low, mechanical sigh with nothing inside but a chipped glass jar of something unidentifiable. The cupboards yielded a few dusty plates, some tarnished silverware, and what might've once been tea leaves.

She opened the oven out of sheer hope. Cold. Empty.

Her stomach groaned again.

"Right. Car snacks it is."

Vivienne stepped out into the fog-bleached morning. The air was damp and cool but less heavy than the night before. As she crossed the gravel toward her car, the wind shifted— and that's when she smelled it.

Warm bread. Bacon. And... was that coffee?

She stopped in her tracks.

Her keys were already in hand, but her feet pivoted instinctively toward the scent. It wasn't coming from the main house. She turned slowly, following the warm, buttery trail past the overgrown hedges and around the crumbling remnants of a stone wall.

A narrow footpath, barely visible beneath a tangle of weeds and moss, curved away from the main drive. The scent grew stronger. Fresh. Earthy. Real.

She followed it.

After about fifty yards, the path opened to a small clearing bordered by ancient trees. At its center stood a weathered stone cottage, smoke curling lazily from the crooked chimney. Ivy crept up one side of the walls, and an old wind chime tinkled faintly near the porch—made of spoons and rusted keys.

Vivienne blinked.

The front door was ajar, and from within came the unmistakable clatter of pans and the low hum of someone whistling.

She hesitated.

Then her stomach growled again—loudly.

"Great," she muttered. "Now I'm tracking food like a cartoon bear."

She approached the door and knocked lightly on the frame. It creaked open further.

A voice from inside—familiar, casual—called out over the sound of sizzling bacon.

"You look worse in the daylight."

Callum stood barefoot in the small kitchen, sleeves rolled up, a cast iron pan in one hand and a half-cooked strip of bacon dangling from the tines of a fork.

He raised a brow. "You're still here"

Vivienne stepped inside, scowling. "So this is *your* little corner of the Hollow."

He raised a brow. "Told you I lived here."

"Yeah, I remember," she said, arms crossing. "Just didn't expect it to smell like a bakery from a fairy tale."

He nodded toward the windowsill, where a fresh loaf of bread cooled next to a chipped pot of honey. "Perk of being the groundskeeper. I feed myself."

"And insult houseguests before breakfast, apparently."

Callum smirked. "Only the fainting ones."

Vivienne opened her mouth, then thought better of it. Her stomach betrayed her again with another audible groan. She eyed the food, then him.

# Chapter 11

They ate in silence.

Not an awkward silence—just a silence that seemed to grow between them like moss. Callum didn't press her with questions. He didn't try to explain himself, or the Hollow. He simply poured coffee into mismatched mugs and passed her a plate like they'd done this a hundred times before.

Vivienne didn't know whether to be grateful or unnerved.

The bread was warm. The eggs fluffy. The bacon just shy of burnt—exactly the way she liked it.

She hated that she liked it.

When her plate was empty and her mug half full, Vivienne pushed back her chair and stood.

"Well," she said, brushing imaginary crumbs from her palms, "Thank you… for breakfast. And for not being a complete lunatic."

Callum looked up from his coffee, unbothered. "You're welcome."

She hesitated. "But I'm leaving. Today. I'll call the solicitor once I have a signal, get the paperwork started to sell the estate. Whatever this place is… it's not something I need or want."

Callum didn't move. Didn't blink. Just sipped his coffee and said, "If you say so."

Vivienne narrowed her eyes. "You're not going to say told you so?"

He finally looked at her—calm, steady, unreadable. "Doesn't matter now does it."

She hated how measured his voice was. How he didn't try to stop her or argue. As if he already knew she wouldn't make it past the night.

Vivienne muttered something under her breath and turned, letting the door slam behind her.

The fog had thinned, and patches of weak morning sun filtered through the trees. Gravel crunched under her boots as she made her way to the car. Her fingers closed around the key.

She slid into the driver's seat and exhaled sharply, as if that might clear her head. "Arrogant bastard!"

The engine didn't respond.

She tried again.

Click. Nothing.

"No. No, no, no. Don't you dare."

She turned the key again, harder this time.

Still nothing. Not even a whine.

Vivienne banged the heel of her hand against the steering wheel. "You have got to be kidding me."

Outside, the wind picked up slightly, rustling the trees. A crow cawed from somewhere deep in the woods.

She tried one more time. Dead.

Vivienne dropped her head onto the steering wheel with a groan. "Of course. Of course the car won't start. Why would it?"

The silence that followed wasn't quiet—it pulsed.

Vivienne stared out the windshield at the curling mist, her breath fogging the glass.

Somewhere across the estate, hidden behind the trees and stone paths, Callum Grey was probably finishing his coffee. Calm. Collected. Like he'd already known this was exactly how the morning would go.

And somehow… that made her even angrier.

She tried the ignition again.

Click.

Nothing.

The dash stayed black, like the car had simply given up.

Vivienne sat back, crossing her arms tightly over her chest. "Dead battery? Or sabotage?" she muttered, then immediately shook her head. "Don't be ridiculous. He wouldn't…"

But the thought trailed off before it could settle.

She popped the hood and climbed out, her boots crunching over gravel as she circled to the front of the car. Lifting the hood took effort—it groaned like it hadn't been opened in years. She squinted down at the engine, but beyond the basics, she had no idea what she was looking for.

Cables were attached. Nothing smoking. Nothing obviously disconnected.

Just… dead.

She shut the hood a little harder than necessary and looked around.

Fog still clung to the tree line. The estate felt utterly isolated—like she'd driven off the map and into some half-forgotten dream. No neighbors. No cell service. No random passersby.

No escape.

She climbed back into the car, slamming the door harder than she meant to. The silence that followed made it worse—like the Hollow itself was holding its breath, waiting for her next move.

"No phone," she muttered, gripping the steering wheel. "No food. No signal. No ride. No damn way off this property."

She thumped her head gently against the headrest, eyes closed.

"Trapped. I am literally trapped on some cursed gothic estate with a guy who talks like a riddle and smells like bacon."

"Oh, perfect. Stranded in a fog-choked horror movie. What's next, messages in blood?"

"This is how people snap. This is how they end up wandering around in nightgowns whispering to wallpaper."

She glanced at the house looming in the rearview mirror, its spires just barely visible through the morning fog. Her reflection stared back at her—disheveled hair, smudged mascara, and a look in her eyes she didn't recognize.

Not fear.

Something closer to fury.

Vivienne exhaled and climbed out of the car again, slamming the door with finality. Her boots crunched across the gravel as she headed toward the front steps—not because she had a plan, but because standing still was no longer an option.

If she was stuck here, then so be it.

# Chapter 12

The front door creaked shut behind her, muffling the wind like a sigh swallowed by stone.

Vivienne stood in the foyer for a long moment, her hand resting on the cold banister. She wasn't sure what she was looking for—or what was looking for her—but the house felt… different in the daylight. Not less eerie. Just quieter. Patient.

She exhaled and began to walk.

The halls stretched long and shadowed, even with morning light filtering through stained-glass panels in fractured rainbows. Dust motes swirled like secrets in the air. She passed doors left ajar, some sealed tight. Her boots echoed softly against hardwood, a steady rhythm of breath and thought and not knowing where she was going.

But the house knew.

As she walked by a door creaked open with a reluctant sigh, revealing a chamber lined wall to wall with mirrors. Some were covered in linen veils. Others bare—reflecting dim, warped versions of herself.

One mirror, taller than the others, framed in gilded wood and ivy carvings, caught her eye. The surface shimmered—not with her reflection, but with flickering images that weren't hers at all. A woman in mourning. Another fleeing down the stairs. A hand clutching a bloodstained letter.

Vivienne stepped back, breath caught in her throat.

At the mirror's base, nestled in dust, sat a small ornate hand mirror—its surface slightly cracked on the edge. The moment she picked it up, the glass shimmered... and then went still. Cold.

She felt something slide behind her eyes. Not a memory. A knowing.

She dropped it into her coat pocket, heart thudding, the weight of the mirror strangely heavy for something so small. When she looked up again, her own reflection blinked back—but something in her eyes seemed older. Not just tired. Inherited.

A sudden creak overhead made her flinch, but nothing followed. The house had settled—or shifted.

Vivienne's gaze swept the chamber once more. There were at least a dozen mirrors, all sizes and styles. Some Art Nouveau. Others ancient enough to have graced Versailles. Beneath one arched full-length glass, the corner of a frame peeked out from under a velvet drape. Curiosity nudged her forward. She tugged the cloth free.

A carved wooden plaque was mounted to the wall beside it. Dust clung to the engraving, but the script was still legible beneath years of neglect.

THE MIRROR ROOM
— Consecrated in 1812 —
Dedicated to Seraphina Vexley
Bearer of the Word of Knowledge
Let that which was be seen,
And that which is forgotten, remember itself.

Vivienne ran her fingers over the inscription, her skin prickling with the weight of the words. "Word of Knowledge?" she murmured aloud. It sounded like something from scripture—or a secret society.

Below the plaque, someone had etched a crude symbol into the wood. A circle divided into nine equal parts, with a different object sketched into each slice. She could make out a mirror, a lamp, a bell, and what looked like an hourglass. The rest had faded or chipped away with time.

"What is this…" Vivienne whispered.

Beneath the sigil, faint lettering—nearly worn away—read:

The Nine Sacred Objects—Each Holds a Gift.

To Know One is to Awaken the House.

To Know All is to See Beyond the Veil.

She stepped back, her breath misting slightly in the air. A chill crept down her spine, not from cold—but from realization. This was no ordinary heirloom. No antique collection.

This room had purpose.

Seraphina Vexley—whoever she had been—had dedicated this space to memory. And if the mirror was any indication, it wasn't just her own.

Vivienne turned toward the mirror again, the tall one framed in ivy. Her reflection waited patiently.

She glanced once more at the plaque, the etched circle, and the list of objects now imprinted in her mind.

Nine sacred objects.

Nine gifts.

Nine rooms?

She didn't have answers—not yet—but the question had already rooted itself deep. The ornate mirror in her pocket felt like a key. Not to unlock a door, but something deeper.

Behind her, one of the veiled mirrors shifted—its cloth falling to the ground without a sound.

Vivienne froze.

In the revealed glass, her reflection flickered… and someone else stood behind her.

Not Callum.

A woman. Pale. Dark eyes sunken with secrets. Hair twisted in an old-fashioned chignon. Lips parted, as though whispering something just out of earshot.

Vivienne spun around.

No one there.

She turned back. The mirror was empty.

Only her own wide eyes stared back now.

She backed toward the door.

The plaque's words echoed in her skull:
Let that which was be seen,
And that which is forgotten, remember itself.

Vivienne pressed her hand against her coat, feeling the cold mirror through the fabric.

Something had awakened.

And she had a feeling—it had just begun.

By late afternoon, the fog had lifted enough for Vivienne to walk the gardens.

Or what remained of them.

Overgrown hedges clawed at once-manicured paths. Rose bushes bloomed wild and tangled beneath iron archways, their petals drooping with dew. The greenhouse at the far end of the property stood in silhouette—its glass panels fogged and fractured like old memory. A marble statue of a woman missing her head leaned precariously near the edge of a reflecting pool gone stagnant.

Still, something about it all felt… honest. The decay didn't frighten her. Not like the house had. Not like Callum had.

Here, nature had been allowed to tell its truth.

By the time she returned to the house, dusk had spread like ink across the grounds. The last light glimmered through the stained-glass window above the foyer, setting the dust dancing again.

Vivienne climbed the stairs without hesitation this time. Her boots no longer faltered on the creaking steps. She made her way back to the bedroom she'd used the night before—drawn by something she couldn't name.

The door was ajar.

Inside, the bed had been remade. The thick comforter turned down, the fire in the hearth quietly smoldering.

And waiting on the small table by the window… was a tray.

Slices of crusty bread. A wedge of aged cheese. Cured meats folded into delicate shapes. A glass of chilled white wine caught the candlelight, its pale gold glinting softly.

No note. No sound from the hall.

But she knew who had left it.

Vivienne stared for a long moment, one hand on the back of the chair, the other against her chest as if to calm the unexpected ache there. She didn't know what to make of him—Callum Grey—but she wasn't ready to make him into a friend.

Not yet.

She sat.

She ate.

And when she curled beneath the covers later, stomach warm, body heavy, she expected the dreams to come. Expected ghosts, or rooms that whispered, or mirrors that showed too much.

But nothing came.

Only the sound of the fire. The weight of the blankets.

And a sleep so deep it felt like falling into the hollow itself.

# Chapter 13

A sharp, deliberate knock startled Vivienne from sleep.

She bolted upright, heart thudding. For a moment, she wasn't sure where she was. The room was still dim, the fire burned out—but the knock came again. Loud. Echoing.

Clank—clank—clank

She threw off the covers, slipped her feet into her boots, and grabbed her phone. No missed calls. No signal.

Descending the grand staircase with quick, cautious steps, she hesitated at the front door. The sharp echo of metal against metal still reverberated faintly—a sign whoever knocked had done so with purpose.

She pulled the door open.

A tall, lanky man stood just beyond the threshold. Early thirties, maybe younger, in a crisp gray overcoat two sizes too big for his narrow frame. Wire-rimmed glasses slid slightly down his nose, and he blinked as though unused to natural light.

"Miss Ashcroft?" he asked, voice clipped and proper.

"Bellamy."

"Right. I'm Edwin Withers—assistant to Mr. Alcott, the solicitor." He adjusted his glasses, then extended a long, pale hand. "Apologies for the early hour. I have an appointment in Penbury shortly, but I was instructed to deliver this to you personally. It should have arrived with the first documents. Apparently, there was… a filing oversight."

He produced a thick cream envelope, sealed with an embossed wax crest—Ashcroft Hollow faintly stamped into its face.

Vivienne took it slowly. The envelope was heavier than it looked.

"There's another key inside," Edwin added. "The estate's master key. Unlocks every door on the property. As well as… a letter."

Vivienne looked up, brows drawn. "A letter?"

"Yes. From your grandmother, Genevieve Ashcroft." He glanced at a slim watch on his wrist. "She asked it be delivered only once the heir had returned to the Hollow."

Vivienne held the envelope tighter.

"I… see," she said quietly.

"If you'll excuse me," Edwin said abruptly, already stepping backward, "I'm dreadfully late as it is."

"Wait—could you possibly give me a lift into town? I need to—"

"I'm afraid not," he said, offering a fleeting, apologetic smile as he turned. "Strict schedule today. Another appointment. I do hope you enjoy your stay, Miss Ashcroft."

"Bellamy," she corrected again.

And just like that, he was gone.

Vivienne stood at the door, envelope pressed to her chest, watching as the little black car disappeared down the long, tree-lined drive without so much as a backward glance. No goodbye. No explanation.

Just fog swallowing the road again.

She shut the door slowly, heart unsteady, and turned the envelope over in her hands. The wax seal broke with a quiet crack. Inside:

A brass skeleton key, darker than the one she'd already received—engraved faintly with the Ashcroft crest.

A folded letter, yellowed slightly with age, ink curling in elegant strokes.

And a handful of old photographs.

She carried it all into the library and sat in the same chair she'd occupied the night before.

Hands trembling, she unfolded the letter first.

*My dearest granddaughter,*
*If you are reading this, it means you have come home—and I am no longer of this world.*
*How I wish I could have met you. I prayed for that more times than I can count. But your mother... she vanished from my life long ago. I do not know what stories she told you, only that pain can twist the truth into silence.*
*Ashcroft Hollow has always chosen its heir. And though your mother turned away, the house has not forgotten. Nor have I.*
*There are truths hidden in these walls. Some beautiful, some bitter. I hope you will stay long enough to find them.*
*I left you this key so that no door may keep you out. The rest... is yours to uncover.*
*With love I could never give in person,*
*—Genevieve Ashcroft*

Vivienne read the letter twice before she even looked at the photographs.

When she did, her breath caught.

There was her mother—no older than ten—standing in front of the mirror room's stained-glass window. Another of her playing in the garden, sunlight in her dark curls. Another beside a tall, stern woman who looked hauntingly like Vivienne herself.

She touched one of the photographs with her fingertips. "Mom, you lived here," she whispered. "You knew this place.

And you never told me."

Vivienne looked up at the manor around her, the letter still open in her hand.

The silence felt heavier now.

Like the house was waiting.

# Chapter 14

Vivienne found him in the garden— kneeling beside a patch of wild rosemary, sleeves rolled up, hands already dirt-streaked despite the early hour.

"I need a favor," she called, arms crossed.

Callum looked up slowly, shielding his eyes from the rising sun. "That so?"

She ignored the jab of irritation his calm tone stirred. "I need to go into town. Groceries, coffee, someone who knows how to get the power properly connected. And maybe someone who can bring this place into the twenty-first century with an actual phone line."

He sat back on his heels, brushing off his palms. "Thought you were leaving."

"I was," she said, chin lifting. "But my car had other plans."

He smirked faintly but didn't press it. "And you're asking me to play chauffeur?"

"I don't see anyone else around," she said, biting the edge of each word. "Unless the hedges take requests."

Callum stood, slow and deliberate. "Town's thirty minutes down winding roads. No signal until about halfway. You sure you're up for that?"

"I'm wearing boots and holding a list," Vivienne said. "I'm up for anything that leads to caffeine and civilization."

He gave her a long look, unreadable. Then he nodded once.

"I'll grab my truck."

The truck was older than she expected. A battered green beast with a dented fender and the faint scent of tobacco and cedar lingering in the cab. It rumbled to life with a cough and a snort, and Callum didn't speak as he pulled away from the Hollow's gates.

Vivienne stared out the window, arms folded, eyes scanning the winding road as it curved between towering trees and thick fog that hadn't yet burned off.

They drove in silence for nearly ten minutes before her curiosity finally cracked.

"So… where exactly is town?"

"North Hollow Ridge," Callum replied, eyes on the road. "Population under eight hundred. Two diners, one grocer, and an antiques shop run by a woman who swears her cat talks to ghosts."

Vivienne raised a brow. "Sounds charming."

"It's something."

When they finally emerged from the trees, the fog thinned and gave way to a sleepy little street flanked by clapboard buildings and crooked signs. She spotted a faded post office, a gas station with a single pump, and a general store with a handwritten chalkboard promising fresh sourdough and eggs.

He parked without asking, turning off the ignition and sliding out of the truck.

Vivienne followed. "This'll do."

Inside the grocer's, she grabbed the basics—coffee, eggs, bread, butter, a few canned soups, and a box of matches just in case the power still wasn't reliable. The shopkeeper, a white-haired man named Earl with a voice like sandpaper, barely blinked at her name or the mention of Ashcroft Hollow. But his smile faltered when she mentioned hooking up a landline.

"Only two fellas around here that still do that," Earl muttered, ringing up her items. "One retired. The other… let's just say he's particular."

"Particular how?" she asked.

"He believes some places shouldn't be… connected."

Vivienne blinked. "That's helpful."

"You're better off asking Maggie at the hardware store," Earl added, handing over her change. "She's got more pull."

She returned to the truck, her arms loaded with brown paper bags.

As Callum started the engine, Vivienne said, "Does everyone here treat Ashcroft Hollow like it's cursed, or is that just small-town charm?"

Callum's expression didn't change. "They have their reasons."

She narrowed her eyes at him but said instead, "I need to go see Maggie."

Callum didn't reply at first—just kept driving, the crunch of gravel and the occasional bird call filling the space between them. He didn't even glance her way, just let the silence settle like dust.

"And after that," Vivienne added, shifting the bags in her lap, "I need to find someone to fix my truck."

"That'd be me," Callum said casually.

Vivienne blinked. "Excuse me?"

"I fix things," he said with a shrug.

"You've known since yesterday that I was planning to leave," she snapped. "You sat there, sipping your coffee, letting me panic about being stranded while you knew damn well *you* could fix it?"

He finally looked at her, calm as still water. "You didn't ask."

Vivienne let out a sharp laugh. "Unbelievable."

He pulled up outside a narrow storefront with a blue-and-white awning that read *Maggie's Hardware & Repair.*

Vivienne stormed out of the truck, slamming the door harder than necessary, muttering under her breath, "I didn't ask because I assumed the guy living in a cabin on my land would tell me if he was a damn mechanic."

Callum didn't follow. He stayed behind the wheel, drumming his fingers on the steering wheel like a man with all the time in the world.

Inside the shop, the air smelled of cedar, paint, and motor oil. Tools lined the walls like art, and a large orange cat blinked lazily from the countertop.

"Morning," came a voice from the back. A woman in her sixties with short, silver-streaked curls appeared, wiping her hands on a rag. "You must be Ashcroft's granddaughter."

Vivienne offered a half-smile. "How did you know?"

Maggie grinned. "You've got her stubborn eyes."

Vivienne let out a breath. "I need help getting Ashcroft Hollow properly connected. Power. Phone line. Internet, if that's even possible."

Maggie didn't flinch. "Possible? Sure. Easy? No. Folks've been avoiding that place for years. Ghost stories, bad luck, talk of disappearances. People spook easy out here."

Vivienne raised a brow. "You spooked?"

"Not even a little." Maggie winked. "I like a good mystery."

Vivienne smiled in spite of herself. "Then you'll love that the guy living on the estate neglected to mention he's a mechanic until just now."

Maggie snorted. "That sounds like Callum. Stubborn mule with a martyr complex."

Vivienne leaned against the counter. "You've known him long?"

"Yep and his grandfather. Knew your grandmother too. Ashcroft Hollow's got a way of tangling people together whether they want it or not."

Vivienne chewed her lip. "I just want the house to function. No flickering lights, no broken water heater, no creepy wind that sounds like whispers."

"I'll make some calls," Maggie said, scribbling something on a notepad. "But it might take a few days. Things move slow around here. Especially when the Hollow's involved."

Vivienne nodded, then looked out the window to the truck where Callum still waited, unmoving.

"I might kill him before the week's out," she muttered.

Maggie smiled. "He's a teddy bear when you get to know him."

Vivienne didn't respond to Maggie's comment. She just offered a tight-lipped smile, grabbed the old rotary phone Maggie insisted would still work with a proper landline—and turned for the door.

Outside, Callum was leaning against the truck now, arms crossed, looking like a man who had nothing to prove.

"Handled?" he asked as she approached.

"For now," she muttered, tossing the bag onto the seat and yanking the door open. "Maggie's making some calls."

Callum didn't move until she was already in the passenger seat. Then he rounded the hood and climbed behind the wheel.

They rode in silence for several miles, the tires crunching over country gravel, wind whistling faintly through the cracked window on Vivienne's side. The estate grew closer with every turn, the trees thickening, the fog returning like breath on glass.

"You could've told me," she said at last, not looking at him. "About being able to fix my car."

"I could've," Callum said, his voice calm, unreadable. "Didn't seem like you wanted anything from me."

"I didn't want to be stranded!"

"And yet," he said, one brow lifting as he glanced her way, "Here you are."

Vivienne's hands curled into fists in her lap. "You are impossible."

"Most people are."

She turned to glare at him, but he didn't look back. Just kept his eyes on the road, steering one-handed like they weren't driving straight back toward a house that creaked when no one touched it, whispered in empty halls, and served meals without a trace of a cook.

The Hollow came into view—gray, looming, eternal.

# Chapter 15

The next morning broke with a reluctant sun, casting pale light through the lace curtains of the second-floor bedroom. Vivienne rose slowly, every muscle stiff from the drafty air and the weight of the Hollow's silence.

She'd just made it downstairs—barefoot, coffee-less, grumbling—when the sharp rap of knuckles echoed against the front door.

Not the brass knocker this time.

More casual. Human.

Vivienne peeked through the leaded glass and saw a man in a tan work jacket, toolbox in hand, shifting from one foot to the other like he wasn't used to waiting long.

She cracked open the door.

"Vivienne Ashcroft?" he asked, already smiling. "Name's Theo Grey. Maggie sent me."

"Bellamy," Vivienne blinked. "Grey?"

He chuckled, stepping back so she could see the van parked on the long gravel drive. GREY ELECTRICAL—RURAL INSTALLATION scrawled across the side in blue vinyl. "I'm the guy she called about hooking up the landline. You'll have to talk to the county about internet—maybe—but I can get you a dial tone."

She hesitated, then opened the door wider. "Come in."

Theo stepped inside, eyes immediately scanning the interior like it was a museum exhibit. "Haven't been inside since I was a teenager."

Vivienne frowned. "You knew my grandmother?"

"Well enough," he said, setting his toolbox down beside the entry table. "I'm Callum's cousin. My dad and his were brothers."

"Of course you are," Vivienne muttered.

Theo didn't seem to notice the edge in her voice. "Isolde—your grandmother—she kept to herself, but she had a soft spot for us neighborhood kids. Let us rake leaves for quarters, sometimes made lemonade even in the cold months. Odd lady, but kind. Always had a story ready."

Vivienne frowned. "You mean Genevieve."

"Right, right." He scratched the back of his neck. "Sorry. My dad always mixed them up.

Isolde was Genevieve's mother, wasn't she? Names get tangled out here."

Vivienne leaned against the bannister, watching as he moved to the corner of the foyer and began inspecting the old phone line hardware near the baseboard.

"She used to tell us the house picked favorites," he added with a grin. "Said it never let the wrong person in. We thought she meant it had a lock, but—who knows? People say things when they get old."

Vivienne didn't answer.

Theo shrugged, pulling out a coil of wire. "Back then? Sure. When someone tells you a house breathes, you believe it—until you grow up and realize it's just creaky wood and bad insulation."

He worked in silence for a few minutes, efficiently tracing the old connections. Vivienne watched, arms crossed.

"So," she said eventually, "This is just a favor for Maggie?"

"I owed her a few." Theo smiled. "Plus, she thought you'd appreciate having a working phone. Said you'd been... isolated."

"That's one word for it."

He finished tightening the wall plate, gave the cord a tug, and stood. "You'll have a dial tone by the end of the day—assuming the old lines haven't corroded underground. If they have, well…" He gestured vaguely toward the woods. "Might take a little more magic."

Vivienne managed a tight smile. "Thanks."

"Don't thank me. Just don't let the Hollow eat you alive." He winked, shouldered his toolbox, and added as he opened the door, "If you need anything else, I'm in the book."

She watched him disappear down the path, boots crunching the gravel.

Once the door clicked shut, Vivienne leaned her head against it and exhaled.

Another Grey. Another story. Another thread tying her to this place whether she liked it or not.

And now—finally—a phone.

Even if she wasn't quite sure who she'd call.

Vivienne stalked through the garden paths, gravel crunching beneath her boots, a familiar fire simmering in her chest. She found Callum near the greenhouse, sleeves rolled up, working a rusted hinge back into place with a stubborn sort of grace that irritated her more than it should have.

"Callum!" she called, arms crossed tight across her chest.

He straightened slowly, brushing dust from his hands before turning to face her. "Morning."

"Your cousin was here," she said, eyes narrowing. "The one who just happened to hook up the landline like it was no big deal."

Callum raised a brow, unfazed. "Theo stopped by, did he?"

"Yes, he did. Installed the phone in less than an hour. Had a lot to say about my grandmother too. Talked like he'd known her for years."

"He did." Callum shrugged. "Everyone did. Hollow's not exactly bursting with strangers."

Vivienne took a step closer, jaw tightening. "And you didn't think to mention that you had family who could help? That someone you knew could've hooked up the damn phone days ago?"

He glanced back at the hinge, calm as ever. "You didn't ask."

"Oh, for—" She stopped herself. "You knew my truck wasn't going anywhere. You knew I was stuck. You didn't even offer. Again."

"I figured you would ask," he said with maddening ease.

Vivienne let out a short, humorless snort. "You're impossible."

He met her eyes. "And you're still here."

They stared at each other for a long beat, something unspoken passing between them—foolish, irritating, and charged.

"Oh, and by the way," he added casually, wiping his hands on a rag, "Another cousin, Liam will be by tomorrow to look at the power. He's better with the wiring than I am."

Her mouth fell open. "You already lined someone up for electricity?"

He shrugged. "Takes a day or two to find the right breaker boxes. House this old—things are wired like a drunken maze. Figured we'd save you from electrocuting yourself."

Vivienne blinked. "And you were going to tell me this when?"

"When you asked."

"You're impossible."

He offered a half-smile. "So you keep saying."

"Next time, maybe try helping instead of watching me flail." She turned to leave, biting back everything else she wanted to say, but his voice followed her—low and unreadable.

"You're not flailing, Vivienne. You're just awakening."

She didn't know how to respond to that.

# Chapter 16

The morning sun broke through a tangle of clouds, gilding Ashcroft Hollow in a soft golden light that made everything seem—if only for a moment—almost normal.

Vivienne stepped out onto the back porch, blinking against the brightness. The fog had lifted, revealing rolling green pastures and woods that stretched far beyond what she had explored. The air was crisp and fresh, scented faintly with pine, damp earth, and wildflowers.

She followed a narrow footpath that twisted past the old garden walls and down a slope dotted with moss-covered stones. The estate was sprawling in ways she hadn't fully grasped—alive in a different way beneath the daylight. Birds called in the trees, and in the distance, she heard the soft rush of a stream.

Eventually, she reached a weathered wooden gate partially open and followed it through to a wide clearing.

A stable.

The structure was solid but worn, the white paint peeling in places, ivy climbing the side. A rusted horseshoe hung above the entrance like a charm too stubborn to fall.

She stepped inside cautiously, the earthy scent of hay and leather thick in the air. A soft nicker echoed from one of the stalls, and then—

There it was.

A magnificent mustang—dappled gray with a streak of midnight down its back, mane wild and dark as smoke. Its eyes met hers with intelligent calm. Vivienne moved slowly, reaching out a tentative hand, heart unexpectedly full.

"Hey, there," she murmured. "Aren't you a surprise."

The mustang leaned forward, bumping her hand gently with its muzzle. She smiled and let her fingers trace the velvet softness of its nose.

"He's usually not that friendly."

She jumped, spinning to find Callum behind her, holding a pair of water pails in one hand and a feed bucket in the other.

"Seriously?" she snapped. "Do you practice sneaking up on people?"

He just grinned, stepping past her to hang the buckets on hooks. The horses stirred with interest.

"What is this place?" she asked, brushing straw from her sleeve. "Why didn't I see it on the map that came with the deed?"

"I wonder what else they missed," Callum laughed. "The stables have been here longer than your grandparents."

She glanced back at the mustang. "Is he yours?"

Callum paused.

"They're yours."

Vivienne blinked. "Mine?"

"Came with the estate," he said, casually dumping feed into the troughs. "Your grandmother kept a few over the years. This one—his name's Rook—was the last she bought. Stubborn thing, but loyal once he likes you."

She stared at the horse, then back at Callum. "So let me get this straight: I inherited a haunted house, an emotionally cryptic groundskeeper—slash cousin, and now a horse?"

"Three, actually," he said, pointing to the other stalls. "But yeah. That about sums it up."

She turned back to Rook, who had rested his chin lightly on the edge of the stall as if claiming her.

"You're joking," she muttered, but her voice lacked conviction.

"Nope."

She sighed, then smirked faintly. "Of course I own a damn horse. Why not?"

Vivienne gave Rook one more affectionate stroke before glancing sideways at Callum. "Do you ride?"

He didn't answer right away, busying himself with the feed. When he finally did speak, his voice was low, casual. "Been riding since before I could walk."

"Of course you have," she muttered under her breath, earning the faintest curve of a smirk from him.

She brushed a strand of hair out of her face. "Well… do you still ride?"

"From time to time," he said. "Why?"

Vivienne leaned an elbow on the stall door. "Because I think I want to."

His eyes flicked up to meet hers. "You ride?"

"Not since summer camp when I was eleven," she admitted. "But I remember the basics. I think. Why—do you only allow seasoned riders near your ghost horses?"

He chuckled under his breath and walked toward the tack room. "They're not ghost horses. But they've got spirit."

"I can handle spirit," she said quickly.

"You sure about that?" he called back.

Vivienne straightened. "Is that another challenge?"

He reappeared a moment later with a worn but well-kept saddle in one arm and a bridle in the other. "More like a warning."

She ignored the twist of nerves in her stomach and lifted her chin. "Let's ride, Callum Grey."

A flicker of something passed through his expression—surprise, maybe—but he nodded and set to work with efficient ease. "Alright then. Rook will carry you. He's strong, steady… if you don't piss him off."

Vivienne arched a brow. "Sound familiar."

He didn't answer that, but she swore she caught the hint of a grin before he turned away.

The wind rushed past her cheeks, and Vivienne threw her head back with a laugh— loud, unfiltered, the first in days. Sunlight dappled through the trees, and the golden warmth on her skin felt like some kind of baptism.

She hadn't laughed like that since—

Since before the will.

Before the house.

Before everything changed.

The trail opened into a wide meadow, and for a few stolen moments, it was just her and the horse. Her legs hugged Rook's sides as he galloped through the tall grass. Her heart was light. Her smile real.

Freedom.

That was the word.

Not just fresh air or open space. But real freedom—uncaged, unhurried.

And then it hit her like a gut punch.

Boston. Her apartment. Her job. Her unpaid bills. Her plants—were the fish even still alive?

She gasped.

This place had... taken hold of her. Not just her time or her thoughts, but something deeper. Like the Hollow had reached inside her and wound its fingers around her will, muffling the noise of everything she used to care about.

As if sensing the shift in her, Rook tensed.

"Hey—whoa," she said, trying to steady him.

Too late.

With a sudden jolt, the mustang surged forward—hooves thundering, mane whipping.

A stump appeared ahead, and Vivienne's heart leapt into her throat.

"Rook!"

The horse leapt.

She didn't.

Her grip slipped. Her balance failed.

The sky spun—

—and then black.

When she woke, everything was soft and dim. Something cold pressed gently against her forehead.

"Easy now," a voice murmured. "You're alright."

Vivienne blinked hard, her vision swimming before focusing on Callum's face. He was crouched beside her, dabbing a cloth to a cut near her hairline.

She was on the settee in the parlor, a blanket over her legs. Her head throbbed. Her mouth was dry.

"What... happened?" she croaked.

"You took a fall," Callum said, quiet. "Rook jumped. You didn't."

She winced, both from the memory and the pain. "Figures."

"You're lucky it wasn't worse," he added, examining the cut. "No fracture, just a decent knock. You were out for a bit."

Vivienne reached up to touch the bandage but stopped short, meeting his eyes instead. "You brought me here?"

"I did."

A beat passed. She swallowed.

"Thanks," she said, her voice softer than she meant.

He gave a small nod, not gloating. Just steady. Present.

Vivienne closed her eyes.

# Chapter 17

Vivienne woke with the taste of damp stone and forgotten memories in her mouth.

The room was quiet—no birdsong, no creaking beams or wind against the windows. Just stillness. Sunlight filtered through the lace curtains, casting delicate patterns across the ceiling like ghosts in mid-dance.

She blinked against the morning haze. Her forehead ached, and when she touched it, the bandage reminded her that yesterday hadn't been a dream. The ride. The fall. Callum carrying her back.

The sofa's blanket had slipped down her side. Someone—Callum, no doubt—had made sure she was warm. Her boots were by the hearth, neatly aligned.

She sat up slowly, the ache in her muscles grounding her in the present.

Yet something… pulled. A whisper in the chest. A quiet nudge behind her ribcage.

It wasn't hunger. It wasn't fear.

It was an eery calling.

She padded barefoot down the hallway, the old house still cold on her feet. As she turned the corner near the grand staircase, her eyes caught movement—a flicker of shadow or light. She paused, listening. Nothing. But then—

Click.

A door.

Just ahead, one of the rooms she had explored that first strange day caught her eye again.

The Mirror Room.

Its door stood ajar once more, the iron handle faintly glinting in the morning light. Last time, it had shown her images— memories, maybe—not her own. And the hand mirror she'd taken still sat wrapped in cloth at the bottom of her coat pocket, quiet since that day.

She hesitated at the threshold.

The room was unchanged: circular, lined with antique mirrors in ornate frames. Some cracked, others covered, a few polished to perfection. But this time, something was different. The air was colder. Still.

She stepped inside.

None of the mirrors moved. No flickering visions. No knowing. Just her own reflection staring back—warily, curiously. Whole.

Vivienne let out a breath.

"Nothing?" she whispered to the room. "Not today?"

But something in her gut said it wasn't over. The Mirror Room had more to reveal.

One mirror stood at the far end, framed in gold so worn it looked more like bone than metal.

It drew her like gravity.

She crossed the room and stood before it.

Her reflection looked back—sleepy, bruised, older somehow.

Then it shifted.

Vivienne's heart jumped.

The mirror shimmered. Her reflection dissolved—and in its place, she saw a girl. Maybe eight or nine. Dark curls, an apron smudged with flour, laughter in her eyes. She was standing right where Vivienne stood now… only the room was brighter, filled with music and chatter.

A woman's voice—faint and distant—called her name.

"Genevieve…"

Vivienne's breath hitched. Her grandmother.

She stepped closer, as if she could push herself through the glass.

But the image faded, melting back into her own reflection.

Silence.

Just her. Just now.

She stood there a long moment, her palms lightly pressed to the surface.

Then she turned and walked slowly back toward the door.

With a soft sigh, she closed her eyes.

She didn't know what was happening here, not really.

The day passed strangely.

Vivienne kept busy—cleaning a little, exploring more rooms, scribbling half-thoughts in the notebook she found tucked in an old drawer. But her mind remained in the Mirror Room, replaying the flicker of her grandmother as a girl… and that voice. That name. Genevieve.

By late afternoon, storm clouds began to gather in the west. The air felt heavy—thick with the kind of silence that came before a downpour. She stood by the tall windows in the parlor, sipping lukewarm tea, when she heard:

Knock. Knock. Knock.

Not the heavy brass door knocker. No— this was softer. More rhythmic.

She turned, heartbeat spiking.

Nothing.

Then again.

But not from the front door. It was… inside.

She followed the sound down the corridor, toward the eastern hall she hadn't explored yet.

Knock. Knock.

The hallway narrowed as Vivienne moved deeper into the east wing, her boots muffled against stone instead of wood now. The air cooled, carrying the faint, resinous scent of frankincense—dry, lingering, as though a service had ended moments ago… or a century past.

She stopped before a heavy oak door bound with black iron hinges. A small, arched window of rippled glass let in only a thread of light. She pushed the door open.

The space beyond was small, almost intimate—yet it carried a weight that pressed against her ribs. Shadows clung to the corners, but the walls themselves seemed to hum faintly, as though they were holding back whispers.

A row of narrow benches faced a modest altar carved from pale stone. On its surface sat a brass oil lamp, tarnished but unbroken. No wick. No fuel. Just an empty bowl of metal, as if waiting.

Above the altar, mounted to the wall, hung another plaque. Its script was the same elegant, flowing hand she had seen in the Mirror Room. Dust softened the edges of the letters, but she could still make them out.

THE EAST CHAPEL

— Consecrated in 1938 —

Dedicated to Lady Isolde Ashcroft

Bearer of the Gift of Faith

In Silence, Light is Given.

Let the prayer be unspoken,

And the flame shall answer.

Vivienne's gaze lingered on the word faith. It felt out of place here—not in meaning, but in weight.

She stepped closer, noticing the faint etching of the same nine-sectioned circle at the bottom of the plaque. One segment—this one unmistakably marked with the brass oil lamp—was outlined more boldly, as though someone had traced over it.

Beneath the sigil, smaller words had been chiseled into the stone:

The Nine Sacred Objects—Each Holds a Gift.

Guarded in Their Chosen Place.

Gathered Together, They Shall Open the Way.

Vivienne reached out, her fingers brushing the cool surface of the lamp. A tremor of… something… moved through her. Not heat exactly. Not light. Just the suggestion of both, like a spark waiting for permission.

She glanced toward the chapel's single stained-glass window, depicting a woman kneeling with hands clasped, her head bowed. The face was worn by time, but the poise— the devotion—reminded Vivienne of the portraits in the hall. Was that Isolde?

Her fingertips lingered on the lamp, and for the briefest heartbeat, a faint glow shimmered in its bowl—no flame, just a soft pulse of gold.

She jerked her hand back. The light vanished.

The walls seemed to sigh.

Vivienne took one step toward the door, but her eyes kept pulling back to the plaque, to that bold outline in the nine-part circle.

That was two she'd found now.

She still didn't know what the "way" was.

But the house clearly intended her to find out.

—

Later, as evening approached, she heard Callum's truck pull up.

Vivienne met him halfway down the stairs.

"You didn't mention there was a chapel in the house," she said.

He arched a brow. "Didn't think it was unlocked."

"It is now."

Callum studied her face, then looked toward the eastern wing. "Some doors open when they want to."

She crossed her arms. "That's comforting."

He half-smiled. "This place doesn't care much about comfort. But it does have purpose."

Vivienne didn't reply. Instead, she said, "By the way, your cousin did a decent job with the landline. No sparks, no electrocution."

Callum smirked. "Of course he did."

She gave him a long look. "Anything else I should expect? A cousin who installs Wi-Fi? A brother who exorcises ghosts?"

His eyes didn't flinch. "Wouldn't rule it out."

That night, the rain came down hard, drumming against the windows like a warning. Vivienne sat curled in the parlor with a blanket and a journal, the fire flickering low.

Somewhere above her, the old house breathed and shifted.

# Chapter 18

Vivienne awoke before dawn.

Not from a dream—just a sudden, inexplicable awareness. Like something had shifted. Or opened.

The house was still. Even the rain had stopped, leaving only the ticking of the grandfather clock in the hall, echoing like a heartbeat in the silence.

She pulled on her robe and slippers, grabbed the old brass main key from the nightstand, and stepped into the corridor. The air felt different. Charged. Like the space between lightning and thunder.

The eastern wing again.

The corridor curved again, as though the house had decided straight lines were overrated. Vivienne kept one hand on the wall, the plaster cold and faintly damp beneath her fingertips. Somewhere ahead, she heard a faint tick… tick…

As she passed the chapel door, she paused—expecting a hum, a glow, anything. But it remained quiet now. Peaceful.

The sound drew her like a thread. She turned another corner and found a door painted midnight blue, its surface speckled faintly with silver flecks that looked like stars in the dim light. The brass knob was cold when she grasped it, almost biting to the touch.

She pushed it open.

The room beyond was bathed in pale light that didn't seem to come from any window— just a lingering silver glow that shifted like moonlight through water. Tall shelves lined the walls, crammed with astrological charts, brittle and curling with age. Dream journals, their leather spines faded, were stacked in precarious towers on every surface.

In the center of the room stood a pedestal draped with black velvet. Upon it rested a silver hourglass locket, its glass chambers frozen—no sand moved between them. The chain coiled beside it like a serpent in waiting.

The ticking she'd heard stopped the moment she stepped inside.

On the far wall, above a cluster of stopped clocks, hung another plaque. She stepped closer, brushing dust from the engraved words.

THE MOON ROOM
— Established in 1974 —
Dedicated to Lady Genevieve Ashcroft
Bearer of the Gift of Prophecy
In the Hour Between Breaths, Dreams Cross the Veil.
Wear the glass, and another's vision shall be yours.

At the bottom, etched in the same elegant hand as the plaques in the Mirror Room and East Chapel, was the nine-sectioned circle. This segment was marked with the shape of the hourglass locket, its outline sharp and deliberate.

And beneath, the same inscription:
The Nine Sacred Objects—Each Holds a Gift.
Guarded in Their Chosen Place.
Gathered Together, They Shall Open the Way.

Vivienne reached for the locket. The moment her fingers closed around it, the air in the room shifted—cooler, heavier.

Her vision swam.

Vivienne gasped and dropped to her knees as another dream—not hers—poured through her.

A woman stood at the cliff's edge—wind in her long, dark hair, the full moon blazing behind her. Her hands clutched a folded letter. She read it once. Then again. Then crumpled it in her fist as a single tear tracked down her cheek.

Then she vanished.

Gone.

The vision ended.

Vivienne was on the floor, the hourglass locket gently ticking in her palm now.

The clocks around her… all shifted forward by one minute.

She assumed the woman was Genevieve, her grandmother.

But the grief in her chest was real. It wasn't hers. And yet… it clung to her like an inheritance.

Vivienne slid it into her pocket beside the ornate hand mirror.

Three objects now. Three rooms. Three women's names.

And the house was far from finished with her.

—

Later that morning, over coffee Callum had wordlessly brought to the main house, Vivienne said:

"Another room opened for me."

He looked up. "Which one?"

"The Moon Room."

He hesitated. "Ah. Genevieve's. Let me guess—prophecy?"

"You knew about the room?"

Callum nodded once. "*Our* grandmother saw things in dreams. Most of them came true."

Vivienne's fingers wrapped around the locket in her robe pocket. "I think I saw one of hers."

"Or one of your own," he said quietly.

She frowned. "What do you mean?"

But he only shook his head, rose from the table, and went to feed the horses.

Alone again, Vivienne returned to the Moon Room.

The clocks had stopped ticking.

Vivienne lingered outside the Moon Room for a long time before going in. The hallway was quiet, too quiet, the kind that made your thoughts sound louder than your footsteps.

Her fingers brushed the locket in her pocket—still cold, still closed. As if it had been dreaming and didn't want to be woken.

When she finally stepped inside, the air held a hush, like the room was listening.

The tall arched windows spilled silver light across the floor, though the sky outside was clouded. Dust motes swirled like constellations in the glow. The walls were lined with astrological charts, faded lunar diagrams, and maps of constellations she didn't recognize.

She drifted toward the writing desk in the corner—curved mahogany, polished in places where hands had rested too often. Dream journals were stacked in uneven piles. Many were locked shut. But one lay open.

Her eyes skimmed the page.

*February 3rd. The girl with the hollow eyes returns again. She does not knock. She does not speak. But I feel her grief like ash in my mouth.*

Vivienne's fingers twitched. She flipped the page. More entries—some legible, others frantic, scrawled sideways in margins or blacked out entirely.

*March 19th. The stars go still when he enters the room.*

*April 10th. The gate is closing. She must come soon.*

She swallowed hard and turned another page. A different hand this time. Familiar.

The ink was finer, the script more fluid— neither as aged nor as frantic as the previous entries. Whoever had written it had a steadier touch, more thoughtful. More recent?

**I saw her again. The little girl. She stands in the Moon Room like she belongs here. Like she always has.**

Vivienne's brow furrowed. The date on the page was faded, but couldn't have been from Geneive's time.

Was it… her grandmother's?

She scanned the nearby pages for a name. None. Just more entries—short, careful, almost meditative. Observations more than prophecies. Feelings woven into fragments.

She sat on the edge of the chaise beneath the window, the journal trembling in her hands. Her mind reeled. The little girl… was it her? Had someone been dreaming of her before she even arrived?

Or had someone else seen something in this house—a future unfolding?

She pulled the locket from her pocket. It clicked open, though she hadn't touched the clasp.

Inside, instead of a photograph, a tiny hourglass rotated—its grains of silver sand drifting upward, not down.

Then, stillness.

No ticking. No whispers. Just the heavy hush of a room holding its breath.

Vivienne closed the locket and slipped it around her neck.

"I'm listening," she whispered.

And for a moment, she thought she felt the room exhale.

# Chapter 19

Callum didn't say anything as he wiped his hands on a rag, then lowered the hood of her car with a soft metallic click.

"It's fixed," he said simply.

Vivienne stood a few feet away, arms crossed, her overnight bag already tossed into the backseat. The morning sun stretched long shadows across the gravel, golden and indifferent.

She stared at the car like it was the answer to her prayers.

"You're sure?" she asked, not looking at him.

He nodded once. "Won't win any races, but it'll get you where you need to go."

Where she needed to go.

Vivienne exhaled slowly, dragging her fingers through her hair. A twitch of nostalgia. But logic whispered—about overdue bills, a dwindling bank account, unanswered emails, and a life she'd left paused far too long.

"I have to," she said, mostly to herself. "I need money. Work. My apartment's probably buried in mail. And I left the fish with just a few days worth of food, but…" She winced. "God, I don't even know if it's still alive."

Callum leaned against the fence, arms folded, unreadable. "So go."

That stung more than she thought it would.

"I'm not leaving because I am scared," she snapped, then winced again. "I mean—I'm not. I just… need to get back to my life."

"No one is holding you back," he said. "But leave knowing this place won't stop being yours just because you walk away for a bit."

She blinked, thrown off by the softness in his voice.

"We'll see," she whispered.

Callum gave a small nod, then handed her something.

The key.

Not the brass one, or the one to her car. The iron one—the one her grandmother left her. The one that opened everything.

"You keep it," he said. "For now."

Vivienne took it carefully, her fingers closing around the cool weight.

She climbed into the car.

For a moment, she just sat there, staring at the house in the rearview mirror. The stained-glass window caught the light just right, casting a prism across the gravel. The wind moved through the trees like a hush.

"Ashcroft Hollow," she murmured.

Then she turned the key in the ignition. The engine rumbled to life.

As she pulled out onto the winding road, Vivienne didn't look back. But the house—*Ashcroft Hollow*—watched her go.

And deep within its walls, a door clicked softly open.

# Chapter 20

Boston smelled like damp pavement and burnt coffee.

The moment Vivienne stepped through the door of her apartment, it was like stepping into a life that no longer quite fit. The place was exactly as she left it—a half-written grocery list on the fridge, and her blue betta fish, Edgar, gliding lazily in his bowl, all was the same—except for the unwatered plant slumped in the window.

"Hey, buddy," she said, setting her bag down and crouching beside him. He was alive, thank God. But he looked unimpressed.

The fish flicked his tail and swam the other way.

She sighed.

Work was a blur the next day. Emails stacked like bricks. Her editor wanted updates. Deadlines she'd long ignored now screamed with urgency. Coworkers noticed the new gray in her eyes. The city moved at a pace she could no longer match. Horns blared. The elevator smelled like onions. Even the corner coffee shop felt too loud, too crowded, too fluorescent.

She was here… home… her home, but part of her was still there.

Ashcroft Hollow lingered behind her eyes. The way the air smelled of moss and memory. The creak of old floorboards. The whisper of wind through the chapel walls.

Callum.

Damn him.

He hadn't tried to contact her. Not that she gave him her number. Not that she would've answered if he had.

She told herself she was glad to be back.

That night, she was happy to sleep in her own bed. But the sheets felt sterile. The silence felt wrong. Even Edgar's slow swimming didn't soothe her.

And then—somewhere between dreaming and not—she was back.

Ashcroft Hollow.

Fog curled against the windows. A bell chimed once, faint and far.

She stood barefoot in the foyer, the wallpaper pulsing faintly with candlelight.

A voice whispered from the walls. Not loud. Not frightening. Just… waiting.

"Come home."

Vivienne bolted upright in bed, heart hammering, breath caught in her throat.

The room was still dark.

Boston still pressed around her.

But inside her chest?

Ashcroft Hollow called for her.

# Chapter 21

The office of Alcott & Associates smelled of lemon polish and paper too old to ever be fresh again. Vivienne sat across from the solicitor, her arms folded tight against her chest, as though bracing against the weight of what was coming.

Mr. Alcott adjusted his spectacles and opened a leather folio embossed with a crest she had nearly forgotten existed—the Ashcroft crest. Its lines were faded, but still sharp enough to make her throat tighten.

"Thank you for coming, Miss Bellamy," he began, voice clipped, formal. "There are a few remaining matters we need to discuss."

Vivienne folded her arms. "You mean besides the house that's falling apart and haunted?"

His mouth twitched in what might have been a smile, though it didn't reach his eyes. "Quite." He slid a folder toward her. "Your grandmother left you a private account.

Accessible immediately. The balance is just over seven hundred and forty thousand dollars. The Hollow itself is free of debt— taxes paid for the next five years."

Vivienne's brow furrowed. "Seven hundred and forty thousand," she repeated slowly. "That's… fine. But after everything I've seen of this house—this family—are you telling me there isn't a trust? No deeper accounts? Nothing else?"

For a heartbeat, silence stretched. Then he gave a careful nod. "There is… more."

Vivienne's arms tightened. "Start talking."

"There is an ancestral trust tied to the estate," he said slowly. "It dates back to the early 1800s—established by Genevieve's great-great…grandmother. The house, the land, and certain heirlooms are protected under this structure. You are now the named beneficiary."

"A trust," Vivienne repeated, her voice flat. "How much are we talking about?"

Alcott folded his hands. "That's… complicated. What you've already received— the liquid funds—are separate. The trust itself holds ownership of Ashcroft Hollow, the surrounding lands, and certain accounts. Some are very old. Bonds, holdings, ledgers that haven't been reviewed in decades. No one truly knows their current value."

Vivienne frowned. "Why not?"

"Because parts of it are not visible in the ordinary sense," Alcott said, his tone careful. "Your grandmother believed the land itself carried worth—something beyond currency. She insisted it not be sold, no matter the temptation."

Vivienne exhaled slowly. "So I'm tied to the Hollow whether I like it or not."

"You're not trapped," he assured her. "But you've inherited more than a house. You've inherited a legacy—and the obligations bound to it."

Her pulse quickened. "Then I want the full will. Every word. About me. About Callum Grey. And why my mother was left out."

Without hesitation, Alcott drew a second file. "Genevieve amended the trust six months before her death. You are sole heir of Ashcroft Hollow, its contents, and its fortune. Callum Grey was granted the North Cottage, where he currently resides, and a monthly stipend to maintain the grounds."

Vivienne narrowed her eyes. "Why him?"

"Because Genevieve raised him for part of his youth after Everett Grey—her second husband—passed away. Though not related by blood, she considered Callum family. He remained at the Hollow after her death to fulfill the promise he made—to protect the estate."

Vivienne's voice dropped. "And my mother?"

Alcott hesitated before speaking. "Your mother, Adele Bellamy, was written out of the will almost thirty years ago. Genevieve declared her estranged. When Adele left Ashcroft Hollow, she severed all ties. Letters unanswered, calls unreturned. Over time, Genevieve ceased trying. Legally, Adele was removed from estate matters."

Vivienne's jaw clenched. "Estranged from her, maybe. But not from me."

Alcott inclined his head. "Yes. We see that now. But from your grandmother's perspective, Adele was... gone. She spoke of her in the past tense, as though she had been lost, not living."

Vivienne's chest tightened. "She didn't even know I existed?"

Another pause. "That remains unclear. There is no mention of you in her early records. Not until only a few years ago, when she amended the trust to include your name."

A silence fell heavy between them.

Vivienne sat back slowly. "My mother's alive. She's just... traveling."

"That is what I've heard," Alcott said softly. "The last address she left was a villa in Spain. She appears to have chosen solitude. Perhaps she wished for the past to stay buried."

Vivienne stared at the polished wood of his desk. No death. No tragedy. Just distance— and silence that had curdled into something darker.

"And my father?" she asked at last.

Alcott shook his head. "There is no record. Genevieve never named him. Adele never filed anything. As far as the law is concerned, Adele raised you alone."

Vivienne rose, her voice quiet but steady. "That much I already knew."

# Chapter 22

The Spanish sun drifted through gauzy linen curtains, scattering golden dust across the tiled floor. Adele Bellamy sipped her espresso slowly, the bitterness grounding her as the sea whispered just beyond the balcony. Another slow, warm morning.

She had been painting again—just in her sketchbook, this time. Loose watercolors of cliffs and vines, washed-out figures in windblown dresses. They always looked vaguely familiar. Like someone she had once been. Or someone she left behind.

The night Genevieve died, Adele had dreamed of the Hollow for the first time in decades.

She hadn't meant to. She never let herself. But dreams didn't ask permission.

In the vision, the house loomed under a violet sky, silent and watching. Its windows glowed with a light that shouldn't have existed—golden, pulsing, alive. The orchard wind had carried whispers. Not words... memories.

Genevieve stood on the stone terrace in her black mourning dress. Unchanged. Regal. Cold.

But her eyes had softened. And she smiled—smiled—as a younger woman stepped through the door behind her.

Vivienne.

They didn't speak.

But the dream ended with Genevieve placing a hand on Vivienne's shoulder... and then walking into the fog.

Gone.

Adele had woken with her heart pounding and her cheeks wet with tears she hadn't shed in years.

That morning, she booked out of the small villa on the Spanish coast.

She didn't want to be found. But yet she also knew—Vivienne would feel it.

The shift. The pull. The opening of something buried.

And her daughter's... message. Simple. Sweet. Direct.

*How you doing? Call when you get time. Miss you mom. Lots to catch up on.*

Adele swallowed hard, thumb trembling over the screen.

She had raised her daughter to be strong enough to stand alone. But not to be left behind.

It was time to stop running from the ghosts of Hollow's past.

Maybe—just maybe—Vivienne could face them better with the whole story.

And maybe… Adele was finally ready to tell it.

She typed slowly:

*I'm okay, sweetheart. I miss you too. I'll call tomorrow when it's early enough your time. Let's catch up. Finally.*

*Love you. Always have.*

Send.

She let the phone rest in her palm, heavy as truth.

Outside, the tide pulled in.

And far across the ocean, the Hollow breathed.

# Chapter 23

Vivienne sat on the windowsill of the small apartment she'd called home for years—feet tucked under her, coffee cooling on the radiator beside her.

Morning light filtered through gauzy curtains. The city noise, once familiar and oddly comforting, now felt like static.

Her phone buzzed.

She didn't expect much—some spam, a calendar reminder, maybe a work email.

It was from her mother.

She opened the message with cautious fingers.

*I'm okay, sweetheart. I miss you too. I'll call tomorrow when it's early enough your time. Let's catch up. Finally.*

*Love you. Always have.*

Vivienne stared at the word.

Finally.

It echoed.

Rang louder than it should've.

It was just one word. But it held weight.
Years of silence.
Decades of questions.
Whole histories neither of them had dared to unpack.

She read it again.

Finally.

Not *soon*. Not *eventually*. Not *someday*.

It meant *now*.

It meant *ready*.

It meant the unspoken might finally be spoken.

Vivienne's throat tightened. A hundred responses buzzed in her chest, but she typed none of them. Instead, she placed the phone on the windowsill and let herself sit with the silence. The truth.

Everything was shifting.
The Hollow had started it.
But this—*this*—was the real beginning.

She turned toward the glass, watching the morning traffic slide past, and whispered to the wind:

"Finally."

The phone rang again—not a buzz, not a notification. A real call.

Vivienne blinked at the screen.
Mark Whitaker.
She hadn't spoken to him in weeks.

They'd shared a few late-night drinks after long shifts. A dinner here and there. Once, a stolen kiss on her fire escape that felt more like curiosity than chemistry.

Still, she answered.

"Mark," she said, trying to keep her tone light. "Hey."

"Well, well," he replied with a smirk she could practically hear. "She lives. I was starting to think you'd joined a cult or vanished into the woods."

She gave a soft laugh. "Not far off."

"I figured," he said. "I stopped by your building a few times. Fish still look alive, so someone's been feeding them. But you? Totally MIA."

"I had… family stuff," Vivienne answered vaguely. "Things I didn't see coming."

"Everything okay?"

"Yes. No. It's complicated."

It *was* complicated. In a way Mark couldn't possibly understand.

"You know, if you needed to disappear, you could've just invited me," he said, teasing.

She didn't respond right away.

Because suddenly—unexpectedly—*Callum's* face rose in her mind.

His quiet intensity. The way his sleeves were always half-rolled, like he never quite stopped working. The subtle way he listened, really listened, even when he didn't respond. The smell of bread and ash and earth that clung to his clothes.

That ridiculous way he'd just *known* she was coming.

"Vivienne?"

"Hmm?"

"You disappeared again. You okay?"

She cleared her throat. "Yeah. I'm just... not really in the city headspace right now."

There was a pause. A beat too long.

"You seeing someone out there?" Mark asked, half-joking.

"No," she said automatically.

Then:

"...I don't know."

But she did.

The image of Callum brushing a strand of hair from her forehead when she was injured came back with such force it almost made her breath catch.

How he hadn't made a move. Hadn't said a word. But *had* stayed.

Mark exhaled, sensing her drift. "Well, I won't keep you. Just wanted to make sure you were alive."

"I appreciate it," she said honestly.

"Take care of yourself, Vivienne."

"You too."

She ended the call and stared at the phone for a long moment.

Then slowly turned it face down and set it aside.

Her tea had gone cold.

Outside, a breeze stirred the curtains, carrying with it the scent of something damp and wild—like moss, and old stone, and distant rain.

Like Ashcroft Hollow.

Like *him*.

And for the first time, Vivienne wasn't sure where "home" really was anymore.

# Chapter 24

The fluorescent lights buzzed overhead, their cold glare bouncing off the sleek white desk where Vivienne sat, fingers frozen above her keyboard.

She had opened the same campaign brief five times that morning. Typed three versions of the opening line for a skincare brand's holiday email. Deleted them all.

Her inbox was a battlefield—client edits, last-minute changes, urgent "Can we hop on a call?" requests. Two meetings down, three to go. Her manager had already stopped by twice, hinting—without actually saying—that deadlines were slipping.

But her mind wasn't here.

Not in Boston.

Not in this glass-walled office where creativity was measured in click-through rates and word counts.

It was still back in Maine.

In the Hollow.

With Callum.

"Earth to Vivienne," came a voice over the cubicle wall.

Vivienne glanced up just as her best friend, Jessie Morgan, popped her head around the corner, a half-empty latte in hand and a suspiciously knowing grin on her face.

"You've been back for a week and haven't told me anything," Jessie said, sliding into the spare chair at Vivienne's desk. "I've been patient. I didn't pry. I even brought you that ridiculously overpriced almond croissant from that place you love. But it's officially time— you owe me details."

Vivienne smiled weakly. "I'm just… adjusting."

Jessie narrowed her eyes. "Adjusting? This from the woman who used to color-code her closet and carry a backup planner in case her first one got a coffee stain?"

"I don't carry two planners," Vivienne muttered.

"You did last year," Jessie said, smirking. "So. Tell me. What was it like? Creepy and cobwebby? Old money haunted? Or was there a brooding gardener with secrets and a jawline like a romance novel cover?"

Vivienne blinked. Her cheeks betrayed her with a flush.

Jessie gasped. "Oh my god. *There was.*"

"It's not like that," Vivienne said too quickly.

Jessie sat back, eyebrows raised. "Didn't say it *was*. But now I'm listening."

Vivienne hesitated. She wasn't ready to explain Callum. Or the mirrors. Or the Moon Room. Or how the wind on the cliffs whispered her name like it knew her story better than she did.

Instead, she glanced out the window—where steel buildings scraped the sky and taxis honked in protest of lunch-hour traffic—and whispered, "I miss it."

Jessie's teasing expression softened. "You miss the house?"

Vivienne nodded. "The quiet. The land. The… space to think. Something about it just—" she faltered, searching for the right words, "—got into me. Like it opened a part of me I didn't know existed."

Jessie didn't joke this time. "Maybe that's the part you're supposed to pay attention to."

Vivienne offered a half-smile, appreciating her friend's intuition. But the sound of a calendar notification broke the moment.

"Meeting in five," Vivienne muttered, closing her laptop a little too hard.

Jessie rose, but leaned in to squeeze her shoulder. "You don't have to have all the answers yet. Just don't ignore the ones that whisper instead of shout."

Vivienne watched her go. The office buzzed on. Deadlines loomed.

But her heart still stood barefoot on wild earth, somewhere between crumbling walls and untamed fields.

And that night, just as she began to wonder whether Ashcroft Hollow would haunt her dreams again…

There was a knock at her door.

Vivienne wasn't expecting company.

The evening had settled quietly around her apartment—dim city light filtered through gauzy curtains, and the muted hum of passing cars played background to her thoughts. She'd just reheated leftovers and was about to ignore them when the knock came.

Three measured raps.

Firm. Familiar.

But not impatient.

Her heart jumped.

Mark.

Of course. He probably felt their call hadn't ended cleanly. She sighed, crossing the floor with the beginnings of an apology already forming on her lips.

She pulled the door open.

And froze.

It wasn't Mark.

"Surprise," the woman said, her voice soft and trembling with emotion.

"Mom?"

Adele Bellamy stood in the hallway—sun-kissed, windswept, and utterly out of place beneath the flickering city hallway light. Her suitcase leaned beside her like it had been dropped the moment she got to the door.

Before Vivienne could speak, her mother pulled her into a tight hug.

Vivienne didn't move at first. Her brain hadn't caught up.

Then, slowly, her arms lifted to return the embrace—one that smelled of citrus shampoo and salt air, just like it always had when she was younger.

"I know," her mother whispered into her hair. "You have a lot of questions."

Vivienne pulled back slightly, blinking away tears she didn't know she'd been holding. "You're supposed to be in Spain."

"I was." Adele offered a sheepish smile. "Then I had a dream about a house I hadn't seen in decades. I woke up shaking and *booked the next flight home.* Something told me I had to be here."

Vivienne swallowed hard. "I didn't mean come home."

"I know." Her eyes softened. "But it felt like you were calling me home."

Vivienne stared at her for a long second. Not angry. Not relieved. Just overwhelmed.

"Come in," she said finally, stepping aside.

Adele wheeled her suitcase into the apartment. The door clicked shut behind them, sealing out the buzz of the world.

As her mother took in the space—half-lived-in, half-forgotten since Vivienne's return from Ashcroft Hollow—she turned back to her daughter with a kind of quiet resolve.

"I think it's time I told you everything," she said.

Vivienne nodded, her throat thick.

She didn't know whether to be afraid… or finally ready.

# Chapter 25

Vivienne poured two glasses of Chardonnay—her grandmother's favorite, though she wasn't sure how she knew that. She passed one to her mother, who accepted it with a quiet nod.

They moved to the couch. Vivienne curled her legs beneath her, glass in hand, eyes steady. Her mother sat more rigidly at the other end, hands wrapped around the stem of the wineglass like it might anchor her to the moment.

"I'm guessing your grandmother died," Adele said softly, not quite a question.

Vivienne took a slow sip before answering. "I thought she was dead *long* ago."

A pause. A flicker of something in her mother's eyes—regret, maybe. Or guilt.

"What happened?" Vivienne asked. "What could possibly have made you leave your mother and never go back? Never *tell me* she even existed?"

Adele closed her eyes briefly, as if bracing herself.

"I was twenty-three," she said finally. "Pregnant. No husband. And suffocating."

Vivienne's fingers tightened slightly on her glass.

"She loved that house," Adele continued. "But not the people in it. Not even me, after a while. Not really. She loved control. Tradition. Legacy. I didn't want to become another ghost in her gallery of expectations."

"So you ran," Vivienne said, voice cool.

"I *chose*," Adele corrected gently. "I chose you. I chose a life where I could breathe. Where I could raise you without… that house watching over us."

Vivienne's gaze narrowed. "And you didn't think I had the right to know where I came from?"

"I *wanted* to tell you." Adele looked down at her wine, her voice growing quieter. "But every time I tried, something stopped me. Guilt, maybe. Or fear that it would pull you in—pull me back."

"It *did* pull us back."

Adele met her daughter's eyes. "I know."

Another silence fell between them. But this one wasn't empty—it was full. Of years unsaid, letters unwritten, memories never shared.

"She left me everything," Vivienne said eventually. "The house. The land. Even a trust."

Adele looked genuinely surprised. "I never returned her calls after I left. I knew she'd... closed the door forever."

"She did. But she left it open for me."

Adele nodded, a little brokenly. "That sounds like her."

Vivienne looked at her mother. Really looked at her. The crow's feet, the freckles faded by sun and time. A woman who had chosen escape over inheritance. A woman who had raised her with love—but also silence.

"There's more, isn't there?" Vivienne asked quietly.

Her mother's lips parted.

"Yes," she said. "So much more."

And Vivienne knew—tonight was just the beginning.

The wineglass felt heavier in Vivienne's hand than it should've. She let the silence stretch a little longer, not to punish her mother, but to steady herself for the question that had hovered for years.

She tilted her head, voice quiet but firm. "What about my father?"

Adele's smile faltered. She looked down into her glass, swirling the pale liquid slowly, as though it might conjure a gentler version of the truth.

Vivienne waited.

"I told you we were married," Adele said softly. "That he died when you were little. That he was some great love I lost too soon."

Vivienne nodded once. "I remember. You even kept a wedding photo."

Adele winced. "Staged. I had a friend take it. Just me, in a secondhand dress. I needed the story to look real."

Vivienne's chest tightened. "So... there was no wedding?"

"No." Adele looked up now, her eyes clear but heavy. "There was a man. He was... someone I cared for, once. But it wasn't love. And it wasn't safe."

Vivienne's breath caught. "What do you mean?"

Adele set the wineglass down gently on the coffee table. Her hands were suddenly folded in her lap, as if she were bracing herself for confession.

"He was charming. Intense. Older than me by at least fifteen years. I met him during one of my many escape attempts from the

Hollow." She paused. "Genevieve didn't approve. Of anyone. But especially not him."

Vivienne leaned forward, the words slicing closer to bone now.

"He wasn't violent, not exactly," Adele said. "But he had a way of pulling me in, making me doubt myself. When I got pregnant, I told him... and he vanished."

Vivienne stared, stunned. "He just left?"

Adele gave a brittle smile. "I think he was never really *there*, Vivienne. Just a fantasy I clung to. And when I realized I was going to raise you alone, I panicked. I couldn't bring you back to Ashcroft Hollow—not with the judgment, the rules, the expectations. So I made up the marriage. Gave you a name, a story."

"*Bellamy*," Vivienne whispered.

Adele nodded. "It's not his. It was a friend of mine grandmother's maiden name. I wanted you to feel like you belonged to something... even if it was a lie."

Vivienne sat back, dazed. "All this time..."

"I know," Adele said. "I should have told you. But I didn't want you to feel... less than. Or like you came from pain."

Vivienne's eyes burned, though no tears fell. "I didn't need perfect. I just needed *truth*."

"I know," Adele whispered. "And I'm so sorry."

They sat in silence for a long moment, the weight of decades coiled between them.

Finally, Vivienne set her wineglass beside her mother's and leaned back on the couch.

"So... who *am* I?" she asked, not accusingly, but curiously. "If not the daughter of a man in a wedding photo... if not a Bellamy... who am I?"

Adele looked at her then, eyes full of something soft and deep.

"You're the girl who was born under the full moon at Ashcroft Hollow," she said. "The one who made me brave enough to leave everything behind. You're Vivienne. Mine. And now... hers too, I suppose."

Vivienne exhaled slowly.

And for the first time in a long while, she didn't feel angry.

Just... open.

Vivienne was quiet for a long time. The clock ticked softly in the background, measuring the space between wine-sweet truth and memories now laid bare.

Then, softly—

"Do I get to know his name?"

Adele looked at her over the rim of her glass. Her lips parted... but no words came at first.

Vivienne tilted her head. "You do remember it, don't you?"

"I do," her mother said quietly. "I've never forgotten it. But for a long time, I tried to pretend I had."

"Why?"

Adele set the glass down again and folded her hands. "Because saying his name meant giving him a place in your story. And I didn't believe he deserved that."

Vivienne's brows drew together.

"He was never violent," Adele said again. "But he wasn't... right, either. He made me feel invisible and then like I was the only person in the world, all in the same breath. You know that kind of charm that curdles when you see what's behind it?"

Vivienne nodded slowly. She'd met that kind of man once or twice.

Adele sighed. "His name was Dominic. Said he was an archivist—collected rare documents and family histories. Traveled constantly, always chasing some old ledger or crumbling map. I never saw much proof of it, though— just stories."

"Did he know about me?"

"I told him. He didn't care. Said I'd be better off without him. And honestly... he wasn't wrong." Adele's voice cracked slightly, but she didn't look away. "But if you want to know more, I kept some things. An old letter he sent after he left. A photograph he gave me when we first met. I kept them locked away. I never knew if you'd want them."

Vivienne's eyes caught on the name, and the air in the room seemed to tighten. Dominic Grey.

The words pulsed on the page, as if the ink itself remembered him. A cold rush slid through her veins, and her breath hitched. Grey—Callum's name.

The connection hit like a jolt, sharp enough to make her fingers curl tighter around the paper. Somewhere deep in the Hollow, a floorboard creaked, low and deliberate, as though the house had stirred at her discovery.

Shadows shifted in the corners, and a faint shiver traced her spine.

This wasn't just a coincidence.

The Hollow had been waiting for her to see it.

"Any relation to Callum Grey?" she asked, her voice sharper than she intended. *He said he wasn't related to me.*

"Who? Never heard of him."

"Never mind…" Vivienne let the words hang, then drew in a slow breath. "I think I do want them. Not because I need him to be a part of me—" her gaze lingered on the name,

"—but because I need to see the whole picture. Even the messy parts."

Adele nodded, but this time with a faint, almost sheepish smile. "It's here, actually. In your hall closet."

Vivienne blinked. "It is here?"

"Remember, I left a few things behind when I sold everything and took off to see the world. It is in one of the boxes. I didn't think I'd ever open it again." She looked toward the hallway. "But I guess some ghosts don't stay packed away forever."

Vivienne stood slowly, her curiosity pulling her toward the closet door. "Let's see it, then."

Adele followed, and together they knelt on the floor as she reached past spare coats and a stack of old books to pull out a dusty, tape-worn box marked only with a single word:

"Before."

Vivienne ran her fingers over the label. The weight of that one word pressed into her like a breath she hadn't realized she'd been holding.

Inside—answers waited.

They sat in silence again, two women bound not just by blood, but by fractured truths and the healing that only comes when all the shadows are named.

Vivienne wasn't sure if she'd ever meet this Dominic Grey—or if he was even still alive—but now, at least, she had a name.

And sometimes, that was the first key to unlocking everything else.

# Chapter 26

Adele carefully peeled back the flaps of the old box. The scent of aged paper and cedar drifted out—a quiet memory of time stored and forgotten. She reached in gently, as though unearthing something sacred, and drew out a small stack of belongings wrapped in a pale silk scarf.

The first item she placed on the coffee table was a photo.

"Here," she said softly, passing it to Vivienne.

Vivienne took it with both hands, already feeling the tremble in her fingertips. The photo was sun-warmed and slightly faded, but the joy in it was unmistakable.

Her mother—so young—sat astride a dappled gray mare, laughing mid-motion as she looked toward the man beside her. Her long auburn hair whipped in the wind, and there was a wild, unburdened freedom in her smile that Vivienne had never seen before.

The man beside her sat taller in the saddle, one hand resting casually on the reins, the other on the saddle horn. His eyes were shaded beneath the brim of a worn riding hat, but his mouth was caught in a half-smile— sharp, wry, and undeniably handsome. There was something almost aristocratic in the slope of his nose, the way he carried himself with quiet confidence. He wore a dark, unbuttoned riding jacket and riding boots that had clearly seen use.

But it was the stables behind them that made Vivienne's breath hitch.

Ashcroft Hollow.

She recognized the wooden beams, the slope of the paddock gate, even the ancient oak tree in the background. It was the same place she'd found the mustang. The same barn Callum had led her through just days ago.

Her eyes returned to the man in the photo. There was something about him… not just his expression, or the way he seemed to look through the camera—but something else.

Something familiar.

"I've seen him," she murmured.

Adele looked up sharply. "You have?"

Vivienne shook her head, not quite certain. "No. I mean… maybe. I don't know. He just feels—" she trailed off, still staring. "Like a memory I don't have."

"That's Dominic," Adele said quietly. "Your father."

Vivienne looked up, the weight of the photo suddenly immense in her hands.

Adele's gaze drifted to the past. "We rode every morning that summer. Before everything changed."

Vivienne looked back down at the photo, trying to map the man's features onto her own reflection—searching for resemblance, for proof.

"Was he from there?" she asked, voice softer now.

Adele hesitated. "Sort of. He… came and went. Like the wind. But yes, Ashcroft Hollow was where we met. And where I left everything behind."

Vivienne's grip tightened slightly on the edges of the photo. The man in the image stared back, half-shadowed, as though holding onto secrets even in stillness.

And something about his face still pulled at her.

As though part of her had known him all along.

Adele reached deeper into the box and pulled out a folded piece of parchment—aged, yellowed, and sealed with wax long broken.

"I never understood this one," she said, handing it carefully to Vivienne. "He left it for me the day he vanished. I only found it after I'd packed everything up. I read it a hundred times and still… it never made much sense."

Vivienne took it reverently. The parchment was heavier than it looked, the ink faded but still legible in a looping, confident hand.

She unfolded it slowly.

*My Dearest Adele,*

*If you are reading this, I am gone.*

*Gone, but not in the way people mean when they say goodbye. I am simply… where I must be. For now.*

*You always asked what I was running from. The truth is—I wasn't running. I was waiting. For time to catch up. For the Hollow to open again. For the next to rise.*

*The house knows who she is. It always has.*

*You never believed me about the mirrors. Or the rooms. Or what I saw in the hour between dusk and memory. But I never lied to you. I only protected you—from all of it.*

*Ashcroft Hollow is not a place, Adele.*

*It is a keyhole.*

*And the women who've passed through it—the Keepers, the Dreamers, the Watchers of the Moon—*

*each of them unlocked something the world was not
ready to see.*

*Genevieve knew this. As did Elspeth before her.
And soon… someone else will too.*

*There is a map, but not the kind you can fold.
You'll find the first mark where shadow meets silver.
Trust the hollow tree and the mirror that doesn't show
your face.*

*The girl in the photograph has your fire. She will
walk between things. Tell her to listen for the ticking.*

*I loved you. In the only way I knew how.*

*Forgive the silence.*

*—D*

Vivienne sat stunned, the paper trembling
lightly in her hands.

"The house knows who she is…" she
whispered aloud, her eyes scanning the lines
again. "The Hollow is a keyhole?"

Adele shrugged helplessly. "I told you.
Nonsense. I assumed it was just a metaphor—
he always spoke in riddles. History buffs."

But Vivienne wasn't so sure.

Because the line—"Trust the hollow tree
and the mirror that doesn't show your face"—
pierced something in her. A memory.

The tree by the barn.

And the mirror in the Moon Room… the
one that shimmered with someone else's
dreams.

Her pulse quickened.

There were too many pieces to ignore now. The women. The rooms. The letter.

The locket around her neck ticked once—so softly she almost missed it.

Vivienne stood slowly, letter still clutched in her hand.

"I need to go back," she said quietly.

Adele looked up, surprised. "To Ashcroft Hollow?"

Vivienne nodded, eyes already distant.

"To find what he left behind."

# Chapter 27

Vivienne stood outside her boss's office door, heart knocking a little too loudly in her chest. She'd written and rewritten what she planned to say during the commute, but now that she was here, it felt heavier than she expected.

A few moments later, she stepped in.

"Hey, Vivienne," her boss said, glancing up from a cluttered desk. "Everything okay?"

She nodded, then shook her head. "Yes… and no. I wanted to talk to you in person."

He leaned back, brows knitting. "Go on."

"I have to take a leave," she said, voice steady despite the ache behind it. "There's something going on with my family. My grandmother passed away recently, and I inherited her estate. But it's more than that. It's… I need time to sort through it. Figure some things out."

He was quiet for a beat, then gave a small nod. "You've always been solid here, Vivienne. You've got personal days saved up, and then some. Take what you need."

"Thank you," she said, meaning it. "I don't know exactly how long I'll be gone. But I'll keep you updated."

She turned to leave—and nearly collided with Jessie her closest friend and coworker, carrying two coffees and a donut in her mouth.

"Hey!" Jessie grinned, muffled by pastry. "You ditching me already?"

Vivienne laughed and took the donut from her. "I'm heading out of town for a while."

Jessie's expression shifted. "Oh. Is everything okay?"

Vivienne nodded. "I think it will be. I just… need some time away. Somewhere quiet. No reception. No internet."

Jessie rolled her eyes playfully. "So medieval."

"More like timeless," Vivienne said with a smile. She hugged her tightly. "I'll call when I can. Promise."

"Better," Jessie murmured into her shoulder. "And bring me back something spooky and antique."

"Deal."

That night, Vivienne packed lightly—just a few bags, her laptop even though it would be mostly useless, and the box with the letter from Dominic, tucked carefully between sweaters.

She came downstairs to find her mom standing in the kitchen, stirring tea.

"You're really going back," Adele said without turning around.

"I am. First thing in the morning."

Adele turned then, meeting her daughter's eyes with quiet resolve. "Then I'm coming with you."

Vivienne blinked. "What? You don't have to—"

"I want to," her mother said firmly. "There's more I need to remember. More I think I need to face. And something tells me you shouldn't be there alone."

Vivienne hesitated, then gave a slow nod.

"Okay. We leave at the crack of dawn."

# Chapter 28

The tires crunched over the gravel driveway, slower now as the trees closed in like a living tunnel. Vivienne eased off the gas, the faint glow of headlights sweeping across the old iron gates as they creaked open on their own.

Adele gripped the door handle beside her. "That's… new."

"I guess it knows I am home," Vivienne whispered.

They drove in silence up the winding drive, the great hulking house rising from the mist like a forgotten castle. Ashcroft Hollow stood waiting, windows like eyes that had never stopped watching.

As Vivienne put the car in park, a gust of wind swept across the lawn, and every porch lantern flared to life.

Adele jumped. "Vivienne, that's not normal."

Vivienne stepped out slowly, the air charged and humming against her skin. Her boots hit the ground, and the wind stopped instantly. Not even the trees moved.

Adele hesitated before following, her eyes scanning the gables, the balconies, the dark windows above. "It was never like this when I lived here," she said. "It was just... cold. Empty. Your grandmother was distant. Silent. The rooms were dark, and the help barely spoke to me."

Vivienne went to the door and pushed it open.

No key. No resistance.

Just a long breath of warm, cinnamon-scented air, like the house itself was exhaling.

Lights flickered on in the foyer. The chandelier above trembled, prisms casting fractured rainbows across the high walls. The stairs curved up like a spine, and somewhere deep in the house, a clock began ticking. It hadn't done that before.

"It's awake," Vivienne said softly.

Adele stepped inside slowly, her breath catching. "This can't be real. It never did this. Never."

"Not for you," Vivienne said, looking around. "But for me... it does."

Thunder rumbled low in the distance, though the sky outside remained clear. Adele's hand drifted to her heart. "I think I saw something here once," she murmured. "When I was a very young girl. I was exploring—curious, bored. It was near the attic. I heard voices, Vivienne. Not people. Echoes. And one of the mirrors in a room? It didn't reflect me."

Vivienne turned sharply. "The Mirror Room?"

Adele nodded. "Yes. But I never found the room again after that day. I thought I'd imagined it."

"You didn't."

Her mother looked at her with wide eyes. "How do you know?"

Vivienne's hand closed around the locket at her throat. "Because I've seen it too."

They stood in the silence for a beat, the ticking clock filling the space between generations.

A whisper passed through the house—just a breath, like someone saying a name too softly to hear.

Adele shivered. "This house… it feels different."

Vivienne nodded. "Hmm. And I think… it's been waiting for us both to come home."

A door slammed far off down the hall. The chandelier flickered once, then steadied.

Adele looked like she might bolt.

Vivienne turned toward the stairs.

"Come on," she said. "Let's go find your room."

Vivienne led the way up the grand staircase, its carved banister gleaming faintly in the low light. The steps creaked under her weight, not in protest, but in a slow, deliberate recognition—welcoming her back. Above, the ceiling arched higher than she remembered, shadowed beams stretching like the ribs of some ancient cathedral.

The Hollow was immense—part Victorian manor, part Gothic relic—its corridors long enough to lose yourself in, its ceilings soaring high enough to swallow whispers.

Adele followed a pace behind, her gaze darting between the ancestral portraits that lined the walls and the flickering sconces, each flame trembling as if stirred by their breath. "Viv," she whispered, "This place feels… different."

Vivienne paused halfway up, resting her hand on the polished rail. "I have to admit, it's a bit spooky. I've seen reflections that didn't match, mirrors that echoed something else. I can't believe my grandmother lived here her

entire life—that you grew up in these halls—
and never felt the eeriness."

Adele's brows knit together. "I wonder why
it never responded to me?"

Vivienne touched the locket resting warm
against her collarbone. "I don't know. Maybe
it only opens to those who are ready to see.
You were young... maybe afraid. Maybe it
closed itself to protect you."

Adele gave a faint, skeptical laugh—but
there was sorrow beneath it.

At the landing, Vivienne stopped before the
second door on the right.

The Moon Room.

The door stood ajar, its velvet curtains
drifting gently despite the absence of open
windows. Silver light filtered down from the
circular skylight above, casting delicate moon-
shadows across the floor. The same celestial
symbols were etched into the wood beneath
their feet—stars, spirals, and phases of the
moon, faded but still pulsing with quiet
power. Clocks lined the walls, their hands
frozen, as if time itself had stopped to listen.

Adele stepped into the room and went still.

Her breath caught. "This room..."

Vivienne turned toward her. "You
recognize it?"

"Not exactly." Adele's eyes were wide. "I
dreamed of it—the night Genevieve died. I

saw a girl standing there." She pointed toward the crescent-shaped chaise beneath the skylight. "I think it was me. And your grandmother… she was mourning. Not crying—mourning. It felt like the end of something. Or maybe a warning."

Vivienne stepped into the center of the room. "I've seen things here too. Not quite memories… more like impressions. Echoes. The room shows what was, or what could be. I think it chooses what to reveal."

Adele stepped back, her shoulders tense. "It's too much, Vivienne."

"I don't think it is meant to scare you," Vivienne said gently. "The women who lived here… I think they were keepers of something. This place remembers. And now… it wants to show me. Us."

Adele's voice broke. "Your grandmother never told me. Not one word."

"Maybe she couldn't," Vivienne said softly. "Because you were already gone."

Adele shook her head, tears welling. "No. She left me long before I ever left this place."

The air shifted—curtains falling still, the room briefly breathless.

Vivienne reached for her mother's hand. "Then maybe it's time we both stopped running."

A soft chime rang out—from deep within the room. The clocks ticked in unison... once.

Adele startled.

Vivienne smiled faintly. "You heard it too."

Her mother nodded, slow and shaken.

They left the Moon Room together.

Out in the hallway, a door they had never seen open before now stood ajar—its iron handle gleaming faintly.

Adele froze. "That was never open before."

Vivienne cast her a knowing glance. "Maybe it's been waiting for your return."

# Chapter 29

Adele's breath caught as she stepped closer. The door, heavy oak with inlaid vines and faded silver scrollwork, looked as though it hadn't been touched in decades. And yet—it beckoned.

She hesitated, one hand rising toward the handle. "I don't remember this room."

Vivienne stood beside her. "I don't think you were meant to. Not then."

Together, they pushed the door open.

The hinges groaned, but the sound felt more like a sigh—long-held breath released at last.

Inside, the air was cool and thick with lavender and old paper. Dust motes danced in golden shafts of candlelight—though no candle had been lit. A round window let in the last glimmer of twilight, casting the room in a soft mauve glow.

The walls were lined with shelves—hundreds of books, all worn and hand-bound, with spines etched in gold ink. Sigils. Symbols. Names.

And in the center of the room stood a writing desk, carved in a style older than anything else in the house. Upon it sat a mirror framed in wrought silver and moonstone, and beneath the mirror… a journal. Closed. Waiting.

Adele's knees faltered slightly. "This was her study," she whispered. "Genevieve's. I thought she only used the front sitting room…"

Vivienne approached the journal. Her hand hovered above the cover, heart racing.

"I think this was her real work," she said. "Not the garden. Not the guests. This."

Adele ran her fingers along the nearest bookshelf. "I dreamed of a place like this once. When I was a girl. I thought it was just imagination."

Vivienne's fingers finally touched the journal's leather binding. At her touch, the mirror above it shimmered—not with a reflection, but with light. Shifting. Revealing something deeper within.

She opened the journal.

The first page was blank—except for a single sentence in careful script.

*"To the one who hears the house: You are not the first. But you may be the last."*

Vivienne turned the page. Symbols filled the margins. Diagrams of constellations, tinctures, rituals. Names of women she didn't recognize—some crossed out, some circled. Notes in Genevieve's hand... and, curiously, others in a different script.

Adele stepped behind her. "That's not her writing," she murmured. "That's older."

Vivienne looked up at the mirror again. For a moment, a face flickered there—not hers. Not her mother's. Someone else. Familiar.

She blinked. It vanished.

Her voice trembled as she said, "There's more going on here than either of us can imagine."

Adele nodded slowly.

Vivienne whispered, "I hope we are ready for it."

The mirror pulsed faintly again, like a heartbeat.

The Hollow had opened its next door.

And it was no longer whispering.

It was calling.

The spine of the old journal cracked as Vivienne opened it again that evening. She'd read it already, twice, but something tugged at her—an edge of memory or intuition whispering to return.

As she flipped a page near the end, something thin and yellowed slipped out from between the sheets.

It fluttered to the floor.

Vivienne knelt, heart suddenly racing. The paper had been folded many times and sealed with a faint wax crest—almost faded to nothing. She lifted it gently.

No name on the outside. No date.

She broke the seal.

Inside was a single page… handwritten, like the others, but the handwriting was not her grandmother's. It was angular, swift—bold.

The salutation stopped her breath.

*Genevieve,*

*Blood binds. But it also blinds. I understand now why you kept your silence, why the truth was not meant to be passed from mouth to ear, but through blood… and through the Hollow itself.*

*You said the house chooses. That it remembers. I believe you now.*

*I traced the line, as you asked. Back through names forgotten by most. Enclosed is what I've uncovered. It confirms what you feared. The patterns. The women. The ones who stayed, and the ones who disappeared.*

*My connection—through Everett Grey—makes me a cousin of sorts, I suppose. But that isn't what matters. The men were never meant to hold the line. Only guard it. Only pass the key.*

*I loved Adele. You knew that. You saw it. You warned me... but I didn't listen. I thought love would be enough to break the cycle.*

*I was wrong.*

*I'm leaving this letter in case I don't return. If the house calls again, I hope it's for her. Or for the child.*

*You know what to do, if it does.*

*— Dominic*

Beneath the letter, something else had been tucked—neatly folded and yellowed with time. A diagram. Hand-drawn.

A family tree.

But unlike any Vivienne had seen before, the women's names formed the spine—bold, central—while the men's names clung to the margins like afterthoughts.

It began with:

Seraphina Vexley

↓

Cordelia Ashcroft

↓

Isaldora Ashcroft

↓

↓

↓

Genevieve Ashcroft

→ Adele Bellamy (née Ashcroft)
→ Vivienne Bellamy

Off to the side, written in smaller, slanted ink:

Everett Grey – second husband to Genevieve. Dominic Grey—the elusive "Archivist of the Hollow, tied to Everett."

Vivienne's breath stilled. Dominic Grey. Her father.

And there it was again—the name that haunted her since the moment she'd first heard it. *Grey*. Callum's name.

The memory of that first realization whispered through her like a draft in an empty corridor, raising the fine hairs at her neck. She wanted to dismiss it as coincidence, yet the Hollow had a way of turning coincidences into curses. What if the thread between them ran deeper than she dared imagine?

She stared at the names. The Ashcroft line was purely matrilineal—the legacy never passed to men. The Greys had always been near, but never in the line. Bound to protect, to keep the records, to guard the keys.

She swallowed, feeling the weight of the Hollow around her, as if the house itself leaned in to see what she'd uncovered. There were no accidents in Ashcroft Hollow. Only waiting truths.

Vivienne sat cross-legged on the Moon Room floor long after the house had gone still again, Dominic's letter trembling in her hands. The edges were soft, the ink faded but steady. The family tree lay open beside her, candlelight flickering across the names—some unfamiliar until tonight.

Footsteps whispered down the hall. The Moon Room door creaked.

Adele stepped in, two mugs of tea in hand, her earlier tension softened but not gone. "You okay?" she asked gently.

Vivienne lifted the letter. "You need to see this."

Adele crossed to her, setting one mug down before lowering herself to the edge of the chaise—the same spot Vivienne remembered from childhood dreams. Her eyes fell to the aged paper.

"Who's it from?" she asked, though her voice suggested she already knew.

Vivienne handed her the letter, pointing to the signature.

Adele's breath hitched. "'Dominic'…"

She read in silence, each line settling heavy in her chest. When she reached I loved Adele. You knew that, her fingers trembled. She set the mug aside, untouched.

Vivienne slid the family tree closer. "He traced it," she said quietly. "Your side. All the way back to Cordelia Ashcroft. Did you know the Greys were tied to the Hollow?"

Adele shook her head slowly. "No. She never told me about knowing any of them… never told me they were keepers of anything." Her voice cracked. "She certainly never told me they were guarding the women's legacy."

Vivienne tapped the margin where Dominic's name was written. "He wasn't in the bloodline. But he was part of it. He knew the secrets."

Adele's eyes softened, grief and something like regret stirring. "And he never said anything. Just… left."

Vivienne covered her mother's hand. "He left this. For us. Maybe especially for you."

Adele's gaze dropped to the letter again, her voice a whisper. "Vivienne… if the Hollow chose you, if the magic in these walls is waking now… I'm afraid of what that means."

"I'm not," Vivienne said, her voice steady. "Not anymore."

Adele leaned in, resting her head on Vivienne's shoulder. "Then lead the way, sweetheart. Because I think we're just getting started."

Outside, the wind stirred the trees. Inside, the Moon Room gave a low, contented hum—listening. Waiting.

# Chapter 30

The rich scent of brewed coffee wafted up the stairs before the sun had fully risen. Adele stirred first, blinking in the early morning light filtering through lace-curtained windows. She had fallen asleep in the same bed as Vivienne—insisting she didn't want to spend the night alone in the house yet, not after everything they'd heard and seen.

Vivienne was already slipping a sweater over her nightshirt when Adele's voice broke the quiet.

"Did you make coffee?"

Vivienne shook her head, a curious smile tugging at her lips. "No. But I think I know who did."

They padded barefoot through the halls, following the warm scent into the sunlit kitchen. Two mugs waited on the counter, steam curling into the morning air. A plate of thick toast, farm butter, and raspberry preserves sat beside a small dish of wild honey.

Adele blinked. "A mystery cook?"

Vivienne laughed softly. "Apparently."

They drank their coffee and sat at the table, but Vivienne's eyes kept drifting to the window—toward the barn.

"I'm going to find him—the cook," Vivienne said after a few sips, setting her mug down with quiet determination.

Adele raised an eyebrow. "The cook?"

Vivienne smirked faintly. "Well… he left us breakfast, didn't he? His name's Callum. You must remember him. He was your mother's second husband's grandson."

Adele blinked, surprise flickering in her eyes. "I never met him. Or the second husband, for that matter."

Vivienne looked at her, confused. "Really?"

"I left before that chapter of her life began," Adele said quietly, wrapping her hands around the warm mug. "She never told me anything about him."

Vivienne's expression grew thoughtful. "Well, he left behind a grandson who knows more about this place than he lets on."

She stood. "We need to talk."

Then she slipped out the door, heading toward the stables with the morning light at her back and questions burning in her chest.

Vivienne found Callum behind the stables, brushing down one of the horses, his sleeves rolled to the elbows, forearms dusted with hay and dried sweat. The old horse leaned into the rhythm of his movements, eyes half-lidded in trust.

She stopped short.

Her breath caught—just for a moment—as if her heart had forgotten its own rhythm.

She hadn't expected the sight of him to do anything to her. Especially with the possibility—unwelcome and unspoken—that they shared more than history. Not like that. Not with the morning sun catching in his hair and the quiet strength in the way his hands moved—steady, unhurried, sure. There was something grounding about him, something real, like the earth itself had shaped him for this place.

He glanced over his shoulder at her then, not startled, just aware—and offered a slow, crooked smile.

"Didn't hear you coming," he said.

Vivienne swallowed. "I wasn't trying to be quiet."

He laughed softly, brushing a hand down the horse's flank. "Still, you always move like someone with secrets."

She took a step closer, feeling the strange pull again—the one that whispered of memories she couldn't name, and futures she hadn't dared imagine.

Maple nickered softly at her presence.

Vivienne didn't smile. Instead, she handed Callum the letter. "I found this in one of my grandmother's journals. It's from Dominic. And this—" she unfolded the lineage and pressed it into his free hand, "—was with it."

Callum took them both, his brow furrowing as he read. The horse huffed gently beside them, as if waiting, too.

When he finished, he looked up at her. "So you know."

"I know a little," Vivienne replied. "Enough to be confused. Enough to know I need more."

She folded her arms. "So I'm asking you now—what do you know, Callum?"

His expression was unreadable. The silence stretched between them like a taut wire.

Vivienne stepped closer. "You grew up here. You knew my grandmother. You knew Dominic. You promised to protect the land."

Her voice softened, but her eyes didn't waver. "What haven't you told me?"

Callum looked past her, toward the house—toward the rooms that had started to breathe again. "It's not just land, Vivienne. And it's not just a house."

"Then what is it?"

He hesitated.

"What questions," she asked, "Should I be asking you?"

He looked at her then, truly looked. His voice was quiet, weighted. "Ask why the men in this lineage are always on the outside. Ask why no one remembers the Ashcroft sons— but everyone remembers the women."

Vivienne's heart skipped. "So this legacy… it doesn't pass through blood alone."

"No," Callum said. "It passes through power. Through knowing. Through choice."

She swallowed. "And me?"

"You were chosen the moment you returned," he said. "But the Hollow's been waiting longer than that."

Vivienne stared at him. "Then tell me everything, Callum. Start from the beginning. No more riddles."

Callum glanced at the papers again, then folded them neatly and handed them back.

"Not here," he said. "Not outside. Tonight. In the East Wing."

Vivienne's brow arched. "What's in the East Wing?"

His eyes darkened. "Answers. And maybe… a few ghosts."

# Chapter 31

Vivienne turned away from the paddock, still bristling but quieter now.

She found her mother seated at the small breakfast table in the sunroom, coffee in hand, gazing out at the fields like they might suddenly whisper back.

"You ride?" Vivienne asked, grabbing her own mug from the counter.

Adele turned. "Haven't in years. Why?"

"Callum's saddling up the horses. He said… we should all go."

Adele blinked. "All?"

Vivienne gave a slow nod. "Apparently, the Hollow's calling you too."

Adele hesitated, looking down at her cup. "I'm not sure I'm ready."

"You don't have to be," Vivienne said, heading toward the back door. "Just… come."

A few minutes later, bundled in Adele's borrowed boots and one of Genevieve's old riding coats, they approached the paddock where Callum waited. The horses were already saddled, their coats gleaming in the soft morning light.

"I wasn't sure she'd come," Callum said, offering Adele a hand.

"She wasn't either," Vivienne muttered.

Adele ignored them both as she placed one foot in the stirrup and swung into the saddle with more grace than either expected.

Callum raised an eyebrow. "You sure you haven't ridden in a while?"

Adele gave him a cool glance. "I used to spend hours sneaking out with the horses. They were the only ones who didn't keep secrets."

That silenced everyone.

Vivienne mounted, suddenly aware of the weight of the letter in her coat pocket.

They rode in silence at first, the horses' hooves soft against the earth, the morning light spilling through the trees. Ashcroft Hollow opened before them—not just the house, but the land itself. Mist clung low along the grass, and through the veil, shapes hinted at themselves: old stone markers, a weathered bench, the foundation of a greenhouse long gone.

The air felt charged.

Vivienne looked over at Callum. "Tell me what you know. About the house. About the letter. About Dominic."

He didn't answer right away.

Then: "Not here. Not yet."

Vivienne sighed. "You keep saying that."

"Because this place has its own way of revealing the truth," he said. "You've already noticed. The rooms... the dreams... the locks that only open when someone's ready. This isn't a mystery to be solved like a riddle. It's a legacy that has to be remembered."

"Then help me *remember*," Vivienne snapped. "Because I don't want to keep tripping over ghosts."

Callum slowed his horse as they reached a low rise where the Hollow stretched in all directions. The wind stirred, brushing across their faces like a whisper too old to understand.

"Dominic wasn't just your mother's lover," he said finally, turning to Vivienne. "He was meant to protect this place. And if I'm reading that letter right... he believed you'd be the one to finish what they started."

Vivienne's chest tightened.

"And what exactly is it," she asked, "That I've supposedly inherited?"

Callum met her gaze.

"That," he said, "Is what you have to find out."

Adele trailed a few paces behind them, her horse moving at a slower gait. The distance seemed intentional—as if the land, or perhaps the moment, needed Vivienne and Callum alone in the lead.

Vivienne glanced over at him, mind still whirring from his cryptic answer. But then something tugged at her, and she turned in the saddle to look back at her mother.

Adele rode quietly, eyes half-lowered, one hand resting lightly on the reins. She looked lost in thought—or maybe in memory.

Vivienne frowned. There were still so many questions. So many stories she'd never been told.

She pulled her horse into a slower pace, letting Callum ride on ahead. When she matched her mother's side, she spoke softly.

"Mom…"

Adele looked up, startled from wherever she'd been.

"I need to know something," Vivienne said. "About your grandfather. My great grandfather. I don't know anything about him."

Adele blinked, then gave a small, dry laugh. "Not many do."

They rode in silence for a few seconds more, the rhythm of the horses filling the space between them.

"What was his name?" Vivienne asked.

Adele sighed, "Lord Malrick Vexmoor."

"Vexmoor?" Vivienne repeated. "I don't recognize that name from anything in the house."

"Malrick Vexmoor," Adele said again, the name rolling off her tongue like old wine soured in the cask—rich once, but tainted by something that had aged in the dark too long.

Vivienne tilted her head. "Vexmoor? Then… why do we have the Ashcroft name?"

Adele gave a bittersweet smile. "Because it was never his. It was Isolde's."

Vivienne blinked. "She kept her name?"

"She insisted. Said it was about legacy, about the Hollow. Malrick argued but lost in the end. He loved her family's money—and position. He was never truly accepted by Evadne or her mother, Anastasia."

Vivienne's throat tightened. "Tell me about him."

Adele's gaze turned distant, her voice low. "He died before I was born. I was told that he wasn't from here. Malrick Vexmoor… he came from the coast of Maine. No one knew much about his past, and he never offered it. That he arrived one summer under the guise of restoring the chapel woodwork, but it was clear he wanted more than a commission."

Vivienne waited.

"I was told that he had this charm—restless, magnetic—but there was a shadow in him. That he'd vanish for hours, sometimes days, walking the cliffs alone. Said the sea spoke to him. I never knew if I was being told as poetry... or a warning. The staff whispered he was drawn to the Hollow's oldest rooms, the ones no one entered after dark. That he asked too many questions about the family's history—about the women who came before."

They rode in silence for a moment, only the rhythm of hooves filling the air.

Vivienne nudged her horse forward to ride alongside Callum again. The trail had narrowed, the trees closing in like watchful sentries. Adele remained just a few paces behind, but Vivienne knew she could hear every word.

She glanced at Callum, her voice low but steady.

"What was he like—your grandfather, Everett Grey?"

For a moment, Callum didn't answer. The reins slid faintly through his gloved fingers as his gaze locked on the trail ahead.

"He wasn't the kind of man people wrote poems about," he said at last. "Quiet. Exacting. He understood land better than people. Numbers, ledgers, boundaries—those were his languages. Everything was measured in gain or loss."

Vivienne studied his profile, searching for the shadow behind his words. "So why Genevieve?"

"She'd already lost Julien Marlow by then," Callum said. "He was the one people whispered about—the artist who saw her as more than the Hollow's heir. When he died, the estate teetered. Old families were circling, the town was restless. Everett had Hollow blood, distantly—enough to silence the talk. Marrying him was a calculation. It kept the Ashcroft name on the gates."

From behind them, Adele's voice cut through the hush of the trees.

"She loved a man who set her heart on fire," she said softly. "And then she chose one who would never let it burn."

Callum's jaw tightened. "She never mentioned Julien to me. Only duty. Heritage. Bloodlines."

"So, she buried him," Adele said, "Not just in the ground, but in silence."

Vivienne's breath caught. "Was Everett cruel?"

"No," Callum replied slowly. "Just… private. Efficient. He kept the Hollow running, made deals behind closed doors. And then, one day, he was gone. Stroke, they said."

Adele's brow furrowed. "She never told me my father died. Never told me she remarried."

"She couldn't," Callum said. "By then, you were already gone. And she'd lost more than she could bear to speak of."

The horses walked on, their hooves muffled in damp leaves. Vivienne felt the weight of all that had been unspoken for decades—lives lived in rooms behind locked doors, names erased from family trees, love remembered only in paint and smoke.

She reached into her pocket, fingers brushing the folded letter from Dominic again.

"There's still more to this story," she murmured. "I can feel it."

Callum's gaze flickered, something unreadable behind his eyes. "Probably," he said. Then, after a beat, "But you might wish you hadn't asked."

# Chapter 32

The fire crackled low in the hearth, casting long shadows across the worn tapestries of the East Wing drawing room. This part of the house felt older than the rest—untouched by modern light switches or thermostats. The air itself held memory, the scent of beeswax and cedar lingering like breath on a mirror.

Vivienne sat cross-legged on the rug, the letter from Dominic unfolded between her and the others. Adele perched on the old settee, wine glass in hand, though she hadn't taken a sip. Callum leaned against the mantel, arms crossed, his eyes fixed on the parchment like it might come alive.

"This is where she kept the real things," Adele said softly. "Genevieve. The things she didn't want seen."

"She trusted Dominic," Vivienne said, her fingers brushing the faded ink. "Enough to leave him this."

Callum stepped closer, boots creaking on the wooden floor. "He was part of the family, but not by blood. Not in the way you'd expect."

Vivienne looked up at him. "Then how?"

Callum hesitated. "He kept the books, handled what Genevieve couldn't—or wouldn't. The land disputes, the whispered debts, the letters that arrived without return addresses. He had a way of making problems disappear before anyone else even knew they existed. Genevieve welcomed him easily… but I think it was you she was waiting for, Vivienne. Or maybe what you'd uncover. The Hollow has a way of holding its breath for the right person to ask the wrong questions—and Dominic… Dominic was here to make sure those questions found their way to you."

Vivienne furrowed her brow. "What do you mean?"

Callum met her eyes. "You ask the right questions. That's why she kept the journal going through him. Why the letter ended up in your hands."

Adele's voice cut through the stillness, brittle as frost. "Ask yourself why the men in this family are always on the edges of the story. Why no one remembers the Ashcroft sons—but every woman's name endures."

Vivienne's eyes narrowed. She'd heard this before, whispered in half-truths and warnings. "What are you saying?"

Adele set her untouched glass aside, the crystal ringing faintly on the table. "My father, Julien—erased. The men before? Just a shadow in the ledgers. Dominic? Tucked into the margins like a footnote. But Genevieve, her mother… even me? We're remembered. Marked. Carried forward."

Callum's gaze lingered on Vivienne. "There's a reason. The Ashcroft line has never belonged to the men. The women were the keepers—of the land, the house, the legacy. This place responds to them… it chooses them."

"The house chooses," Vivienne repeated, her voice barely a whisper, as if afraid the walls might hear.

Callum stepped forward and gently laid an aged slip of paper beside the letter. Another page—half-burned at the edges. "I found this tucked behind one of the portrait frames in the library," he said. "I think it was meant to go with the letter."

Vivienne unfolded it carefully. Ink faded but legible.

*"To the women of Ashcroft Hollow.*
*If you're reading this, then the Hollow has awakened again.*

*It does not sleep—it waits. And it will only open its truth to one who bears its name not just in blood, but in burden.*
*The sons are stewards. The daughters are the flame."*

Vivienne stared at the line, the words ringing through her.

"I thought I was just… cleaning out a house," she said, her voice shaking. "I didn't know I was walking into a legacy."

Adele's eyes glistened. "None of us did."

Callum crouched beside her. "Dominic knew. He left this for you because he believed you'd finish what was started generations ago."

Vivienne looked at him. "What was started?"

Callum hesitated. "A breaking. A severing. A refusal to let the wrong power hold the Hollow. You're not here to fix the house, Vivienne. You're here to heal it."

A silence settled over them, heavy and sacred.

Then the fire hissed, a log collapsing inward. Sparks rose, and for a moment, the room flickered brighter—illuminating the old portraits on the walls. One of the women, a stern face in shadows, seemed to almost smirk.

Vivienne exhaled slowly.

"Then I need to know everything. About the women. About the house. About me."

# Chapter 33

Vivienne sat back on her heels, the folded letter resting in her lap like a relic that had been waiting to be read for decades. The flicker of the hearth played across her face, but her attention was fixed on her mother. The room had fallen quiet, save for the soft crackle of embers and the occasional shift of wind outside the stained-glass windows.

"Tell me something," she said gently. "How did you meet my father?"

Adele blinked, startled by the question. "Dominic?"

Vivienne nodded, her voice barely above a whisper. "You never told me about him. Not really. But I need to know. All of it."

Adele reached for her wine glass—not to drink, but to anchor herself. Her fingers wrapped around the stem like it might keep her steady against something long buried.

"I was nineteen when Julien died," she began. "And everything changed. The house... the Hollow... it felt like it swallowed itself after the fire. Genevieve retreated. The light went out of everything."

She stared into the glass as if it could rewind time.

"I ran off to Boston for a few years— needed space to breathe. But I came back for a couple weeks. I don't even remember why. Maybe I thought I'd find something still alive here. Something to hold on to."

Vivienne waited, heart aching.

"That's when I met him," Adele continued. "Dominic. He was already here when I arrived—said he was helping the Greys with estate records. Tall, quiet, unreadable. The kind of man who said little but noticed everything."

She gave a soft, bitter laugh. "At first, I thought he was just another ghost the house had summoned."

Vivienne's brow furrowed. "So you didn't know him before?"

"No," Adele said, "But it felt like I did. We spent afternoons wandering the old orchard, poking through the collapsed greenhouse, watching storms roll in from the cliffs. He never asked questions. He just listened."

"And then?" Vivienne asked.

"It happened slowly. Then all at once." Adele's voice cracked. "He made me feel like I could breathe again. Like the house didn't own every part of me. We were careful. Or thought we were."

Vivienne looked down at the letter. "Did Genevieve know?"

Adele smiled faintly. "Probably. But she never interfered. She just watched him. Like the wind watches fire."

Vivienne's voice softened. "And when you found out you were pregnant?"

Adele's eyes turned flinty. "I was back in Boston. I told him. He changed. It was like I'd broken some unspoken contract. He said he wasn't the kind of man who could raise a child—especially not here. Not under this roof."

"He walked away?" Vivienne guessed.

"He disappeared," Adele whispered. "Sent a note. Said he was sorry. Said it would be easier for everyone if he was gone."

Vivienne stared into the fire. "But he left these letters. To me. Not you."

Adele's gaze fell to the folded parchment. "Maybe he regretted it. Or maybe he was trying to make peace with the Hollow before it swallowed him too."

The silence that followed was thick with old grief and half-healed wounds.

Callum, quiet until now, shifted beside the fireplace. "There's something else," he said.

He handed Vivienne another letter.

As she opened it, something shifted in the air—like the Hollow was listening.

She read aloud, slowly.

*"If you're reading this, I've already broken every promise I made to your mother. But you were never meant to be ordinary. Not with her fire. Not with what you carry.*

*There are rooms in this house that open only for the right blood. The right intention. They've waited, just like I waited. Just like she waited.*

*Maybe now… you'll understand why no one remembers the Ashcroft sons. Only the women remain."*

Vivienne looked up. "Why only the women?"

Callum's expression darkened. "My grandfather said something once—that the Hollow never needed men for long. That it used them, then erased them."

Vivienne whispered, "Like watchers. Witnesses."

Adele flinched slightly. "Your father said that too—near the end.

Callum continued, "He kept a notebook, you know. After Genevieve died. Filled with symbols he said came to him in dreams. Repeating patterns. Like he was remembering something he hadn't lived yet."

Vivienne felt a chill move through her. "Do you think they are still here?"

Callum nodded. "Upstairs. In the old study. He kept it hidden."

Vivienne touched the folded letters. "Then that's where I need to go next. If these are more than just apologies—if they're clues…"

Callum leaned forward. "Then you're already closer than anyone's ever been."

The flames in the fireplace sputtered, then flared brighter for a heartbeat, as if in agreement.

Vivienne stood, suddenly alert. "Something's about to shift. I can feel it."

And somewhere above them, in the east turret, a door they thought forgotten stirred with the breath of the Hollow.

# Chapter 34

Vivienne couldn't sleep.

Not because of the storm—it had passed hours ago—but because the Hollow itself felt too awake. The walls hummed faintly. The windows pulsed with moonlight. Shadows stretched longer than they should have.

The letter still sat beside her bed, edges worn from rereading. But it wasn't the only thing that called her now.

She rose, silent as breath, and slipped into one of Genevieve's old housecoats. Something told her not to wake Adele. This was a path she had to walk alone.

Down the hall, past the locked study, she paused at the corner where the air always felt colder. She remembered Callum's words: This place doesn't give answers unless you ask the right questions.

So she whispered one aloud. "What haven't I seen yet?"

The hallway creaked in response.

Vivienne followed the sensation, past the tapestry of the Ashcroft family tree, until she reached the east wing stairwell—the one that led to the turret. No one had gone up there in years.

The knob stuck at first, then gave way with a groan.

Dust spiraled in the moonlight as she ascended the narrow steps. At the top, a warped door stood slightly ajar.

Vivienne stepped into the round turret room. It was smaller than she imagined, with windows on all sides and a domed ceiling painted in faded celestial patterns.

A cracked leather journal lay on the floor.

She knelt, brushing the cover. I. *Ashcroft.* Isolde.

Vivienne opened it. The first few entries were dreamy, poetic. Musings on the wind through the orchard. Her husband Malrick Vexmoor's fascination with the veil between worlds. But the tone soon shifted.

*I saw her again last night. The other me. Her eyes are mine, but older. Wiser—or more worn. She speaks in riddles. Calls me "anchor" and says I've forgotten something important. But how can I forget what hasn't happened yet?*

Vivienne's heart quickened.

She flipped through more pages. Sketches of mirrored doors, maps of underground tunnels, rituals circled in smudged ink. There was a phrase repeated several times, scrawled in red pencil.

*The Mirror Room must never be opened without blood to bind it.*

She kept reading until a gust of wind slammed the turret window. Vivienne jolted— and realized she wasn't alone.

Adele stood in the doorway, arms folded.

"You shouldn't be up here alone," she said quietly.

Vivienne held up the journal. "Did you know about this? About Isolde?"

Adele entered slowly, brushing her fingers along the curved wall.

"I knew my grandmother was called mad. That she claimed to speak with herself across lifetimes. Genevieve never spoke of her. Said it was best not to feed shadows."

Vivienne studied her mother's face. "And the séance room? Did you know that was real?"

Adele hesitated. "Only in whispers. A room behind the mirrored library. My father once joked it was where the Hollow did its dreaming. But I always thought it was just legend."

"It's not," Vivienne said. "This journal… it talks about it. About time loops. Mirrors. Bloodline rituals."

She handed it over. Adele flipped to a random page and blanched.

*Malrick says the men are keepers. But I think they are watchers. They die young, or go missing. I asked the house why. It whispered: Because they do not belong. Not here. Not in this story.*

Adele looked up slowly. "I've read something like this before."

"Where?"

She didn't answer at first.

Then, in a voice wrapped in memory: "Your father used to keep a notebook. He said the Hollow spoke to him too, but not in words. In symbols. He started drawing the same sigils over and over again. Like he was trying to remember something he'd never lived."

Vivienne's throat tightened.

"I think it's time I saw those notes," she said.

Adele nodded. "Are you sure?"

"Yes." Vivienne watched as her mother left the turret, then turned back toward the window. Below, the orchard was still. But she felt it now—subtle as breath—the house

shifting around her. Doors unlocking.
Waiting.

# Chapter 35

Morning came gray and slow, like the Hollow was trying to decide whether to keep sleeping.

Vivienne stood in front of the study door, barefoot, hair unbrushed, the hem of Genevieve's old housecoat trailing behind her like a shadow. Adele had already unlocked the door but left her to enter alone.

The air inside was still. Dust floated in slanted light through the narrow windows. Nothing had been moved in years. Stacks of paper yellowed with age. Books with cracked spines. The lingering scent of cedar, ink… and something older.

Dominic used her great-grandfather's desk which sat against the far wall, a brass lamp frozen mid-swing above it. His chair—an old thing with torn upholstery and clawed feet— seemed to lean forward as if expecting her.

Vivienne approached slowly. One of the desk drawers was already pulled halfway out, left open on purpose.

Inside, wrapped in oilskin, was the notebook.

She unwrapped it carefully.

The cover was simple—matte black, worn at the edges—but the first page stopped her breath.

Dozens of sigils. Some familiar—variations of alchemical and occult symbols—but others felt… older. Curved in ways that pulled at her subconscious. Dreamlike. Primal.

She flipped to the next page. A single line written in her father's neat, deliberate hand:

*"They are not memories. They are warnings."*

The next pages were filled with sketches, strange patterns repeating across generations—spirals, mirrored arches, eyes within mirrors. In the margins, he'd scribbled fragmented thoughts:

*"Why only the daughters?"*

*"She watches from the mirror. But it's not her."*

*"This house is a clock."*

Vivienne's fingers trembled. It reminded her of Isolde's journal—only this felt sharper. Less poetic. More frantic. Like her father was racing against something unseen.

Another page held nine interlocking circles. In the center: a mirror, cracked.

Around it, small symbols she recognized: the rosary, the comb, the singing bell, the oil lamp.

Her breath caught. The Nine Sacred Objects.

But her father had never seen them. How could he have known?

A voice behind her.

"Try page 43."

She jumped—Callum stood in the doorway, holding two mugs of tea. His voice was quiet, rough from sleep.

She obeyed.

Page 43 held a hand-drawn diagram of the Hollow's floorplan—but overlaid with thin, red lines that didn't match the architecture. A lattice of energy. Tunnels, maybe? Ley lines?

And in the center, circled in gold ink:

The Séance Room.

Vivienne looked up at him. "How did you know about this page?"

Callum crossed the room, set the mugs down, and ran a hand through his hair.

"I've seen it before," he said. "My uncle— he worked on the estate when your father was still around. He saw Dominic drawing these symbols, mumbling to himself. Said it was like he was trying to map something... under the house."

Vivienne sat back. "So the séance room is real. And my father was trying to find it?"

Callum nodded. "Maybe more than that. Maybe he was trying to stop it."

Vivienne's eyes snapped to him.

"What do you mean?"

Callum hesitated, then pulled something from his jacket pocket. A thin, folded slip of paper. "My uncle kept this. Told me never to read it unless something woke up again."

Vivienne unfolded it.

It was a sigil. Hand-drawn. The same one from the center of the book—the cracked mirror inside the nine circles.

Underneath it, in her father's handwriting:

*"If she reaches the mirror too soon, the cycle repeats."*

Vivienne's voice was barely a whisper. "What cycle?"

Callum looked at her, and for the first time, she saw fear in his eyes.

"I think your father tried to end something. Something this house has done before. Over and over."

Vivienne clutched the notebook. Her fingers stained faintly red from the ink. "And now it's my turn."

—

Most of the rooms in this house unsettled her.

Even before she knew what was in them, but the Mirror Room was the creepiest.

Frames of gold and splintered wood lined the walls, their warped glass either fractured or veiled in velvet. The shelves offered no books—only mirrors. Some antique, some modern. No two the same. Some reflected too brightly. Others… not quite enough.

Vivienne entered alone.

She held her father's notebook close, its weight somehow heavier now. As if the pages themselves had absorbed fear.

The door creaked shut behind her. The temperature dropped a degree.

She stopped at the center of the room.

Nine mirrors faced inward, creating a fractured circle. She turned slowly, heart thudding. One of them shimmered faintly— not like glass but like water.

*"The séance room is where the Hollow does its dreaming."*

Her mother's words echoed in her head.

Vivienne opened the notebook again. Page 43—the floorplan, the cracked mirror sigil, the hidden room.

She looked back up and whispered, "Where are you?"

Nothing.

She stepped forward.

One mirror—a tall, Victorian frame with curling iron roses—flickered as she neared. Her reflection bent unnaturally. In the glass, her lips moved… but she hadn't spoken.

She gasped, stepped back.

The reflection stayed still.

Wrong.

Then, slowly, it raised its hand—and pointed to the right.

Vivienne turned. The mirror directly beside it—a simple rectangular pane with a blackened silver edge—rippled like heat. She reached out and pressed her palm against it.

Warm.

She pushed.

The glass didn't shatter. It sank.

A sound like a sigh filled the room, followed by a low, mechanical groan.

The mirror slid inward, revealing a hidden doorway. Dust billowed. A stairwell spiraled down into darkness.

Vivienne stared into it.

The Hollow had moved again.

She didn't hesitate.

She descended the narrow stairs, heart pounding with each step. The air grew thick with frankincense and old smoke. Her fingers brushed against stone as the walls narrowed, then widened again into…

A circular chamber.

No windows. No furniture. Just candles—dozens of them—flickering though none were lit. At the center stood a table of carved obsidian etched with sigils she now recognized. Nine chairs circled it. One was overturned.

Above the table, hanging from invisible threads, was a mirror.

Perfectly round. Like an eye.

And behind it—Vivienne swore she saw it—a flicker of movement.

She stepped closer.

A breath on her neck.

She turned.

Callum stood behind her, pale, silent.

"I followed the sound," he said. "I shouldn't have let you come alone."

Vivienne swallowed hard. "I think we found it."

He nodded. "Or it found you."

She held up the notebook. "This is where it starts, isn't it? Whatever my father tried to stop. Whatever Isolde saw coming."

Callum looked around the room. "There's something else here. I can feel it."

Vivienne's gaze drifted to the center of the table.

There, nestled in a carved depression, was a single object.

A silver key, cold to the touch, shaped like a crescent moon.

She picked it up.

The mirror above the table cracked straight through the center.

And far, far away—through the walls of Ashcroft Hollow—the tower clock struck 3:03 a.m.

The moment the clock chimed 3:03, the room breathed.

Not in metaphor.

It inhaled.

The candles flared to life—dozens of tiny flames blooming in unison without a single spark.

Vivienne froze, the silver key still in her palm. The cracked mirror above the obsidian table hummed with a low, pulsing sound—like distant thunder echoing underwater.

Callum reached for her. "Vivienne…"

But she couldn't move. Her gaze was locked on the mirror.

The crack in the glass widened with a slow, deliberate screech. Behind it, a silvery mist swirled—not a reflection but something else. A veil. A window.

No—a door.

Suddenly, her father's notebook grew hot against her chest. She yanked it out, flipping to the center page. New ink bled through the paper, forming an unfamiliar symbol. A circle with nine spokes.

She gasped. "It's reacting."

The air thickened.

The chairs scraped back—on their own. Empty, yet animated by unseen forces.

Callum stepped in front of her. "We need to go. Now."

But the table pulsed again, and the flames dimmed. In the flickering dark, a voice—faint and feminine—whispered from the mirror:

"Anchor…"

Vivienne staggered.

"Key-bearer…"

Callum turned, eyes wide.

"She comes again."

Vivienne shook her head. "Who are you?"

The mist in the mirror condensed— forming a vague silhouette. A woman, draped in shadow, her face shrouded. But her voice… it was layered. Not one speaker. Many. A chorus of echoes.

"Nine have passed. Nine will awaken. But not all will survive."

The room trembled.

"The Hollow remembers. But do you?"

Vivienne stumbled backward. "This is a warning."

"No," Callum said, his voice low. "It's a summons."

Suddenly, the table split down the center—and the silver key jumped from her palm, landing in the center of the sigil with a metallic clang. Every candle extinguished.

Darkness swallowed them.

Then… silence.

Just before the flames flickered back to life, Vivienne heard it—

A heartbeat.

Not hers.

Not Callum's.

The house.

The Hollow was awake.

# Chapter 36

Vivienne couldn't tell if her eyes were open.

The darkness was so complete it felt soft—velvety, almost warm—but it pressed on her from every side.

And then, a flicker.

Not light.

Memory.

Except… not hers.

She stood in the séance room, but it had changed. The table was unbroken, gleaming. The mirror whole. Candles burned steadily in ornate holders shaped like hands. Shadows danced across velvet drapes. It was the same room—and yet not.

A dozen figures stood in a circle, hands clasped.

At the head, Lord Malrick Vexmoor, unmistakable in his dark brocade jacket, his eyes sharp and blazing. Beside him, a woman with long hair flowing down her back.

Isolde.
But younger.
They were chanting.
Vivienne stepped forward—but no one saw her. She wasn't truly there. She was inside a memory, a fragment of time held within the walls.
Isolde's eyes fluttered as she swayed, possessed by something greater. "She is close… the soul returns… but the body is not yet formed…"
Malrick placed a hand on her shoulder. "We anchor her. We bind her name. Through the blood, through the Hollow."
One of the men in the circle faltered. "What if she refuses the gift?"
"She never does," Malrick said. "Not truly. She always comes back. Always finds the way."
Vivienne's pulse thundered.
Isolde lifted her head. Her eyes met Vivienne's—truly saw her.
"It is too early for you, child."
Vivienne froze.
"You broke the circle. The veil is thin and listening."
"I don't understand," Vivienne whispered.
But the scene cracked—like glass under pressure. Faces blurred. The walls shook.
Vivienne stumbled back into darkness—

And slammed into something solid.

Callum.

He caught her before she hit the ground, arms wrapped tightly around her.

The séance room was as it had been—cold, still, and empty.

The mirror, however, now bore a perfect handprint in the center of the glass—smudged as if someone had pressed from the inside.

Vivienne gasped. "They were calling me."

Callum looked pale. "You were gone for almost a minute. You weren't breathing."

She clutched the notebook against her chest.

"I think I saw my great grandparents," she whispered.

Vivienne's knees buckled, and Callum eased her down onto the wooden floor. She was trembling—part cold, part terror, part something else she couldn't name.

He held her face between his hands, voice low but firm. "What happened? You just... went still."

She tried to speak, but the words got caught behind everything she'd just witnessed. It hadn't been a dream. It was real—too textured, too loud, too strange to be imagined.

"I was there," she managed finally. "In this room. But it was different. Newer. There were

people. Malrick, Isolde. A circle. They were…
they were calling something into the world. A
soul."

Callum's brows drew together. "A
summoning?"

"No. A return." Her gaze flicked to the
mirror. "They said she always comes back."

Callum followed her eyes to the glass. The
smudged handprint had begun to fade, as if
being absorbed back into the silver. "Who's
she?"

Vivienne's voice cracked. "Me. I think they
meant me."

He was silent for a long moment, only the
tick of the broken wall sconce filling the air.

Then, "You've said before—about the
house feeling familiar. Like it remembers
you."

She nodded slowly. "What if I don't just
carry their blood? What if I've been them? Or
with them, somehow? What if this place is a
tether?"

A soft, mournful creak ran along the walls,
as if the house itself was listening.

Callum stood and walked to the edge of the
room, brushing his hand along the seam
where the mirror met the paneling. He
stopped, then pressed his fingers against the
faintest of gaps.

The wall gave way with a sigh.

A narrow passage, lined with soot-darkened stone, opened behind the mirror.

Vivienne rose slowly. The air pouring out of the tunnel was damp and bitter, like crushed leaves and memory.

She glanced back. The circle table. The extinguished candles. The echo of Malrick's voice in her mind.

This room wasn't just a space. It was a recording.

A trapdoor of time.

Callum turned to her, waiting for a decision.

Vivienne took a breath, closed the notebook, and tucked it under her arm.

"Let's get out of here."

They stepped through the mirror's frame and into the passage, the wall sliding closed behind them with a sound like breath being held.

For a moment, neither of them spoke. The narrow tunnel twisted ahead, lit only by the glow of Vivienne's flashlight and the occasional flicker of strange symbols etched into the stone—sigils she recognized from Dominic's notebook. Some glowed faintly as they passed.

"Vivienne," Callum said, touching her back gently, "What if this house didn't just call you here to remember? What if it needs you to finish something?"

She stopped walking. The question hung heavy in the air.

"Then I need to know what was started," she whispered. "Before it swallows me whole."

They emerged at the far end of the mirrored library—through a panel hidden between two tall bookcases.

As the hidden door clicked shut behind them, a low chime rang through the Hollow.

3:03 a.m.

# Chapter 37

Vivienne didn't sleep.

Even after escaping the séance room, even after the walls settled and the mirrors stopped whispering, her mind stayed sharp—buzzing with fragments of names, symbols, and that one phrase that echoed louder than the rest:

*She always comes back.*

At sunrise, she found Adele already in the kitchen, nursing a cold cup of coffee, the old family Bible opened on the table—not for devotion, but study. A candle flickered beside it, casting soft light across worn pages.

Vivienne dropped the notebook on the table with a quiet thud.

Adele looked up, eyes tired but clear.

"You went into the séance room, didn't you?"

Vivienne nodded.

"It showed me something," she said. "Not just about Isolde. About the house. About me." She paused. "And I think about you too."

Adele didn't flinch. "I've always known there was more. I just… never knew where to look."

"I saw Malrick," Vivienne continued. "And Isolde. They were performing a ritual. Something to do with returning—not summoning. I think… I think I've been here before."

The silence between them thickened.

Then Vivienne leaned forward. "Mom, who built Ashcroft Hollow?"

Adele blinked, caught off guard. "Malrick, I assumed. That's what the records always said. He expanded the estate after marrying Isolde—"

"But did he build it? Or inherit it? Or… take it?"

Vivienne's voice had a new edge—sharp, searching.

"I need to see the original deed. If it still exists."

Adele hesitated, then rose slowly. "There's a drawer in Malrick's study I've never been able to open. It's locked tight. The key's been missing for generations."

Vivienne stood too. "Then let's pick the lock."

The study was cloaked in dust and disuse. Sunlight filtered through stained glass, washing the room in muted ruby and gold. Portraits of men—Ashcroft sons—stared down from the walls, all with strangely identical eyes.

Vivienne crossed to the desk. The lower drawer on the left was different—heavier, reinforced. She knelt and pressed her fingers around the seam. The sigil carved into its face looked familiar—almost identical to the one etched into the séance room floor.

Callum's words from days before echoed in her memory: *"Sometimes it's not about forcing something open. It's about knowing what it's protecting."*

She placed her palm flat against the sigil and whispered, "I need to remember."

The lock clicked.

Inside was a velvet-lined box, wrapped in oilskin.

Vivienne lifted it out gently. A brittle scroll sat inside—a deed, yellowed with age, wax seal unbroken.

She unrolled it carefully, heart pounding.
ASHCROFT HOLLOW ESTATE – TRANSFER OF OWNERSHIP
Year of our Lord 1947
Previous Holder: Seraphina Vexley

To: Lord Malrick Vexmoor

Vivienne's fingers tightened.

"Mom," she whispered, holding it up. "This wasn't his to begin with."

Adele stepped closer, reading the name again. "Seraphina…"

"Do you know her?"

"No. But the name's in the family tree— way back, barely legible."

Vivienne's eyes scanned the fine print— Latin phrases, a symbol stamped beneath the seal. It wasn't just a legal deed.

It was a pact.

"Do you see this?" Vivienne pointed. "This isn't a notary's seal. It's a sigil—same one from Dominic's notebook. Same one on the séance room door. Same one that glows in the tunnels."

Adele's breath caught. "A secret order?"

"Or a covenant," Vivienne said. "Malrick didn't buy the Hollow. He took something sacred. From Seraphina. From all of the women."

The air shimmered.

And suddenly Vivienne knew: this wasn't just a home passed down through generations.

It was a trap.

For the gifted.

For the ones who remembered.

For her.

# Chapter 38

The name *Seraphina Vexley* wouldn't let go.

It clung to Vivienne's thoughts like perfume on a silk sleeve—faint but haunting, familiar in a way that made her skin prickle.

Back in the mirrored library, Vivienne sat surrounded by opened books, crumbling ledgers, and half-translated Latin dictionaries. She had pulled the ancestral journal from its locked cabinet, retrieved Malrick's correspondence.

The seal on the original deed and Dominic's symbols—they were identical.

Three interlocking crescents around a single starburst.

A glyph older than anything Malrick had ever drawn.

Vivienne flipped through Dominic's notebook, breath catching at the margins— filled with drawings he had obsessively copied and re-copied. Some were simple: loops, lines, crosses. But others… others pulsed with meaning. One sketch in particular caught her eye.

Nine circles surrounding a central flame.

Each marked with a different symbol.

Each paired with a name she didn't recognize—except one.

Seraphina.

Vivienne traced the flame at the center. Below it, Dominic had scrawled:

*"We are vessels. Carriers. The Nine must return before the Hollow can sleep."*

A sudden gust of wind hissed across the floor. One of the Latin tomes she'd left open fluttered and fell shut.

Vivienne startled, then frowned.

The room had grown colder.

She pulled the deed closer again, now looking with different eyes. Seraphina Vexley had signed it in blood—not ink. Below her signature was a short line in Latin, nearly illegible:

*Custodes lucis… novem ignis…*

*Guardians of the Light. Keepers of the Nine Flames.*

She stood abruptly, went to the old family tree on the wall—and realized something was wrong.

Seraphina's name wasn't there.

Not as a wife. Not as a daughter. Not as anyone.

And yet she had owned the Hollow.

"Why erase her?" Vivienne murmured. "What was Malrick hiding?"

She opened Dominic's notebook again. Several pages had been paperclipped together. She slid the clip off and found a map—not of the house, but of the land beneath it. Tunnels. Symbols. What looked like a circle with nine chambers.

Dominic had written only two words beside it:

Seraphina's Sanctum.

Vivienne's chest tightened.

*What if Seraphina wasn't just the owner of Ashcroft Hollow—what if she was the origin of the Nine?*

*What if Malrick hadn't created the legacy—but stolen it?*

Vivienne closed the notebook slowly, her fingers trembling around the edges. The Hollow's silence wasn't empty—it felt watchful, like breath held just behind the walls.

She pressed a hand to the deed again, eyes locked on the blood-written name: Seraphina Vexley.

*Why was she erased?*

The question looped through her thoughts as she carried both the notebook and deed into the study. Adele was already there, curled in one of the old velvet chairs with a blanket around her shoulders and tea gone cold beside her.

"I think Dominic knew," Vivienne said, laying the documents down. "About Seraphina. About the Nine. About everything."

Adele looked up, startled. "What do you mean?"

Vivienne opened the deed and pointed to the seal. Then she opened Dominic's notebook to the same symbol.

"I think this house was built on something older. Something sacred. And Seraphina… she wasn't just a relative. She was the founder. The first. And Malrick… may have taken it from her."

Adele paled. "Taken?"

"Look at this." Vivienne turned to the map—the Nine-chambered circle beneath the house. "He built Ashcroft Hollow over it. Maybe to preserve it. Maybe to possess it."

Adele traced the symbol with a finger. "Your father used to dream about tunnels. He'd wake up talking about fire beneath the roots. I thought he was imagining things, but…"

Vivienne nodded. "He wasn't. And the gifts—they aren't bound to the Ashcrofts.

They're older. Malrick didn't create the Nine. He only… inherited them. Or stole them."

Adele sat back, breath shaky. "Then why was Seraphina erased from the family records?"

"Because someone didn't want us to remember her. Or her power. Or the fact that maybe, just maybe…" Vivienne hesitated. "This place doesn't belong to the Ashcrofts at all."

A log shifted in the hearth, sending sparks up the flue.

They both jumped.

Vivienne gathered the documents and turned toward the fireplace mantle, where old portraits still hung. Malrick. Isolde. Genevieve. None smiled. All of them seemed to stare at her now with different intent.

A soft knock at the doorway pulled her back.

Callum stood there, hesitant.

"I heard voices," he said. "Didn't mean to intrude."

"You're not," Vivienne said, a little too quickly.

He stepped inside, glancing at the notebook in her hand. "Is that his? Dominic's?"

Vivienne nodded and passed it to him. "Look at the seal. Same as the one on the deed. And the symbols—some of them match the ones carved into the Music Room window."

Callum's brow furrowed. "I saw this one," he said, pointing, "Etched into a beam in the stables. Hidden behind an old saddle."

Adele inhaled sharply. "He marked the land."

Vivienne felt her heartbeat shift. "Then it's not just in the house. The Hollow spreads wider."

The room pulsed with silence.

Then Callum asked, "Have you ever considered… maybe the Hollow isn't cursed or haunted. Maybe it's guarding something. Or someone."

Vivienne turned to face him fully. "Then we need to find out who."

Their eyes held for a long, quiet moment—something unspoken stretching between them.

Adele rose slowly. "I'll leave you two to this," she said, her voice soft. "But Vivienne—be careful. Every time we ask for truth here, something answers."

Vivienne nodded, watching her mother disappear down the hall.

She turned back to Callum, who hadn't moved.

"Do you believe it?" she asked. "About the Nine? About Seraphina?"

"I believe this house doesn't play by ordinary rules," he said quietly.

And in the stillness that followed, the flames in the hearth flared—just once—as if stirred by breath.

# Chapter 39

The fire had gone out hours ago, but Vivienne sat in the library still, the deed on her lap like it was warm to the touch. It wasn't—but something about it was. It hummed with an energy she didn't recognize, but couldn't deny. The seal etched into the parchment matched the one Dominic used to sketch—looping, ancient lines shaped like an infinity knot wrapped in thorns.

He hadn't just imagined them.

Her thumb brushed the ink again. He knew. Somehow, he'd known before her. Before Adele. Before any of them were ready to believe.

"Why didn't I ask more questions?" she whispered aloud. "Why didn't I look closer when he—"

A sound pulled her out of her thoughts.

Not from the hallway. From inside the wall.

A faint, dragging scrape. Like a fingertip brushing along wood.

Vivienne stood, blood draining from her face. The room was still dark except for a low wash of moonlight, and yet… the air had thickened. Time bent, pressing in on her.

She stepped back. The bookshelf behind her—one of the mirrored ones—fogged at its center.

A handprint bloomed there.

Fresh.

She didn't scream. She couldn't. Her body froze, rooted. Her breath caught in her chest like something ancient had wrapped fingers around her lungs.

And then—

The mirror *shimmered*. Not cracked, not broken—but like water.

Vivienne blinked.

Her reflection stared back.

But it *wasn't her*.

The woman in the glass looked older, but still in her thirties—same eyes, same mouth— but dressed in pale robes that shimmered like candlelight. Her hair was braided down one side. Her fingers were stained with ink.

Vivienne tried to move. Couldn't.

Then the reflection *spoke*.

"You are not the first to remember."

The voice wasn't her own. It was hers—but distant. Like a future echo.

"You are the doorway, Vivienne."

Vivienne's pulse raced. "What… what does that mean?"

But the reflection only stepped backward, disappearing into the mirrored world.

A voice—*his voice*—rose behind her like smoke curling through time.

"I left pieces in the walls," Dominic said, soft and close. "In the stones. In the orchard. You were always meant to find me."

She turned.

No one was there.

And yet—her hand tingled again. That same phantom pressure from the séance room.

Something brushed her cheek. Not air. Not breeze.

A memory.

And then everything shifted.

The library dissolved.

The orchard was younger, its branches supple and silvered with moonlight. The air smelled of green wood and night-blooming jasmine. She—Genevieve—stood barefoot in a thin white nightgown, her breath rising in pale clouds.

Dominic waited across from her, shirt open at the collar, sleeves rolled, his eyes dark as the spaces between stars.

"You have to forget me," he said, the words thick with strain.

She shook her head, the movement small but fierce. "I won't. I can't."

"If you remember too soon, it unravels. Everything. We'll be back where we started."

"I don't care—"

"You will," he cut in, voice low and certain. "The Hollow takes its price. Every time. Every life."

He closed the distance, his hand warm against her cheek. "But when the moment comes, Vivienne… I'll find you. I always will."

Her lips parted—

And the world split open with a scream. Long, raw, threaded with grief so deep it seemed to shake the trees.

Vivienne gasped awake from the dream.

She was on the floor of the library, heart pounding so hard it echoed in her ears. The deed lay open beside her, the seal still gleaming in the moonlight.

She scrambled up, chest tight.

In the mirror, her reflection stared back, pale and shaken—but normal.

Only one thing was different.

Tucked into the corner of the mirror frame, just behind the glass, was a folded page she *knew* hadn't been there before.

Vivienne reached for it, hands trembling.

It was a page from Dominic's notebook.

Drawn in his careful hand: the seal from the deed.

And beneath it, a single sentence scrawled in faded ink:

*"The Nine began long before us. And they're not finished yet."*

# Chapter 40

The next morning broke heavy with mist.

Vivienne stood at the old desk in the mirrored library, the deed unrolled beneath her fingers. The seal had faded overnight—its ink now dull, as if retreating back into the paper. But the name on the document remained untouched. Written in thick, slanted script:

Seraphina Vexley.

Not Lord Malrick Vexmoor.

Vivienne traced the letters again. Seraphina. A name that echoed in her dreams more than once—always whispered, always distant.

She turned the document over. A faint watermark marked the lower edge, nearly invisible. A symbol that matched the one Dominic had drawn in dozens of variations: a circle of thorns surrounding a single flame.

The seal of The Nine.

She barely had time to process the shock when the air around her shifted again.

Not cold. Not warm.

Just different. Like someone had stepped into the room.

She didn't turn.

"I felt you last night," she said quietly.

The silence answered like breath against her neck.

Vivienne closed her eyes. "Are you... Dominic?"

A pause.

Then a whisper—not from behind her, not from her own mind, but from somewhere in between.

"I'm not what I was."

Vivienne opened her eyes. The mirror in front of her didn't show her reflection this time. It showed him.

Dominic stood in the orchard again, just like in the memory. But this time he was older. Weathered. His shirt was torn at the collar, his boots muddy. His eyes burned like something ancient lived behind them.

"You died," she said.

He tilted his head. "I left."

"But you're here."

"I never left the Hollow. Not really."

"Then what are you?"

His image flickered in the mirror, like a flame in wind. "Bound. By choice. For you."

Vivienne's chest tightened.

"I didn't understand before," she whispered.

"I didn't want you to," he replied. "Not until you were ready."

He looked down.

"The Hollow was Seraphina's before it was ever Malrick's. She built the circle. Drew the lines. The Nine followed her. Worshipped her. Or feared her. Or both."

"Was she one of them?" Vivienne asked.

"She *was* them."

A wind howled suddenly, not outside—but from the walls. Books fluttered. The mirror cracked—not shattered, but enough to ripple the image of Dominic like stone dropped in water.

"She's waking," he said, voice distorted. "The land remembers her. The house remembers. And through you… she will too."

Vivienne stepped closer. "What do I do?"

Dominic's eyes softened, just for a moment.

"Remember who you were before all of this."

The mirror *exploded* into silver dust.

Vivienne fell back, covering her face.

When she opened her eyes again, the library was empty.

No wind. No voice.

Just the page from Dominic's notebook, still clutched in her hand. A new line had been scrawled beneath last night's.

*"She waits in the roots of the Hollow. And the blood remembers the path."*

The page from Dominic's notebook felt warm in her hand, as though inked with something alive.

Vivienne returned to the kitchen table, the deed rolled up beside her, the torn page spread between her and her mother. Callum leaned against the counter, arms crossed, but his eyes never left Vivienne's face.

Adele read the notebook entry aloud, voice barely above a whisper.

"She waits in the roots of the Hollow. And the blood remembers the path."

A pause.

Then Adele looked up. "You're sure it was Dominic?"

Vivienne nodded. "He didn't appear. Not exactly. It was a mirror—his reflection. But it was him. Older. Different. Bound here, somehow."

Callum spoke finally. "Bound to the Hollow? Or to you?"

Vivienne's stomach flipped. She hadn't let herself ask that.

"I don't know," she murmured. "But he said the Hollow was never Malrick's. It was Seraphina's."

Adele straightened. "That name… Seraphina Vexley. I've seen it before."

"Where?"

"In the church records. Ages ago, when I was researching our ancestry for the genealogical society. Vexley was a name tied to the early settlers—maybe even before Ashcroft's time."

Vivienne's heart kicked.

"I want to find out who she was. Why she built this place. Why she was erased."

Callum stepped closer. "Then we go where names last longer than memories."

"Archives?" Vivienne asked.

He nodded. "Town hall first. Then the chapel. If Seraphina Vexley was significant, there's a trail."

—

That afternoon, they sat in the dusty records room at the back of the old municipal hall. Boxes were stacked high, many never digitized. Adele rifled through marriage records while Callum pulled deeds from the early land survey.

Vivienne worked from the only candle-lit corner of the room—scanning old maps and tax registries.

And then she found it.

A map dated 1812. The Hollow wasn't called Ashcroft Hollow then.

It was Ashcroft Hall.

Vivienne stared at the curled script across the central acreage. In the margin, faint but legible, a note scribbled in the same looping hand:

"Land granted to S. Vexley in perpetuity, per order of the Nine."

Her breath caught.

The Nine. They weren't just a myth. They'd been real. A council? A secret society?

She ran her fingers along the ink—and it *flashed* cold beneath her skin.

The floor blurred beneath her. The scent of parchment turned to crushed lavender and soot.

Vivienne blinked—and the room was gone.

—

She stood in a high-vaulted parlor. Candlelight flickered across gilded mirrors. And in the center—

A woman in silver robes.

Hair the color of coal. Eyes dark as ravens. She turned toward Vivienne.

"Welcome back," she said softly. "You were always meant to return."

Vivienne tried to speak but couldn't. Her throat held silence.

"Magic, once rooted, does not forget. You knew the rites. The gates. The cost."

The woman reached out a hand—and Vivienne felt herself walking forward, even without willing it.

"He buried me under his name," the woman whispered. "But blood remembers truth. And now, so do you."

Suddenly, the parlor cracked apart like glass. Light split the floor.

Vivienne fell.

And landed hard—back in the records room, Callum catching her before she hit the ground.

"Vivienne!" he said sharply. "What happened?"

Her hand trembled as she pressed the map to her chest.

"I saw her," she whispered. "Seraphina. She… she knows who I am."

Callum exchanged a glance with Adele, who was pale and silent.

Vivienne looked between them both.

"We need to find out why Seraphina was erased. And what she gave to this land.

Because it wasn't Malrick who made this place
sacred."

She held up the map.

"It was her."

# Chapter 41

The map and deed were tucked away in Vivienne's satchel, the flame of urgency dimmed now to a steady burn beneath her skin.

Adele had gone upstairs to lie down—claiming a headache, though Vivienne suspected her mother needed a moment to process it all. The journals. The Hollow's true owner. Seraphina Vexley.

Vivienne found herself back outside, beneath the orchard trees, the late sun casting golden ribbons through the leaves. She didn't expect Callum to follow.

But he did.

"I thought you might want quiet," he said, stepping beside her with two mugs of tea.

Vivienne accepted hers with a nod. "Quiet's hard to come by in this place."

They stood together for a while, the only sound the occasional rustle of wind through the branches.

"You scared me earlier," Callum said, voice low. "When you fell."

Vivienne sipped. "It wasn't like the other visions. This one… it *pulled* me."

"Into her?"

She nodded. "Seraphina. She called me back. Like I belonged to the Hollow. To her."

Callum looked away, jaw working. "You said Dominic appeared too."

"His reflection. He didn't look like himself, not exactly. But he *felt* the same." She paused. "You believe me, don't you?"

He turned to her then—really looked at her. "Vivienne, this place has changed everything I thought I knew about life and death. About time. I don't just believe you. I'd follow you straight into the séance room again if that's where it led."

That surprised her more than it should have.

She searched his face. "Why?"

He gave a quiet laugh. "Because… this place chose you. And I think—maybe I did too."

Vivienne's breath caught.

Callum stepped closer, slow and deliberate. "When I came here, I was trying to outrun ghosts. I thought helping you settle the estate would be a clean distraction. But nothing about this place is clean. Or easy."

She gave a shaky smile. "No, it really isn't."

He lifted a hand, brushing a strand of hair behind her ear. "But then I met you. And for all the twisted roots and haunted rooms, Vivienne… you make it feel like home's not such a bad thing to want again."

Her heart skittered. She hadn't expected that. Hadn't expected him.

Vivienne set down her mug and looked up at him—eyes searching.

"This place breaks things open," she whispered. "What if it breaks us?"

Callum cupped her face, thumb grazing her cheek. "Then we rebuild. Together."

And before she could second-guess it, Vivienne leaned into him.

The kiss was slow, sure—a tether between storm and silence. It wasn't fireworks or a desperate grasp. It was grounding. Like finding something familiar in the center of the unknown.

When they finally parted, forehead to forehead, the wind stilled around them.

Vivienne exhaled.

"Tomorrow," she said, voice soft, "We find out who Seraphina really was."

Callum nodded, fingers still laced in hers.

"And tonight," he murmured, "We let the house rest."

They walked back toward the Hollow, not speaking—because nothing needed to be said. For once, the walls didn't creak. The orchard didn't whisper. The house seemed to honor the stillness they carried between them.

But above them, behind the high turret, a single window flickered with light. The mirror room. Watching.

Waiting.

# Chapter 42

The knock came just past dawn.

Vivienne was still half-asleep, curled on the velvet settee in the mirrored library with Callum's jacket draped over her like a shield. A fire had long since turned to ash in the grate, and the faint smell of applewood lingered.

She blinked, confused.

The knock came again—steady. Real.

Callum stirred beside her. "Did you hear?"

Another knock. This time from the front door.

They bolted upright.

Vivienne reached the threshold first, heart pounding, every dream from the séance room flashing like lightning in her chest.

She opened the door.

And there he stood.

Dominic.

Older now. A few silver streaks in his dark hair. But his eyes—those familiar, storm-hued eyes—were the same. Haunted. Human.

Vivienne's breath froze.

"Hello, pumpkin," he said quietly, voice thick. "You look just like her."

She didn't realize she'd stepped back until Callum's hand found hers.

Adele appeared at the top of the stairs, one hand on the banister, the other pressed to her mouth. "Dominic?"

"I told you I'd come back," he said. "I just didn't know when."

Vivienne's thoughts raced. "How?"

He stepped inside, slowly, like he remembered the house's pulse and was trying to match it again.

"I don't know exactly," he said, eyes on her. "I don't remember the years. Not in order. But something pulled me back… after you opened the mirror."

Vivienne blinked. "You were trapped in the séance room?"

He hesitated. "I think… part of me was."

Adele moved down the steps, cautious. "You vanished."

Dominic looked at her, eyes soft. "I know. But I wasn't really gone. Just… somewhere else. With her."

"Her?" Vivienne asked.

He nodded slowly. "Seraphina."

Vivienne felt the name tighten in her throat. "You knew her?"

"I saw her," Dominic said, reaching into his coat. "And she showed me this."

He handed Vivienne a folded page—the same one she had seen in the mirror room, the symbols once etched into air now solid in ink. In the center: the same sigil from the deed. A spiral nested inside a triangle, surrounded by seven stars.

Adele paled. "That's the seal from the altar in the séance room."

Vivienne opened the page, and her hands tingled.

"It's a map," she whispered. "A spiritual one. The points… they match the layout of the estate."

Dominic nodded. "Seraphina was the first. The Hollow was hers. Long before Malrick Vexmoor. She bound the land with ritual, with blood and intention. Malrick took it. Stole her work and buried her name."

Vivienne's voice trembled. "So Seraphina is… real?"

"She was more than real," Dominic said. "She was a Guardian. Of something older than any of us. And now—" he paused, glancing between Adele and then to Vivienne "—it's passing to you."

Vivienne swallowed, pulse racing. "Why me?"

Dominic looked at her like it was obvious. "Because Seraphina wasn't just a stranger. She's your blood. And I think… you're her echo."

Silence settled like fog.

Callum stepped forward, gaze unreadable. "What does that mean—'her echo'?"

Dominic exhaled. "It means Vivienne is the next in the line of Keepers. The Hollow didn't just call her back. It created her for this moment."

Vivienne's knees nearly buckled. Callum caught her, steady as ever.

"I need proof," she whispered. "I need to see who she really was."

Dominic nodded. "Then come with me."

He turned toward the east wing—toward the door hidden behind the old clock tower. "There's another room," he said. "One no one's opened since Seraphina's death."

Adele's voice caught. "What room?"

Dominic met her eyes. "The Root Cellar. But it's not for food. It's for memory."

Vivienne tightened her grip on Callum's hand.

They followed Dominic into the shadows, through a door that wasn't there yesterday, and downstairs carved not of stone—but of salt and ash.

The stairwell narrowed the farther they descended, the walls no longer the familiar stone of the Hollow, but something older. Rougher. Salt-crusted and veined with quartz that shimmered faintly in the dark.

Dominic held a lantern, its flame catching strange shapes in the walls—runes maybe, or simply erosion. Vivienne wasn't sure. But the air grew heavier with every step, as if they were sinking not just through the earth but through time itself.

"Why salt?" Callum asked under his breath, his hand steady on Vivienne's back.

"Preservation," Dominic said without turning. "Protection. The old ways used salt to bind energy. What Seraphina sealed here… she didn't want disturbed. Not easily."

Adele gripped the railing, her face pale in the flickering light. "How far down does this go?"

"We're almost there."

The last step opened onto a circular cavern, larger than Vivienne expected. The ceiling arched high above them, carved into a domed vault. Strange symbols lined the curve of it, glowing softly, as if responding to their presence.

At the center stood an altar—not of marble or wood, but obsidian, polished to a mirror sheen. Resting atop it: a thick, leather-bound book sealed shut with a clasp of tarnished silver. The same spiral sigil was etched into the cover.

Vivienne felt it before she touched it.

A hum beneath her skin. A pulse that echoed in her bones.

"This was hers," Dominic said, reverent. "Seraphina's Grimoire."

Vivienne stepped forward slowly. "Why hasn't anyone found this before?"

"Because the Hollow only opens it when it's ready," Dominic replied. "And only for blood that remembers."

She reached for the clasp. As her fingers brushed the metal, it released with a soft click.

A low vibration filled the air. Dust rose from the earth. The lantern flickered.

Then—nothing.

Vivienne opened the book.

The pages were dense with glyphs and looping script, much of it in Latin or something older. But some sections had sketches—ritual circles, a tree with nine roots, and faces. One face—hers—drawn in charcoal, centuries too early.

Callum peered over her shoulder. "That's you."

"No," Vivienne whispered. "That's Seraphina."

Adele reached out to turn the page. Her hand froze midair.

The page turned itself.

Vivienne's vision blurred.

Then—

She wasn't standing in the cavern anymore.

She stood in a sunlit orchard, barefoot, wearing a long emerald dress embroidered in gold thread. The air smelled of honey and smoke. Bells chimed faintly.

People stood before her in a circle, their faces shadowed. One held a ceremonial dagger. Another, a mirror. Another, a bowl of crimson liquid.

She heard her own voice speak—but it wasn't her.

"I offer this binding of light and shadow. Of seed and ash. Let the Hollow remember who we are."

A flash.

She was underground again, the obsidian altar slick with blood. A man—Malrick

Vexmoor, younger and wild-eyed—stood across from her.

"You took it," Seraphina's voice spat. "The land was never yours."

"It answers to power," Malrick replied coldly. "And you've lost yours."

Then pain—flaring white-hot—and everything collapsed into shadow.

Vivienne gasped and fell to her knees.

Callum caught her, shouting her name. Adele was beside her instantly. Dominic steadied the lantern, eyes dark with knowing.

"You saw her," he said gently.

Vivienne nodded, shaking, tears streaking down her face. "She was me. Or… I was her. I think I watched her die."

"Not just die," Dominic said quietly. "She was *erased*. Malrick stole her legacy, her power, and rewrote the Hollow in his name. That's why the men die here. Why the house forgets the sons. It remembers only what she bound it to."

Adele sat back slowly, her expression haunted, as if the truth was pressing in on her from all sides.

"That's why she kept me close," she said at last, voice low. "Why my mother bound me so I couldn't see the gifts… couldn't be tied to them. She thought she was protecting me."

"She loved you," Dominic said. "You were her everything. But Vivienne…" he turned to her. "You're the *return*. The Hollow woke because it knew you had come home."

Vivienne looked at the altar. "So what now?"

Dominic's voice was steady. "Now, you decide what to do with what was stolen."

# Chapter 43

They emerged from the stairwell. No one spoke. The weight of what they'd uncovered lingered—an invisible thread tethered to their chests.

Adele went ahead in silence, needing solitude.

Dominic lingered at the edge of the hallway, where the light from the turret spilled in soft gold. "The Hollow knows what to do next," he said quietly. "But it will test you, Vivienne. It always tests the ones who awaken it."

Vivienne nodded, her mind still heavy with Seraphina's voice, the echo of power and betrayal that pulsed in the bloodline. When she turned, she found Callum watching her.

Not just watching—seeing her.

"Come with me?" he asked, voice low.

She followed him out to the orchard, where dew still clung to the grass and the air smelled of earth and green things. He led her to the edge of the old stone wall near the stables, where a bench overlooked the mist-shrouded hills.

Neither spoke at first.

Finally, Callum broke the silence. "I saw your face when you came back. Like you'd crossed some line and weren't sure if you made it back whole."

"I'm not sure I did," she said. "Everything's unraveling—and knitting back together in ways I don't understand. I saw her die, Callum. And somehow, I know what she felt. The betrayal. The power. The love she lost."

His jaw flexed, his voice soft. "You're not alone in this."

Vivienne gave a small, humorless laugh. "Sometimes I feel like the Hollow's been grooming me my whole life. As if I was meant to walk back into a past I didn't know I lived."

Callum's hand found hers on the bench. Warm. Steady. "Maybe you were. And maybe you were also meant to have someone waiting when you came back."

She looked at him then—really looked— and something in her chest shifted. A flicker of recognition, deep and ancient, collided with the sharp memory of the truth: they shared blood. Not close, but enough. Enough to make her breath catch.

It was like a key turning in a lock she didn't know she carried, a door swinging open to something both comforting and forbidden.

He leaned in slightly. "I don't know much about reincarnation or haunted houses, Vivienne. But I know what it means to be pulled to someone. To want to protect them—even when I shouldn't."

Her pulse raced. She didn't pull away. And just as his lips were to brush hers—

Footsteps crunched on the gravel path.

They sprang apart, and Adele's voice called, "Vivienne?"

Vivienne exhaled, brushing her hair back. "Yeah. I'm here."

Adele emerged from the hedgerow, a slip of paper in her hand. "You need to see this."

Vivienne stood, heart still racing for more than one reason.

"It's a letter," Adele said. "Hand-delivered while we were outside. From someone claiming to be a historical archivist. Says he has documents relating to *the original founding* of Ashcroft Hollow—long before Malrick."

Vivienne frowned. "Coincidence?"

Callum narrowed his eyes. "No such thing anymore."

Adele handed over the envelope. It was sealed with red wax, the symbol pressed into it one Vivienne now recognized from both

Seraphina's book and Dominic's mirror fragment.

The spiral.

Vivienne opened it. A crisp, expensive card. Just a few lines, written in elegant script:

*Miss Ashcroft,*

*I believe your family's history is far older— and far darker—than you've been told.*

*I request an audience. There are matters that concern us both.*

*—Benedict Vale*

Vivienne read it twice. Then looked up.

"Who the hell is Benedict Vale?"

Callum stepped closer, protective again. "More importantly… what does he want with you?"

Vivienne didn't answer.

But somewhere deep in the walls of the Hollow, the house seemed to hold it's breath.

And wait.

# Chapter 44

The Hollow was quiet when Benedict Vale arrived.

Too quiet.

Vivienne watched from the upper window as a black car crunched slowly up the gravel drive. The man who stepped out wore a tailored charcoal coat, the collar slightly turned as if against an unseen wind. He carried a leather folio and wore gloves, despite the mild air.

Callum stood beside her, arms crossed. "That's not a historian's car."

"He said he was with the Historical Preservation Society," Vivienne murmured.

Callum didn't answer. Just watched as Benedict Vale moved with sharp purpose, every motion too measured to be casual.

Vivienne met him at the door, Callum at her side like a silent sentinel.

"Miss Ashcroft," Benedict said with a slight bow. His voice was velvet-smooth, almost old-fashioned. "Thank you for granting me an audience."

She was getting used to being called Miss Ashcroft. "You said you had information about the Hollow."

"I do," he replied, eyes drifting past her toward the grand hallway. "But information is only as useful as the questions being asked. May we speak in private?"

Vivienne hesitated.

Callum didn't. "Anything you have to say, you can say in front of both of us."

Benedict's eyes flicked toward him, and something like a smirk ghosted across his face. "Of course."

They moved into the mirrored library. The sunlight caught on the glass and reflections, turning the room into a labyrinth of selves. Benedict walked the room slowly, fingers trailing the edge of an antique table.

"Do you know the name Seraphina Vexley?" he asked.

Vivienne's pulse quickened. "I do."

He turned, satisfied. "Then you know she was the original owner of this land. Before Lord Malrick Vexmoor. Before the estate was called Ashcroft Hollow."

"She was gifted," Vivienne said carefully. "The journals say she saw between worlds."

Benedict nodded. "She didn't just see. She *bound* them."

He pulled a page from his folio—a fragile parchment with a symbol Vivienne recognized. The spiral, wrapped in serpentine script.

"This was her mark," he continued. "It appears in societies across Europe. The Nine. The Keepers. The Order of the Hollow. All branches of the same root. She was the beginning… and in some ways, the curse."

"What curse?" Callum asked.

"She opened something that was never meant to be opened."

Vivienne stepped closer. "So the Hollow… it's not just haunted. It's *consecrated*."

"To something older than God," Benedict said quietly.

Vivienne swallowed. "And what do you want from me?"

"I want you to understand what you are." He placed the folio down. "You're not just an Ashcroft heir. You're Seraphina's blood. A direct descendant. And this house… it's *alive* because of you."

The silence stretched.

Callum spoke first. "Why now? Why are you here *now*?"

Benedict studied Vivienne for a moment. "Because the seals are weakening. The Mirror Room has reopened. And once all three seals are broken…"

He didn't finish the sentence. He didn't have to.

Vivienne felt it like a thread tightening in her chest.

"Where are the other seals?" she asked.

"Lost," he said. "Or hidden in plain sight. You'll know when it's time."

And then he turned toward the door. "You may find what you need in the town archives. Seraphina left a final letter, never delivered. They wouldn't understand her. But perhaps… you will."

And just like that, he was gone.

Later that afternoon, Vivienne drove into town with Callum beside her, the Hollow shrinking in the rearview mirror.

"You okay?" he asked quietly.

Vivienne nodded, fingers tightening on the steering wheel. "He knew too much."

Callum stared out the window. "He wasn't lying. That part scares me more."

They parked outside the old records hall, the scent of paper and dust thick as they entered. Vivienne moved with purpose— through deeds and death records, birth registries and court transcripts—until she found it.

A fragile, yellowed envelope.

To the One Who Follows

Inside: a letter. Written in looping script, signed by Seraphina.

*If you are reading this, it means I failed—or that I succeeded in a way I could never control.*

*There are three seals that bind what lies beneath. One blood. One mirror. One word.*

*I gave the house my name so it would remember me. But it forgets, over time. Just like people do.*

*The house will test you. But if you are mine, you will remember what I could not.*

*And then, perhaps, we may meet again.*

Vivienne looked up from the letter, breath shallow.

And somewhere behind the rows of dusty tomes, a faint shimmer moved in the air—like a ghost caught between pages.

# Chapter 45

As twilight begun its slow descent, casting long shadows across the orchard and bleeding gold through the towering windows, Dominic walked through the doorway.

He looked more alive than he had in Vivienne's dreams—hair damp from a recent shower, sleeves rolled to his forearms, but still carrying that flicker of something… otherworldly. As if the Hollow had changed him, brought him back not untouched, but marked.

"You found something," he said, even before Vivienne could speak.

She handed him the letter from Seraphina.

Adele appeared behind him, eyes wide as she read over his shoulder. "This… this matches the writing in the oldest pages of Isolde's journal."

"Three seals," Dominic murmured. "One blood. One mirror. One word."

"The Mirror Room is open," Vivienne said, her voice low. "And I think the blood seal might've been the ritual Seraphina hinted at in her early writings… the sacrifice of memory. Or identity."

Callum frowned. "So… we're looking for the *word* now?"

"No," Dominic said slowly. "We're looking for the *second seal*. The mirror was only the key to the séance room. That room was the first veil. The second will be harder."

They stood in the entry hall—the Hollow watching them.

Vivienne turned toward the study. "There's one place we haven't searched. Malrick's study. It was always locked. But after what we found to be true in the séance room… I think it's ready to be opened."

The group moved as one. The heavy door creaked open easily now, as though the house had finally relented.

Inside, the study smelled of old leather and dried ink. Books lined every wall, but it was the desk that drew Vivienne forward.

Dominic moved to the fireplace, eyes scanning the stones. "He wrote here. He watched the orchard from this window. But he also hid things."

Callum examined the bookcases, tapping gently for hollow sounds.

Vivienne opened the desk drawers carefully. Letters. Unsent correspondence. Scraps of strange equations that looked more like alchemical formulas than math.

Then her hand caught on a false bottom.

She pried it up.

A leather-bound book. Smaller than the others. Bound in black with a seal on the cover—a trifold spiral with a serpent winding through it. The same sigil that had appeared in Seraphina's notes.

Vivienne opened it. Inside, a single line was written across the first page:

*"Only memory can open the door below."*

Dominic drew in a sharp breath. "That's the second seal."

Adele frowned. "But what door?"

Callum turned from the bookcase. "There's something behind this wall."

Vivienne and Dominic joined him. Together, they pushed the tall shelf aside. Dust and silence greeted them—but behind it, a faint seam was visible in the wall. Almost like...

"A door," Vivienne whispered.

Dominic pressed the spiral seal to the wood.

Nothing happened.

Vivienne stepped forward. "It said… only memory can open it."

She took a breath, then whispered aloud: "I remember her eyes. Seraphina's. They were my eyes. In the mirror."

The wood pulsed faintly beneath her palm.

A line of light appeared down the center.

Slowly, the door creaked inward, revealing a narrow stone stairwell descending into darkness.

"Should we?" Callum asked, brow furrowed.

Vivienne didn't hesitate. "We're already inside the story. We need to see how it ends."

They descended into the dark with only a lantern in Dominic's hand and the thrum of energy thickening with each step.

The air grew colder.

Then… a landing. A circular room carved from bedrock. At its center: a stone altar. And along the walls—murals. Symbols. Names.

Dominic stepped forward, brushing moss from three names carved into the wall.

Seraphina Vexley. Isolde Ashcroft. Vivienne Ashcroft.

"They knew," he whispered. "They always knew it would come to you."

"But why me?" Vivienne murmured.

Adele touched her shoulder. "Because you remember. Even when the others forgot."

Vivienne stepped to the altar. On its surface was a groove—spiral shaped, and at the center, a small circular indentation.

Dominic drew a folded paper from his coat—the page from his notebook that had appeared in the Mirror Room.

He placed it in the groove.

The stone altar flared with soft golden light. The spiral filled, glowing as though lit from within.

A voice—feminine, echoing—rose from the walls, not quite sound, not quite thought.

*"Two seals broken. One remains. Speak the word, and the Hollow shall open."*

The light faded.

Silence.

Dominic stared at the altar. "It's waiting for the last of us to remember the word that binds it all together."

They stood together in the silence of the earth, breath slow, hearts thudding.

Above them, the Hollow shifted again.

And for the first time, Vivienne wondered not what lay *beneath* the house—but what might be trying to rise *through* it.

# Chapter 46

The storm had finally passed, but the Hollow remained quiet, blanketed in a hush that felt deeper than sleep. Only the fire crackled in the hearth, casting golden shadows across the worn rugs and aged portraits in the drawing room.

Adele sat curled on the settee, knees tucked under her, a wool shawl draped over her shoulders. Her gaze lingered on the flames, but her thoughts were clearly elsewhere—years away.

Dominic entered quietly, a tumbler of whiskey in one hand. He hesitated for a moment, watching her in the firelight. She hadn't heard him yet.

"You still sit like that," he said softly. "Like you're listening to something the rest of us can't hear."

Adele turned, startled—but then softened as she saw him. "Dominic."

He handed her the glass. Their fingers brushed, and for a heartbeat, neither of them moved.

"I never thought I'd see you again," she said, voice low. "Not like this. Not… real."

"I wasn't sure I'd find my way back either," he admitted. "But something—someone—pulled me. Maybe it was you, maybe our daughter."

Adele exhaled a shaky breath, the emotion catching her by surprise. "Vivienne thought I was holding onto a ghost. Maybe I was."

"She's done well because of you," Dominic said, taking the seat beside her, his voice wrapped in warmth and admiration. "Smart. Brave. Stubborn as hell." He gave a crooked smile. "Definitely my daughter."

Adele laughed, and the sound was brighter than anything the Hollow had heard in days.

"She's more like you than you know," he continued. "And you… you've been the anchor since you came back. You've steadied her. Helped her see what was worth holding onto. And somehow, you kept me alive in here—" he touched a hand to his chest, "—even when I was gone."

Her eyes welled, but she blinked them clear. "Memory is a funny thing. Some days it felt like I was cursed."

Dominic shifted closer. His hand moved without thought to the small of her back—familiar, reverent, magnetic.

"I missed you every damn day," he said.

Adele's breath caught as she turned to him fully. "You vanished."

"I didn't want to," he said. "The Hollow… it took something from me. From us. But I never stopped loving you."

His lips found hers.

The kiss was not tentative. It was long-forbidden and full of hunger—of years lost and aching remembered. Her hands gripped his shoulders, drawing him closer, grounding herself in the reality of him—warm, solid, alive.

The fire roared as if echoing the moment.

And for a time, the weight of decades, of secrets, of silence, slipped away.

Just the two of them, rediscovering what the Hollow had once promised—what it had nearly buried.

Love, still burning.

# Chapter 47

Vivienne stood in the mirrored library, light from a single lamp flickering across the glass-paneled walls. Her fingers trailed the edge of the original and newly revealed deed again—the one that bore the name Seraphina Vexley, not Malrick Vexmoor.

But something else had started gnawing at her.

None of the portraits in the hallway depicted Ashcroft men past Malrick. No records of their lives. No journal entries from sons, brothers, or uncles. Just names scratched faintly in family bibles, never spoken aloud.

Adele entered the library quietly, Dominic behind her. They had the ease of new warmth between them, but both looked unsettled.

"I've been thinking," Vivienne began, turning toward them. "Why are the men always forgotten? The family tree barely remembers them. Isolde's journal says they're 'watchers'—that they don't belong. What does that mean?"

Adele exhaled, brow furrowed. "It's true. Even as a girl, I remember my father saying that Ashcroft men rarely made it past middle age. They disappeared, or faded. Like the house never let them root."

Dominic gave a short, humorless laugh. "Maybe I'm proof—another name that slips out of the family's memory until there's nothing left but a shadow in the margins. First you're in the photographs, then you're not. First they tell stories about you, then they tell them as if you were someone else. Eventually, you're just… gone."

"No," Vivienne said firmly. "You came back. That has to mean something."

She stepped over to the fireplace, where she'd left one of Dominic's old journal pages—a sigil drawn in thick graphite, resembling a crescent cradling a key.

"It's more than that," she said. "You said the Hollow called you. That it didn't speak in words, but in symbols. Maybe it doesn't *want* watchers anymore. Maybe it's ready for a seer."

Dominic studied the seal. "Three. There were three seals. I drew them all—just didn't know what they meant back then."

"Two are broken," Vivienne whispered. "And now we know the Hollow predates the Ashcrofts. Maybe Marlick didn't create the magic—maybe he tried to control it."

A silence fell.

Then Adele, barely above a whisper: "What if the men were never *meant* to hold it?"

Vivienne turned toward the portrait of Seraphina that now hung in the corner—*her* eyes piercing, timeless. "We know now that the Hollow was hers from the beginning? And it's been rejecting every man who's tried to claim it since."

Dominic moved closer to the mirror, staring at his own reflection. "I was never married into the family. Never the heir."

Vivienne looked at her father. "But I am."

The air in the library shifted—heavy, electric, waiting.

Vivienne pulled the deed from its leather folder and held it up to the mirror.

There, just beneath Seraphina's name, was an inscription in faded ink.

"Three seals bind the Hollow. One of blood. One of breath. One of name."

Dominic inhaled sharply. "You've broken two. The blood in the séance room... and the breath when the veil opened."

Adele's eyes repeated. "That means only one remains."

Vivienne traced the final line with her fingertip. *Speak the word, and the Hollow shall open.*

She looked into the mirror.

A reflection flickered.

Not hers.

Seraphina, watching.

Then gone.

Vivienne whispered, "We're close."

# Chapter 48

The storm returned at dusk.

Wind howled through the eaves of the Hollow, and lightning cracked like a whip above the orchard. Inside, Vivienne stood at the threshold of Julian Ashcroft's study—door unlocked.

Dominic held the lantern beside her. "You ready for this?"

"No," Vivienne said, voice low. "But we have to."

The study smelled of old tobacco, cedar oil, and forgotten time. Dust clung to the shelves in heavy sheets. Julian's books lined the walls—on spiritualism, geometry, lunar calendars, and mirrored consciousness.

At the center of the room, a desk carved with celestial symbols. A journal sat open on the surface.

Vivienne's fingers trembled as she picked it up.

*March 3rd, 1879 — Midnight approaches. The hour between worlds. I've seen it now—how the mirror thins when the body slows. Seraphina warned me, but she does not see what I see. I must cross. For Isolde. For legacy. The third seal must be broken in name, not blood.*

She turned the page.

*I will speak the Name tonight. Let the Hollow decide if I am worthy.*

A large sigil was drawn on the next page—identical to the one Vivienne had seen in the séance room. And beneath it, three words in Malrick's handwriting, shakier than before:

*It is not mine.*

Suddenly, the lantern flickered. The air tightened.

Vivienne spun toward the far wall—where a faded tapestry hung unevenly. Dominic moved to lift it—and behind it, they found a mirror. Not just a mirror.

A portal.

The glass shimmered like black water, and carved into its frame were three symbols: a drop of blood, a breath swirl, and a blank circle.

Vivienne stared at her reflection—and saw Seraphina standing behind her.

"She's trying to show us," Vivienne whispered.

Adele stepped into the room just then, drawn by the pulsing energy. Her face paled. "This mirror... it was sealed after Malrick died. My grandmother forbade anyone from entering the study after that night."

Dominic turned to her. "What happened?"

Adele swallowed hard. "He collapsed during a ritual. Heart exploded, they said. But Isolde wrote later that he wasn't truly dead. That he was trapped."

Vivienne turned back to the mirror.

"The third seal," she said. "It's not just about saying a name. It's about saying the true name."

She looked at the deed again. *Seraphina Vexley.*

"No," she murmured. "That's not the name that opens it."

Dominic moved beside her, his voice almost reverent. "Then what is?"

Vivienne closed her eyes. The name came like a whisper. One she had only heard in fragments—in dreams, visions, echoed through time.

"Ashcroft."

The mirror flared white.

Wind burst through the room. Pages scattered, the desk shook, and the symbols along the mirror's edge ignited in pale gold light.

Then—silence.

The mirror now shimmered with a soft glow. Beyond the glass, they saw a staircase descending… downward. Not into the cellar—but into *something* else. Somewhere older. Deeper.

Dominic turned toward Vivienne, eyes wide. "You broke the seal."

Vivienne exhaled shakily. "No. *She* did."

They descended together.

Each step pulsed with energy, the walls lined with smooth stone, etched with glyphs that matched Dominic's sketches. At the base, a door—half-buried in earth and time.

Vivienne placed her palm against it.

The wood vibrated with life.

Behind them, Callum appeared—soaked from the storm, chest heaving. "You came down here without me?"

Vivienne's heart skipped at the sight of him. "You're late."

He grinned, stepping forward. "You're insane."

Before she could respond, he reached out, brushing a strand of damp hair from her face. "But I'm not letting you go through that door alone."

Dominic cleared his throat.

Adele smiled faintly. "Let her have this moment."

Callum's hand lingered at her cheek.

Then Vivienne turned away quickly and back to the door.

*Three seals broken.*

*The Hollow shall open.*

She spoke aloud the final line from Malrick's ritual journal.

"Let the House remember."

The door creaked open.

And what lay beyond was older than the Ashcrofts, older than names—waiting to be found.

# Chapter 49

The door groaned open, exhaling a breath of stale, earth-soaked air. Vivienne stepped through first, her lantern casting long shadows over walls of smooth black stone, veined with quartz that glowed faintly from within. The space didn't feel like a basement.

It felt like a tomb.

Or a womb.

The narrow corridor opened into a circular chamber carved directly into the rock. Nine columns circled the perimeter, each etched with a woman's name.

Genevieve

Isolde.

Ophelia.

Evadne.

Anastasia.

Viviette.

Isadora.

Cordelia.

Vivienne moved toward the final pillar. She brushed off the dust. Etched faintly beneath the grime was Seraphina.

Her hand trembled. "Wow…?"

Dominic stepped up beside her, jaw slack. "This wasn't a family crypt. This was a binding circle."

Adele nodded slowly, her voice barely above a whisper. "The Nine. Wasn't just a legend."

In the center of the chamber sat a stone basin—empty, but lined with runes. The walls behind the columns told stories in pictures—hieroglyphic-like murals of women with radiant hands, holding back a dark force that rippled like smoke.

Callum crouched beside the basin. "This was used for something… ritualistic."

Vivienne stared at the murals. "They weren't just gifted. They were the seal."

A flicker in her periphery.

She turned—and saw Seraphina standing just outside the ring of pillars. Her face was luminous, half-shadowed.

"We were never meant to hold it forever," Seraphina said, voice like wind in a keyhole. "But the men were too weak. Malrick tried to open the veil without knowing what was tethered. And now, only the Mirror Soul can end what he began."

Vivienne blinked—and Seraphina was gone.

But a cold truth settled over her like ash.

The Nine were never chosen at random. The Hollow was not a home—it was a vessel, built atop a fracture in the veil between worlds. The women were not protectors.

They were binders.

Each Gift—a key.

Each woman—another layer of the lock.

Dominic stepped forward, pulling something from his coat. A page. Torn. Weathered.

"After you opened the second seal, this slid free from behind the séance room's mirror," he said. "It's one of my drawings… the symbols I thought were meaningless."

He unfolded it carefully. The sketch was of this very room—but from above. A diagram of the pillars, basin, and at the center—

A radiant sigil shaped like an eye and mirror combined.

And beneath it, written in strange but familiar script:

*When the Nine are Named and the Circle made whole, the Hollow shall wake… and ask its due.*

Vivienne's voice was hoarse. "What does that mean—'ask its due'?"

Dominic didn't answer. But Adele's gaze drifted toward her daughter—and then to Callum.

Vivienne noticed too late how still he'd gone.

Callum stepped away from the basin. His eyes shimmered with something dark. Regret. Recognition.

"I didn't tell you," he said softly. "Because I didn't want it to be true. But I've seen this place before. In dreams. Visions. I was always on the outside."

Vivienne's breath caught. "What are you saying?"

"I think… my bloodline was meant to guard this circle," Callum said quietly. "To protect the Nine. But never to stand among them."

He reached toward her—but stopped short, as if the air between them had weight.
"If I stay too long, I don't know what the Hollow will do."

Vivienne felt it too—that magnetic ache pulling her forward, the inevitability of it.
"Then leave," she whispered.

His jaw tightened. "I'd rather break a thousand years of oaths than lose you to this place."

The silence thickened, pressing in on them. Then Vivienne closed the space, her fingers brushing his. The Hollow seemed to pulse in response, a slow, steady beat beneath their feet.

"I don't care if we're family," she said, breath unsteady. "Blood or no blood—damn the rules. I love you."

Dominic's voice cut in sharply. "What are you saying?"

Vivienne turned, looking between Callum and her father. "You and Everett were related. That would make Callum and me—"

"Related?" Dominic's brow furrowed, and then—unexpectedly—he laughed. "You thought you two were related?"

"Yes," she said, almost defensively.

Callum stepped closer. "I told her we weren't."

"But Everett was your father," Vivienne pressed.

"He raised me," Dominic corrected gently. "But not by blood. He was my godfather. My parents died when I was very young, and Everett took me in as his own. I was an Grey in name, not in blood."

Something loosened in her chest— something she hadn't realized she'd been holding.

Behind them, the stone columns shivered faintly, as if the chamber itself had exhaled. Nine women. Nine names. One basin.

Vivienne's gaze swept the circle.

And then—soft as breath, ancient as roots—came the whisper:

Speak the truth, and the Hollow shall breathe.

She reached for Callum's hand again, steady this time. "Then what are we waiting for?"

# Chapter 50

Vivienne stepped into the center of the chamber.

The basin before her hummed faintly, like something beneath it had begun to stir.

The names of the Nine glowed along the pillars, as if waiting.

Adele stood just beyond the circle, beside Dominic, holding the torn page that bore the sigil. Her lips moved in silent prayer—or memory. Dominic's jaw was set, his hand resting protectively on Adele's back.

Callum stood at the outer edge. Watching. Tense. Torn.

Vivienne inhaled deeply. The air inside the chamber thickened, rippling like water. The Hollow itself felt like it was leaning in, waiting.

She didn't have a ritual. No script. Only instinct.

Only truth.

She placed her palm flat against the basin's rim and closed her eyes.

"I call to the Nine.
To the blood oath buried beneath silence.
To the watchers, the whisperers, the weavers.
To the women who were more than wives and mothers—
You were binders. Seals. Flames.
I speak your names."

Vivienne moved slowly, deliberately, around the circle—pausing at each glowing name carved into the stone.

Genevieve
Isolde.
Ophelia.
Evadne.
Anastasia.
Viviette.
Isadora.
Cordelia.

Her voice caught—eyes flicking up to meet her mother's. Adele's expression softened, then nodded, proud and trembling.

"And Seraphina."

A pulse surged through the room—a low thrum that seemed to originate from the stone beneath her feet. The basin lit from within, a golden light rising like dawn through fog.

The air snapped.

The circle around her blazed.

Then… silence.

And something ancient, watching, waiting.

Vivienne swallowed and spoke again, quieter this time:

"I break the final seal.
Let what has been bound come forward.
Let the truth breathe.
Let the Hollow open."

The light inside the basin surged upward like a column of flame—but it wasn't hot. It passed through her like memory, like song. Her body trembled, not in fear—but in remembrance.

She saw them.

Nine women—standing in a circle just like this. Clothed in white. Eyes shining with something more than power—purpose. They turned to her as one, and smiled.

Seraphina stepped forward. Her hair was loose. Her face soft and worn and beautiful.

"You remember now," she whispered. "You've always been the mirror. The bridge."

Vivienne gasped.

"The Hollow is alive," Seraphina said. "And you, child, are its breath."

A great crack split through the chamber walls—not destruction, but unveiling. A panel in the stone behind the basin folded open, revealing a staircase spiraling downward, lit from below with a flickering amber glow.

The vision faded.

Vivienne swayed.

Callum stepped forward just in time to catch her. His arms came around her like instinct—solid, grounding. For a moment, they simply breathed together. His forehead rested gently against hers.

"You okay," he murmured.

"It's not over," she whispered. "It's only just beginning."

Behind them, Adele moved to the stairwell, eyes wide. Dominic followed, hand tightening on her waist as if to say *I'm here this time. You're not alone.*

Vivienne turned to Callum.

"Coming?" she asked.

"Try to stop me."

They descended.

The Hollow exhaled.

The stairs groaned beneath their feet—not with age, but as though reacting to their presence. The Hollow didn't just allow them through.

It was expecting them.

The flickering amber light grew brighter as they descended, winding deeper than Vivienne thought possible. This place hadn't been mapped. Not in Isolde's or Malrick's journals. Not in Dominic's symbols. It was off the page—forgotten by design.

When they reached the base, the air shifted—heavy with musk and ash and something sweeter, like old roses left to dry.

The chamber opened before them.

A vast, circular room carved into the bedrock. Arched stone ribs curved overhead, meeting in a central point like the inside of a cathedral. Strange symbols lined the walls, glowing faintly. A stone dais rose from the center, encircled by another sigil—one Vivienne had seen in Dominic's notebook.

She stepped closer.

Callum stayed beside her, gaze scanning the walls like a sentry, every muscle in his body taut.

Adele and Dominic followed more slowly, hand in hand. Their fingers brushed—two people who had lost everything, now tethered again.

"I've never felt anything like this," Adele whispered. "Not even during the mirror ritual. This is older."

Dominic nodded. "This was here before the Hollow. Before Malrick. He built the newer parts of the house on top of it."

Vivienne knelt at the dais, fingers grazing its surface.

There, carved shallowly into the stone, was a name.

Seraphina Vexley.

"Unbelievable," Vivienne breathed. "This is where it all began."

Dominic stepped forward, pulling something from his coat. A single, weathered page—charcoal sketches and glyphs scribbled around the edges. The same symbol on the ground now glowed softly at their feet.

"This was the last page I ever drew," he said, voice rough with memory. "Before… before the Hollow took me."

"From me," Adele said gently. "It held you. All this time."

He looked at her, eyes softening. "I always loved you."

Vivienne reached for the center of the dais, pressing her palm to the seal.

A pulse.

The ground beneath them vibrated. A low hum rose, building like a storm. The symbols on the walls flared—one by one—until the entire chamber glowed with a light not of this world.

And then it stopped.

Dead silence.

From the stone, a panel slid open.

A book emerged—leatherbound, chained, its cover engraved with three symbols: a heart, a mirror, and a key.

Vivienne's breath caught.

"The Book of the Nine," Dominic whispered.

"Amazing," Adele said, awe-struck.

Callum stepped closer, hand brushing Vivienne's back as if to steady her. "Are you ready for what it says?"

Vivienne turned to him, searching his eyes.

"I don't know," she said honestly. "But I think I was born for this."

He didn't speak—just leaned in and kissed her, slow and steady. No frenzy. No fear. Just two people at the edge of the unknown, choosing each other again.

When they broke apart, Vivienne turned back to the book.

She took the key from around her neck—the one Isolde's journal had led her to weeks ago—and slipped it into the lock.

Click.

The chains fell away.

# Chapter 51

Vivienne slowly unwrapped the chain from around the book. Its leather cover was cracked, soft with age, but it pulsed faintly beneath her fingertips—alive, almost. The symbols on the front shimmered subtly: a heart for love, a mirror for truth, a key for what lies beyond.

She opened it.

The pages inside were thick vellum, handwritten in a graceful, looping script. Not Malrick's hand. Not Isolde's. Something older.

Seraphina Vexley, Keeper of the Hollow. *Binder of Nine. Daughter of Blood and Light. The First to See Across the Veil.*

Vivienne's breath caught.

A sketch followed—of a woman with Vivienne's eyes. Her hair darker, but her expression… was familiar. Watching. Waiting.

"She looked like you," Callum murmured beside her. "Not just similar. Almost exact."

Vivienne nodded, voice catching in her throat. "I think… I know I've dreamt of her before. She used to speak to me when I was little. I thought she was imaginary."

"She wasn't," Dominic said. "She was the first of the line. Not by birth—but by choice."

Vivienne turned the page.

There, scrawled in deeper ink—almost etched—were nine names. All women. All Ashcroft matriarchs. Some Vivienne knew from the family tree. Others had been forgotten.

But Seraphina's name came first.

The Nine Shall Bind What Was Torn. *Each a Gift. Each a Seal. Only Together Can the Hollow Sleep.*

A hand-drawn diagram followed—nine points arranged in a circle. At the center: a mirror, cracked through the middle. Seraphina stood on one side. On the other, a shadow— vague, shifting.

"The Mirror Soul," Adele whispered aloud, reading the faded script. "She who walks both sides, who remembers both lives. She who can close the breach."

Vivienne swallowed hard. "Me."

Dominic nodded slowly. "Seraphina was the first to fragment. To divide her essence across time so she could always return. You're not just descended from her, Vivienne. You *are* her—again.”

“But how is that even possible?” Callum asked. “She’s been gone for decades.”

“The Nine weren’t just gifted,” Adele said. “They were chosen. The Hollow is more than a home—it’s a vessel. It remembers. It holds. It waits.”

“For what?” Vivienne asked.

“For the one who can put the mirror back together.”

Vivienne turned another page—and stopped.

There, drawn with incredible precision, was a symbol she knew too well. The same one that appeared when she bled on the floor in the séance room. The same one on the deed.

The Final Seal. The Heart of the House. The Rift Beneath.

And below it, a warning:

*To open it without the Nine is to invite ruin. To open it without the Mirror Soul is to become lost. But to open it with love… is to be free.*

Vivienne looked up.

“We have to gather them,” she said. “The descendants. The Nine.”

“We don’t know how,” Adele replied.

“Then we search each of the rooms,” Callum said firmly. “We start with the names in the book. We trace the bloodline. We remember them."

Vivienne closed the book gently, pressing her hand to its cover. It pulsed once, as if sealing the moment.

"We're almost there," she whispered. "The Hollow's ready. And so am I."

Callum stepped closer, brushing a strand of hair behind her ear.

"Whatever happens next… I'm with you."

She turned to face him. "Even if it means breaking the rules?"

"Especially then."

Their hands found each other's, fingers twining—not as guardians and heirs, not as fate-bound opposites, but as something simpler. Truer.

The chamber pulsed again, and the symbols on the wall dimmed—waiting.

Vivienne's breath caught. For a heartbeat, the chamber seemed to dissolve around her, replaced by fractured flashes—

…the plaque in the Mirror Room, its inscription curling around a nine-sectioned circle.

…the silvered panel in the Moon Room, marked with the same faint grooves.

…the East Chapel, where candlelight once revealed etchings she thought were ornamental.

Each one shimmered in her mind's eye, the empty sections glowing like lanterns in the dark. Six were unlit. Three burned bright.

She gripped Callum's hand tighter. "I know where to start."

He frowned. "Viv—what did you see?"

"The plaques," she said, the words spilling fast now. "They're not just memorials. They're a map. The nine-sectioned circle—three are already here. The other six… they're out there. We find them, we find the rest of the Nine."

Callum's eyes darkened with resolve. "Then we don't waste another second."

Above them, the Hollow seemed to exhale—timbers groaning, the air rippling with something almost like approval.

The hunt had begun.

# Chapter 52

They almost ran back to the East Chapel.

It greeted them with its usual hush—a silence that felt deeper than mere absence of sound. The faint scent of frankincense clung stubbornly to the air, as though it had seeped into the stone itself. Candlelight flickered against the carved beams overhead, too faint to banish the shadows that pooled in the corners. Dust drifted in slow spirals, disturbed only by their footfalls.

On the far wall, the brass plaque gleamed as if it had been polished since their last visit. Words caught the light like a secret being revealed:

THE NINE SACRED OBJECTS—EACH HOLDS A GIFT

Vivienne's breath caught. She reached out, her fingertips tracing the etched letters. The metal was cool, but beneath it—she swore—there was a faint pulse, as though the plaque itself had a heartbeat.

Her gaze fell to the nine-sectioned circle at the bottom. Each fragment bore a symbol— each a shard of something greater. Slowly, reverently, she touched the first three that seemed to hum under her skin.

Her voice was low, almost lost in the stillness.

"A mirror…" Her eyes unfocused. "The ornate hand mirror from the Mirror Room… Seraphina Vexley's gift—the Word of Knowledge."

Her fingers slid to the next.

"A silver hourglass… the Moon Room," she whispered. "Genevieve Ashcroft… prophecy bound to time itself."

And then—her hand hovered over the third, lingering.

"A lamp," she breathed, tracing the delicate etching of its curve. "Here. Isolde Ashcroft's room… Faith."

The other six symbols waited in silence, their lines catching faint glints of gold: a porcelain doll cradling a hidden scroll, a pressed herb book, a crystal singing bell, a rosary strung with foreign prayers, a jet-black pendant, an ash-dusted comb.

As she brushed each one, her voice dropped lower still—more to herself than the others.

"They're not just objects. They're watching. Waiting."

Adele stepped closer, her gaze fixed on one of the symbols.

"I know this one," she murmured, brushing her fingertips over the tiny etched outline of a book. "The herb book… I used to love going to that room."

Vivienne's head turned sharply toward her. "Where is it?"

"My mother called it the Healing Conservatory," Adele said, a faint smile ghosting her lips. "I can take you there."

They left the East Chapel together, the air growing warmer as they moved down a narrow hallway wreathed in ivy. The scent of dried flowers and something older—earthy, medicinal—met them before they even reached the door.

The Healing Conservatory was exactly as its name promised: walls veiled in ivy, sunlight slanting through glass panes thick with age, and shelves crowded with jars, bundles of herbs, and curling parchment labels. The air was heady with the mingled perfume of rosemary, sage, and lavender—an aroma that felt like both balm and memory.

Against the far wall hung another brass plaque, its surface worn to a soft glow. Vivienne stepped closer, reading aloud:

# THE HEALING CONSERVATORY

— Consecrated in (1833)—
Dedicated to Cordelia Ashcroft
Bearer of the Gifts of Healing
Let what is wounded be mended,
And what is in pain find its rest.

As she finished, her eyes found the book itself—resting on a stand draped with a faded green cloth. She lifted it carefully. The leather binding was supple with age, the gilt lettering barely legible. When she opened it, thin stems and petals lay pressed between the pages, their shapes perfectly preserved. A soft, golden warmth bloomed beneath her fingertips, as if the book recognized her touch.

The others watched in silence as Vivienne's expression shifted—part wonder, part certainty.

"It knows," she whispered. "It knows what's needed… and when."

Vivienne handed the herb book to Callum. "Hold onto this… please." Her voice was quiet, almost distracted, as she turned back to the brass plaque, tracing each etched segment one by one. When her fingers brushed the book symbol again, it pulsed faintly beneath her touch—warm, alive.

"Five more to go," she murmured.

Her hand stilled on the carving of a small bell.

"Where would you find a bell?"

Dominic's gaze sharpened, a faint smile ghosting across his lips. "I used to love the Music Room."

"I remember that," Adele added softly.

Without another word, Dominic led the way, his footsteps echoing down the corridor as if the house itself were leaning in to listen.

THE MUSIC ROOM

— Consecrated in (1851)—

Dedicated to Isaldora Ashcroft

Bearer of the Gift of Tongues

Let voices long silenced rise again,

And languages lost find their way to the living.

The Music Room greeted them with a hush that was anything but empty. Shadows pooled in the corners, the air thick with a faint metallic tang—as if sound itself had left residue behind. A grand piano sat in the center, its lid warped, keys fractured. Yet from somewhere—no one could say where—a low, trembling note seemed to hum, unending.

Above it, on a stand, rested the crystal singing bell. Even without touch, it gave a shiver of sound, like a whisper in a forgotten tongue.

Vivienne approached the crystal singing bell slowly, as if the room itself might object to her getting too close. The faint, unbroken note in the air shifted as she reached out—a ripple through invisible water.

Her fingers brushed the smooth rim. The bell answered with a single, pure chime— no louder than a breath, yet it seemed to shiver through the marrow of her bones.

Her throat constricted, then loosened. And without thought, she spoke.

Not in English.

Not in any language she recognized.

The syllables poured out—sharp and liquid at once, syllables folding into each other like the tide pulling back from a shore. Her voice deepened, layered, as though another spoke through her. Dominic and Adele exchanged startled looks; Callum took an instinctive step back.

The shadows in the corners seemed to lean forward.

When the final word left her lips, the air stilled. The note faded.

Vivienne's eyes blinked rapidly as if waking from a dream.

"What… was that?" she whispered, her voice hoarse.

No one answered, but the bell in her hands pulsed once, like a heartbeat.

# Chapter 53

Dominic's hand hovered protectively near Vivienne's elbow as they left the Music Room, as though the lingering chime still pressed on the air between them. The hall beyond was narrower than she remembered, shadows crowding closer with each step, lit only by the wavering glow of wall sconces.

They descended a short, curved staircase, the kind that felt older than the rest of the house—worn smooth in the center from centuries of passage—until the scent of old paper and waxed oak whispered around them.

A set of towering double doors loomed ahead, painted a deep cobalt.
Vivienne pushed them open.

The Blue Library spread before them— three stories high, shelves rising to a domed ceiling painted with constellations. Blue glass panes filtered the daylight, staining everything in shades of twilight. Dust motes drifted like slow-moving stars.

On the far side, mounted in brass, was another plaque:

THE BLUE LIBRARY

— Consecrated in 1871 —

Dedicated to Viviette Ashcroft

Bearer of the Gift of Interpretation of Tongues

Let every word be known,

And every script be read.

"Mother, what exactly does 'consecrated' mean?"

Adele glanced over, her voice gentle but steady. "It means set apart—made sacred for a purpose. Once something is consecrated, it's no longer ordinary. It belongs to something greater."

"Interesting."

Vivienne's gaze tracked upward until she spotted it—resting in a velvet-lined alcove, the Multilingual Rosary. Its beads glimmered faintly, carved from stones that seemed to shift in hue as she moved—onyx to pearl to sapphire.

When her fingers closed around it, a quiet click echoed in her mind, like the turning of an unseen lock. She glanced at the spines of the nearest books. Titles that had been indecipherable a breath ago now bloomed into meaning—languages she didn't speak, alphabets she couldn't name, unfolding into clear words.

"This is… impossible," she murmured.

But the rosary only warmed in her palm, as if pleased to be understood.

Vivienne let the rosary's last bead slide from her fingers, its quiet weight settling into her pocket as if it had always belonged there.

"Five found," she murmured. "And the next?"

Her gaze caught the faint outline of another symbol on the great brass plaque—the teardrop curve of a pendant. A pull, almost physical, tugged her attention toward the east corridor. The air there felt colder, the shadows less willing to retreat.

Callum noticed. "You feel it too?"

She nodded once. "The next one is waiting… in the Glass Atrium."

They followed her down the hall, the sound of their steps muted by an uncanny stillness. Frosted daylight seeped through cracked panes overhead, casting fractured ribbons of light that quivered across the walls. Somewhere, faint as breath, glass shifted—no wind, no reason, yet it groaned like something restless.

Dominic pushed the warped double doors open, and a plaque waited just inside:

THE GLASS ATRIUM
— Consecrated in 1894 —
Dedicated to Anastasia Ashcroft
Bearer of the Gift of Discerning of Spirits
"Let falsehood be revealed, and the unseen show its face."

As Vivienne stepped inside, she felt the air grow sharp, almost metallic. The atrium smelled faintly of dust and something older—like rain on ancient stone. Overhead, the shattered glass threw splintered light across the marble floor in patterns that seemed to shift if she stared too long.

"Feels wrong in here," Adele whispered.

It was then the doors slammed shut with a booming finality that echoed through the hollow chamber. The latch clicked from the other side.

Dominic rattled the handle. "It's locked."

Callum scanned the shadows, every muscle taut. "Then we're not leaving—at least, not for awhile."

A draft stirred the hanging ferns in the far corner, and something moved in the fractured reflection of the glass above—something that wasn't any of them.

The cold settled in quickly.

Vivienne wrapped her arms around herself, scanning the shattered glass ceiling. Moonlight had replaced the fractured daylight now, spilling in silver and shadow. Each gust of wind rattled the jagged panes, sending a delicate, eerie music through the space—like a thousand tiny chimes just beyond hearing.

"We should find a spot away from the glass," Callum said quietly, eyes on the dark corners where the beams of moonlight failed to reach.

They moved toward the central fountain—a dry, cracked basin, its marble streaked with age. The air there felt heavier, as if something watched from the shadows beyond the ferns.

Adele brushed her fingers against a cold stone bench. "Why would this room be consecrated?" she murmured. "For plants? For light?"

"Not for plants," Vivienne said, her voice low. "For what walks here unseen."

As if summoned by the words, a sudden tap-tap-tap echoed from the far wall. Slow. Measured. Too precise to be wind. Dominic lifted a fallen length of iron from the floor.

The tapping stopped.

Then, in the broken reflection of a cracked glass pane, Vivienne saw it—movement. A pale, blurred figure in the reflection only, its face shifting like smoke, eyes black as the gaps in the ceiling.

Her hand brushed along the cold wall where the plaque had been mounted, fingertips tracing a shallow groove in the stone. Something hard was embedded there, smooth as glass beneath the dust. At first, it was icy, like touching winter water—but as her fingers curled around it, a slow warmth began to seep into her skin. She worked it free, and the faint light caught on a pendant the color of midnight.

It was polished black jet, its surface so flawlessly dark it seemed to swallow the glow from the room. Encased in a delicate silver setting, it hung from a fine, tarnished chain that looked older than any of them could guess. The stone pulsed faintly in her palm— once, twice—and then the warmth surged, sudden and fierce, until it felt as if the pendant itself burned with a hidden fire.

Vivienne hissed, her breath sharp. "It's burning—" She dropped it onto the bench, where it landed with a soft metallic clink, rocking slightly before coming to rest, as if reluctant to be still.

Callum picked it up carefully with the hem of his shirt, keeping his fingers well away from the stone. "You said it burns hot when…"

"When a spirit is malevolent," Vivienne finished—though she had no idea how she knew that. Her gaze flicked back to the fractured glass, where the shadow still lingered, sliding between shards like oil through water.

"Jet's not just a stone," Callum said quietly. "It's fossilized wood—millions of years old. Comes from ancient trees buried under pressure, turned black and hard as obsidian. People have used it for protection since the Middle Ages… charms against curses, mourning jewelry, even talismans to keep away evil." His gaze flicked to the pendant, the chain twisting faintly as if moved by breath. "And if it's heating like that— whatever's here doesn't want us here."

The night dragged on, each hour marked by new sounds—whispers curling through the rafters, cold bursts of air that smelled faintly of rot, and the soft scrape of something circling just beyond the limits of their vision. They huddled together in the center, Dominic gripping the iron bar, Callum keeping the pendant in sight, Adele muttering quiet prayers under her breath.

Then, in the fractured glass overhead, the moonlight seemed to twist. One shard reflected nothing but darkness. Another showed them all sitting together—except there was a fifth figure crouched low between Vivienne and Callum.

It was a woman, or something once shaped like one. Her form shimmered faintly, as though made of water disturbed by a breeze. Strands of hair floated around her face like smoke, her eyes two hollow pools of black that seemed to pull at the edges of thought.

She didn't move in the real room—only in the reflections.

Vivienne's breath hitched. "Don't… turn around," she whispered.

Dominic's grip tightened on the iron bar. "Why?"

"She's behind us," Vivienne said, eyes fixed on the broken pane that showed the thing's head slowly tilting, as if curious.

The pendant near Callum's hand began to glow with a faint, oily sheen. Its heat was no longer a warning—it was a demand, thrumming.

Then the figure's mouth opened. No sound came, but the air in the atrium shifted. The whispers in the rafters coalesced into words— fragments in a language Vivienne didn't know but somehow understood. Not yours. Leave it.

Her eyes darted to the pendant.

The figure's gaze followed.

"Pass me the pendant," she told Callum sharply. "Whatever you do, don't drop it."

The spirit moved—or rather, every reflection of her moved at once, surging forward in the glass. In the real space, the air slammed against them like a wave, rattling the glass and driving a sharp chill through their bones. Adele's prayer rose to a near shout, each word echoing unnaturally as though spoken by a hundred voices at once.

The pendant seared in Vivienne's grasp. The figure stopped mid-lunge, head jerking back, the reflections fracturing into nothing.

Silence.

It was only then that they realized the wind outside had died, and the only sound was their breathing.

For a heartbeat, the silence felt like safety.

Then—tap.

It came from the far corner, soft, deliberate, as if a single fingernail had struck the glass. Vivienne's head whipped toward the sound, but nothing moved.

Tap… tap… tap. Slow. Rhythmic. Closer.

The fractured panes shimmered faintly, not from light, but from movement just beneath their surface—like something swimming behind ice. Shapes pressed against the glass from the inside—faces warped and stretched, their eyes nothing but black hollows.

A cold breath feathered the back of Vivienne's neck. She spun, but there was no one there—only Callum's wide eyes and Adele's white-knuckled grip on the rosary.

The jet pendant throbbed in Vivienne's hand, not just with heat now, but with a slow, pulsing rhythm… like a heartbeat that wasn't hers.

Without warning, every shard in the shattered panes quivered. Reflections began to peel away from their bodies—shadows detaching, moving independently. One leaned forward until its mouth almost touched Vivienne's ear.

"Let us in."

The words were a hiss, but the sound bloomed inside her skull, as if whispered from within her own mind.

The temperature plummeted. Frost began creeping over the edges of the broken panes, and the figures in the glass started to pound— each strike sending a vibration through the floor beneath them.

The pendant flared, almost white-hot now, and Vivienne had to bite back a scream as its heat bit into her skin.

A jagged crack spidered across one of the larger panes with an earsplitting snap. Frost poured from it like smoke, curling into the room. Behind the glass, the faces solidified— no longer vague impressions but gaunt, pallid visages with teeth too long for their mouths and eyes that gleamed wetly in the fractured light.

One pressed her skeletal hands against the glass. The pane bulged inward, bending as if the barrier between worlds were made of water. Another face appeared beside it—this one grinning, lips stretched so far back they split at the corners.

The pounding became deafening.

Callum stumbled back, his voice shaking. "Viv, it's going to—"

The first face lunged, shoving her entire head and shoulders through the glass. Shards hung in the air like suspended droplets, never falling, as if the world itself held its breath. Her hair hung in a slow, underwater drift, and the stench of earth and rot rolled into the room.

Her mouth opened, and the voice that came out was not hers—it was a chorus, layered and discordant.

"Blood and breath, open the way."

The pendant's heat became agony. Vivienne clutched it in both hands, every instinct telling her to drop it, but some deeper compulsion made her hold on tighter. The black jet blazed like a coal, and a vibration hummed up her arms, into her chest.

Light—faint at first—began to leak from the stone, pushing back the frost, the figures, the shadowed edges of the glass. The woman's head twisted sharply, a snarl cutting across her face, and the suspended shards suddenly snapped back into place with a sound like breaking bones.

The figures shrieked, not with sound but with pressure, a psychic force that made their teeth ache and their vision blur. Then, one by one, the faces dissolved into the fractured reflections until nothing but warped glass remained.

The frost retreated. The air stilled.

Only the scorch mark in Vivienne's palm proved it had happened at all.

The silence pressed in, but Vivienne's breath caught when the fractured reflections in the glass began to knit themselves into something else—not the gaunt faces from before, but a single woman's image.

She was tall, with an austere beauty that seemed to belong to another century—dark hair swept into a severe twist, high collar edged in lace, and eyes so sharp they seemed to see through Vivienne. The fractured glass shimmered behind her like a halo of broken light.

"You have passed," the woman said, her voice both near and impossibly far. "The test of discerning spirits is not in seeing them, but in knowing their truth."

Vivienne's pulse thundered in her ears. "Who are you?"

"Anastasia Ashcroft," the figure replied. "Fifth of my line. Guardian of this place. I was bound here to guard the vision you now hold." Her gaze flicked to the jet pendant, still smoldering faintly in Vivienne's palm.

Vivienne swallowed. "What was it? That… thing?"

"A deceiver," Anastasia said, her expression unyielding. "There are spirits who dress themselves in sorrow, who will speak as if they are lost, in need, desperate for your aid. They will offer you glimpses of truth in exchange for something—your time, your will… your soul. Never trust a spirit who asks for payment, no matter how small."

Her eyes narrowed, as if weighing Vivienne's worth. "The highest spirits ask for nothing. They give freely, for their only purpose is to guide, protect, and lift. All others seek to take. Remember this, or the next time, you will not leave the room."

The glass flickered, her form wavered, and for a moment the air was heavy with the scent of violets and candle smoke. Anastasia's last words hung in the stillness:

"Discernment is your shield. Vision is your sword. Use them well."

The vision dissolved like smoke in sunlight, leaving only Vivienne's reflection staring back.

When dawn finally bled through the broken ceiling, the pendant cooled instantly. The locked doors clicked open without a hand laid upon them.

Vivienne was the last to leave. She glanced up once more at the jagged panes, half-expecting those black eyes to reappear. But the glass only held the pale morning sky.

She slipped the pendant over her neck, next to the locket.

# Chapter 54

"Who else is hungry?" Vivienne asked, breaking the heavy silence.

They all moved toward the kitchen, the echo of the night's events clinging like damp air. Callum cracked eggs into a pan, the sizzle loud in the quiet house, while Adele measured coffee grounds with deliberate care, the rich aroma beginning to cut through the lingering chill.

Dominic leaned against the doorway, arms crossed, watching Vivienne. "You know," he said, voice low but steady, "Not every battle is about strength. Last night, you didn't win because you fought harder—you won because you knew what you were facing. That's rarer than you think."

Vivienne met his gaze, unsure how to answer, but the words lodged in her mind like a pebble in a shoe—impossible to ignore.

As they ate, Vivienne's mind wandered back through the night.

The Glass Atrium came first—fractured panes casting restless shards of light, the air prickling with something unseen. In her palm, the jet pendant had grown warm, almost alive, as if recognizing her. It wasn't just a trinket— it was a warning, a way of knowing what eyes alone could never reveal. *Discernment.*

Then the Healing Conservatory—ivy curling over forgotten stone, the scent of dried herbs lingering like a memory that refused to fade. She could almost hear Cordelia's presence there, gentle but unyielding, coaxing life back into whatever was broken. It was more than a place; it was *healing* itself, breathing through the walls.

And the Blue Library—dust thick on the shelves, but the books inside were anything but dead. Even the ones she shouldn't have been able to read had unfolded themselves to her like old friends. There was a current there, an understanding that went deeper than language—*the gift of interpretation*, guiding her to meanings that had been buried for generations.

These rooms weren't simply part of the house. They were keepers of something far older, each holding a thread of power... and the more she pulled, the more she felt the whole tapestry stirring.

Dominic leaned back in his chair, studying her as though he'd been watching the threads take shape himself. "The rooms aren't random, Vivienne," he said quietly. "They're speaking to you. The question is—are you ready to understand what they're asking for?"

He reached into the worn leather folio that rarely left his side and pulled out a sheaf of sketches—charcoal and ink drawings she recognized instantly. Symbols. The same ones carved into the conservatory's lintel, etched into the Blue Library's spine of stone, and faintly scrawled in dust across the Glass Atrium's fractured frame.

Vivienne's breath caught. "You've been there… before me."

"I've been listening," he corrected, sliding the pages toward her. Each drawing matched a room she had entered, but layered with an additional mark—circles, intersecting lines, shapes that hummed with a strange symmetry. Not language, not quite art. Something in-between.

She brushed her fingers over the page, feeling the faint drag of graphite. Her mind began connecting them, unbidden—the healing herb pressed between Cordelia's pages, the burning pendant from Anastasia's atrium, the impossible words the Blue Library had surrendered to her. Different gifts, different bloodlines… all speaking in the same hidden tongue.

Vivienne traced the lines of the sketch again, her fingertip pausing where the pattern broke. Two spaces remained unfinished—two symbols absent. Her gaze flicked up to Dominic.

"You already know which rooms we haven't found yet… don't you?" she asked, her voice low.

Dominic's lips curved, though the expression carried no warmth. "Knowing and finding are not the same thing."

Before she could press him further, Adele's voice cut in like a draft through a half-open door. "Enough for right now. We all need a rest before we push on."

"Mom," Vivienne protested, "We can't stop now—"

"Yes, we can," Adele said firmly. "The rooms will still be here. And you'll see them more clearly after sleep."

Reluctantly, Vivienne let herself be drawn toward the parlor. The moment Callum coaxed a flame to life in the fireplace, the space shifted from cold shadow to a pocket of warmth. The fire crackled and whispered against the hush, its glow painting the walls in a rhythm that seemed almost hypnotic.

She sank into the armchair nearest the hearth. The heat seeped into her bones, loosening every last thread of tension she'd been clinging to. Her eyes grew heavy—not from choice, but as if the house itself had decided rest was not optional. The murmurs of the others blurred into a soft, indistinct hum.

Her last waking thought was of those two missing symbols—unfound, unfinished—and the uneasy certainty that they were waiting for her, just beyond the reach of sleep.

# Chapter 55

Vivienne woke with her heart pounding and the taste of smoke in her mouth.

The dream clung to her like a veil—grey, shifting, impossible to peel away. She had stood in a room swathed in tattered lace and scorched wallpaper, the air thick with the ghost of a fire that refused to die. Ash floated in the stillness like black snow, coating the floorboards and the ornate comb on the vanity.

The bridal gown hung in the corner—yellowed silk scorched along the hem—its bodice intact, but the veil was gone.

She didn't need to wonder what the place was. She knew.

The Bridal Suite.

And she knew, with an absolute certainty that made her breath catch, that the missing veil mattered just as much as the comb.

Not waiting for the others to stir, Vivienne slipped from her chair, the fire in the parlor still crackling softly behind her. She padded through the quiet house, avoiding the boards she'd already learned would creak.

The staircase loomed ahead, its banister cold beneath her hand. Halfway up, she thought she heard a faint rustle behind her—like silk skirts brushing against the wall—but when she glanced over her shoulder, the hallway below lay empty.

The east wing felt different this morning, as if the house itself was holding its breath. A faint, acrid scent curled down the corridor—char and roses, the exact perfume of her dream.

Her fingers grazed the wall, and when she reached the last door on the left, she didn't need to check the tarnished brass plate. She knew.

The door resisted at first, wood swollen in its frame, but then yielded with a sigh.

Inside, the air was cooler, edged with a chill that raised gooseflesh along her arms. Sunlight filtered through a sheer curtain, touching the ash that lay in a fine layer over everything.

The bed was still dressed in bridal white, though its edges were greyed and frayed. On the vanity sat the comb from her dream— delicate, silver-edged, its teeth dusted in soot yet gleaming faintly as if it remembered a time before fire.

The gown hung exactly where she'd seen it, but the veil was nowhere in sight.

She stepped forward, each footfall stirring the ash, her mind flicking to the whispers of the prologue she'd once read in an old ledger. *Seraphina walked into the east wing and never came out.*

Vivienne's fingers hovered over the comb but didn't touch it. Not yet. Something told her the room would react.

Somewhere deep within the walls, a faint crack sounded—like timber shifting. Or… footsteps.

Her fingers hovered over the tarnished brass plate.

**THE BRIDAL SUITE**
— Consecrated in 1913 —
Dedicated to Evadne Ashcroft
Bearer of the Working of Miracles
Let that which is marred be made whole,
And that which is lost be spared from flame.

She didn't need to read it to know. The certainty was already lodged in her chest, heavy and unshakable.

"Vivienne!" Callum's voice echoed down the corridor, urgent. Footsteps followed—more than one set.

"I'm in here," she whispered, not wanting to break the stillness.

A moment later, Callum, Adele, and Dominic filled the doorway. Vivienne stood in the center of the room, a single tear slipping down her cheek.

The Bridal Suite was both beautiful and wrong—walls once white now blotched with pale gray smoke stains that never seemed to fade, no matter how carefully scrubbed. The lace-draped bed sat beneath a canopy warped by heat, the edges forever curled in memory of flame. On a stand nearby rested a wedding dress, untouched by ash… yet missing its veil.

The air shifted, cool and heavy, and a woman's figure shimmered into view—tall, dignified, with eyes like embers that burned from somewhere far away.

Evadne Ashcroft.

Her voice was the sound of memory itself. *"Seraphina Vexley… my great grandmother. She wed Thaddeus Ashcroft in 1807. He died in 1812, and she never remarried. In 1852, she vanished. They searched the house, every inch of it. Two days later, they found her diary—not in her room, not in the study, but beneath the floorboards of the ballroom… wrapped in her wedding veil. The last page was dated for a week yet to come. The final sentence was never finished."*

The words pressed into Vivienne's chest like a weight. She glanced toward the vanity, where an ash-dusted comb lay in perfect stillness. She knew without touching it—hair combed with it would never burn, break, or tangle, even in fire.

But she also knew something else.

She couldn't take it. Not yet.

Not until she found the veil.

Not until she found the diary.

Her gaze shifted to the small circle of nine etched faintly on the wall above the vanity—its segments each holding a unique symbol. One of them now seemed to hum, the faintest outline of a comb flickering within it.

She swallowed hard. *The diary comes first.*

Vivienne straightened her shoulders, her pulse quickening. She'd learned enough in this house to know that not every spirit told the truth—and not every presence had her best interests at heart.

"If you truly are Evadne Ashcroft," she said quietly, "Tell me something only she would know. Something about the night of the fire in this room."

The spirit's eyes softened. *"The fire began in the hearth, not from negligence but from a guest's jealous rage. She pulled the curtains down before the flames reached them… and still, the smoke came. Her hair—" She touched it gently. "—smelled of ash for months. Thaddeus always said it reminded him of the night they first met, by a bonfire."*

Vivienne's breath caught. That detail matched a note she'd seen in one of the Ashcroft family letters—something no wandering spirit could have guessed.

"All right," Vivienne said, her voice steadier. "Then you know why I'm here. I can't take the comb until I find the diary. And the veil."

Evadne's form steadied, the pale shimmer of her gown catching the light from the hall. *"They are together now, but not where they were found. The ballroom floorboards were torn up long ago. The diary and veil were taken… hidden again. This time in a place that hears the heart, yet holds no pulse of its own."*

Vivienne frowned, letting the words sink in. Hears the heart… but no pulse.

Callum shifted beside her, but she barely noticed. "Somewhere quiet?" she murmured. "Somewhere that… listens?"

The spirit's gaze deepened. *"A place where secrets linger in the still air, where even the smallest whisper is kept."* Her voice softened, almost a warning. *"Go there, and you'll find what you seek— wrapped together, as they were before."*

Vivienne's breath caught as her mind landed on it—the small, locked confessional chamber adjoining the old chapel. The one they had walked past earlier, its carved wooden door warped but intact, its hinges untouched for decades.

Before she could ask another question, Evadne began to fade, her outline dissolving into the dimness. *"But be certain, Vivienne… once you find it, you cannot close what it remembers."*

The room grew still.

Vivienne turned to the others, her voice low but resolute. "We're going back to the east chapel."

Though they had stepped inside before, the chapel still met them with its same solemn breath. The faint ghost of candle wax lingered in the air, long since burned away, and the stone walls carried a chill that felt older than memory. Dust hung suspended in the muted light, drifting lazily whenever they moved.

Callum tried the confessional door—it yielded with a long, reluctant groan—but inside there was nothing, only the stale dampness of mildew clinging to the wood.

They searched every pew, lifted every kneeler, ran their fingers along the carved altar rail. Nothing. Not even a stray scrap of cloth.

Frustration tightened Vivienne's chest. She leaned against the tall leaded-glass window to catch her breath. The sun had shifted just enough to catch on something beyond the chapel wall. A flash—small, bright—like sunlight on glass or polished metal.

She narrowed her eyes. Beyond the overgrown hedge stood the ancient oak, its gnarled branches twisted like arthritic fingers. She stepped closer to the glass, angling for a better look. There it was again—a brief sparkle deep in the bark.

"Out there," she whispered.

The four of them made their way through the rear door, the air heavy with the scent of moss and damp earth. The oak loomed above them, its trunk wide enough to swallow a man whole. As Vivienne pressed her hand to the rough bark, she felt it—a shallow hollow, concealed behind a curtain of ivy.

Callum pulled the vines aside. Inside the opening, wrapped in a bundle of yellowed silk, was a length of delicate lace—the wedding veil. Nestled within its folds lay a small, leather-bound book, its cover cracked but intact.

Vivienne's fingers trembled as she lifted it free. The Ashcroft crest was faintly embossed on the front, and though the leather was worn, the clasp still held.

"The diary," she breathed.

The oak seemed to shiver with the wind, though the air around them was perfectly still.

She held it close, almost protectively, feeling its weight as if it carried more than words— perhaps the very breath of the one who had written it.

But now was not the time to read. The spirit's warning lingered in her mind: the diary first… then the comb.

"We have to go back," Vivienne said quietly, her voice edged with urgency. She glanced toward the shadowed silhouette of the manor, its windows like watching eyes. "Before someone… or something… decides we shouldn't."

The others exchanged wary glances, but followed as she turned toward the house. The air felt heavier with each step, as though the Hollow itself knew what they carried.

Inside, the upper hall stretched ahead, every closed door a reminder of what still waited to be found. The Bridal Suite. The Ash-Dusted Comb.

Vivienne's pace quickened. She could almost hear the faint scrape of a comb's teeth through hair, the whisper of silk against floorboards, and the ghost of a vow spoken long ago.

They were close. She could feel it.

# Chapter 56

They crossed the threshold of the upper hall, the polished wood creaking under their combined weight. The air was sharper here, scented faintly of smoke, as though the fire that had once ravaged the Bridal Suite still lingered in the grain of the walls.

Vivienne's fingers tightened around the diary as they reached the last door on the left.

Callum eased the door open. It groaned like something roused from a long, unwilling sleep.

The room beyond hadn't changed since last they where there, it was a mausoleum of beauty—charred edges on the ceiling where flames had once licked, the faint scent of lavender clinging stubbornly to the air. The bed stood dressed in faded ivory, the lace canopy yellowed with age, shadows pooling beneath it like a second veil.

Except the comb.

Vivienne stepped inside, each footfall careful, her gaze scanning for the telltale gleam.

The others fanned out—Callum toward the wardrobe, Dominic to the vanity, Adele to the cracked armoire.

Vivienne felt it before she saw it—an almost imperceptible warmth, drawing her toward the vanity's oval mirror. Its surface was clouded, as though smoke had been trapped beneath the glass. And there, resting before it, was the comb.

It was no ordinary trinket. The silver teeth shimmered faintly, as if dusted with frost and ash in the same breath. Along its spine, tiny etched symbols spiraled into the likeness of one of the nine segments from the circle—a mark Vivienne had seen in the old sketches Dominic had drawn in the margins of his journal and in each of the rooms they found.

Vivienne reached for it, but the mirror's reflection wavered—not following her movements exactly. The reflection of her hand lagged a heartbeat behind.

The temperature dropped. Somewhere behind her, Callum muttered, "Vivienne, don't—"

She closed her hand around the comb. The mirror's surface rippled once, twice… then stilled. The warmth vanished, replaced by a cold so deep it seemed to seep into her bones.

From the mirror's depths, faint as a whisper, a woman's voice sighed: *"Now… we are bound."*

The mirror shuddered. At first it was subtle, a barely-there ripple like breath on water. Then the glass convulsed, twisting their reflections into grotesque mockeries—eyes too wide, smiles stretching where no smile should be.

Vivienne's reflection moved when she did not. Its lips parted, and black smoke curled from its mouth, pressing against the glass as if desperate to escape.

"Put it back," Adele hissed, backing away.

The silver frame groaned under invisible strain, its filigree twisting as though it were alive. Dominic stepped forward, but his reflection didn't follow—it stayed behind in the mirror, staring at him with an expression of pure malice.

A deep vibration rolled through the room, rattling the vanity's drawers. One of the bedposts cracked like a gunshot. The lace canopy above them began to sway though the air was still.

Callum reached for Vivienne, but the mirror lashed out first. A cold wind slammed into them, pulling—no, dragging—them toward the glass. Their reflections' hands pressed against the inside, fingers blackening the silver backing.

Vivienne's breath came fast. Bound. That was the word the voice had used. Bound to what? Or to whom?

She yanked the comb free of the mirror's influence, holding it tight to her chest. The pull weakened, the glass losing its grip with a hiss like steam escaping a kettle. One last ripple swept across the surface, erasing the warped faces and leaving only their pale, shaken reflections.

The silence afterward was deafening.

Dominic exhaled slowly, his voice low and deliberate. "That was no simple haunting. That was a warning."

The four of them left the bridal room without another word, their footsteps echoing through the corridor like reluctant heartbeats.

The parlor welcomed them with its heavy velvet drapes and scent of old tobacco. Callum went straight to the hearth, crouching to coax the embers back to life. Sparks flared, then the fire caught, sending warm light crawling across the walls. Shadows retreated, though not completely—leaving pockets of darkness in the corners as if the house still listened.

Dominic stood by the window, arms crossed, eyes on the shifting glass panes. Adele sank into one of the high-backed chairs, pulling her shawl tighter around her shoulders.

Vivienne set the diary on the low table between them, the comb lying beside it like a silent witness. The Ashcroft crest glimmered faintly in the firelight.

"Let's take stock," Callum said, straightening. "We have the comb from the mirror… the diary we found in the oak… and the veil."

"And each of them is marked," Vivienne added. "One of the nine segments on the circle—the comb, the veil, the diary. Pieces of something bigger."

Dominic's gaze flicked to the diary, his voice quiet but pointed. "Then we should know what's written inside."

Vivienne hesitated only a moment. The clasp gave way with a reluctant snap, as though the book had been holding its breath for more than a century. The leather cover creaked as she opened it, the first page revealing delicate handwriting in faded ink:

*Seraphina Vexley Ashcroft — 1806*

The fire popped, sending a small spray of sparks into the air. She drew a steadying breath, then began to read aloud…

# Chapter 57

Vivienne cleared her throat, the firelight catching the edges of the delicate script. *"April 14th, 1806."* She glanced at the others before continuing.

*Today, I met the man who would alter the course of my days. Father insisted I accompany him to the spring gathering at Whitcombe Hall, though I protested the frivolity of such assemblies. The air was thick with perfume and polite lies, as it always is, and yet... there he stood.*

Her eyes tracked the lines, the voice in her head slowly becoming Seraphina's own.

*Thaddeus Ashcroft was not of our county, nor of our petty gossip. He was taller than most men, with a gaze that saw too much and a stillness that unsettled me. I thought him severe at first—until he spoke. His words were deliberate, each chosen as if it carried weight enough to tip the scales of fate. I should have looked away; instead, I listened.*

The ink grew slightly darker, as if her hand had pressed harder.

*We walked the garden paths that evening, away from the music and the watchful eyes. He spoke of books, of far-off cities, of the sea. He asked nothing of my fortune, my lineage, my dowry—only of what stirred my heart when I was alone. I could not answer at first, for no one had ever cared to ask.*

Vivienne turned the page.

*By winter, his letters had become the highlight of my weeks. By the first thaw, I knew I would marry him. We wed in the chapel of St. Jude on the 3rd of May, 1807. I wore mother's veil, and he placed upon my finger a band of gold etched with the Ashcroft crest. The bells rang for nearly an hour, though it felt like minutes. I was twenty years old, and I believed our days would stretch on forever.*

Vivienne's voice softened, almost faltering.

*I could not know then how brief forever can be.*

She let the silence settle over the room, the fire's crackle the only sound.

Vivienne turned the next page carefully; the script remained elegant, though the ink here was a softer brown, faded with time.

*July 2nd, 1807.*

Father's gift to us was beyond anything I had dared to hope for. He presented Thaddeus and me with a parcel of land—rolling green, bounded by ancient oaks and bordered on one side by the river bend. It was to be ours entirely, a place to shape into the seat of our new life. I asked Thaddeus what we might call it, and without hesitation he said, "Ashcroft Hall."

*We broke ground before the year's end. The plans were grand, perhaps too much so for a pair of newlyweds, yet Thaddeus insisted it should stand for centuries, not merely for us. The work was slow, each stone hauled by hand, every beam cut to measure. In the first winter, only the west wing stood completed—three rooms, a modest kitchen, and a narrow hall that opened to the land like an unfinished thought. We lived there as if it were a palace.*

Vivienne glanced toward the others, her voice lowering as though the fire might carry the words elsewhere.

Vivienne's eyes moved to the next page, the ink here uneven, as though the hand that wrote it trembled.

*December 14th, 1807.*

I write this with a heart heavier than I knew a soul could bear. My beautiful boys—my twins—are gone. Born too soon, too fragile for this world, they slipped away before the first snow could fall. Thaddeus tried to be strong for me, but I saw him weep alone in the half-built hall, his hands clenching the beams as though he could keep the whole house from collapsing beneath the weight of our grief.

I cannot bring myself to enter the nursery we prepared. The little cradles, the blankets my mother stitched, the soft wooden toys—all sit untouched, waiting for hands that will never grasp them. I told the staff the room must remain closed. It is not to be spoken of. Let it be sealed from the world, as if by silence we might keep the ache from swallowing us whole.

Vivienne felt her throat tighten, her voice faltering before she found the strength to continue.

*But God, in His mercy, did not leave me childless for long. In the fall of the following year, 1808, our daughter was born. We named her Cordelia Ashcroft—a name I had dreamed of since I was a girl. Her cry filled the hollow places in my heart, though it could never quite mend the tear the boys had left. Still, she brought light into rooms that had known only shadows.*

Vivienne paused, the fire's warmth seeming dim against the cold that had settled in her chest. Then, with a breath, she turned the page.

*Years passed, and with them the sound of hammers and saws never ceased. By the spring of 1812, five years after we first stepped onto that soil, Ashcroft Hall stood in its full measure—grand windows catching the light, the great staircase sweeping like a river of oak, and the chapel at its heart, consecrated for generations to come.*

*Yet beauty does not safeguard against shadows.*

Vivienne let the last line hang in the warm air of the parlor, the crackle of the fire suddenly feeling too loud, too alive.

Vivienne's eyes lingered on the name *Cordelia Ashcroft*, tracing the letters as though she could feel the woman's life through the ink. But it was the earlier mention of the nursery—sealed, silent, forgotten—that clung to her thoughts.

She set the diary gently on the table, her fingers resting on its worn leather cover. A strange hush seemed to creep into the parlor, the kind that prickled at the back of her neck. She thought she heard something—a faint, high giggle—though the sound was so soft it could have been the wind in the eaves.

Her gaze drifted toward the shadowed hallway, to where the upper floor landing would be just above. She remembered the narrow corridor they had passed days earlier, the door at the very end with its peeling white paint and tarnished brass knob… a door they had never opened.

And then she saw it—through the reflection in the parlor's glass-fronted cabinet—something small and pale moving in the dimness of the hallway, there and gone in the span of a blink.

Vivienne rose abruptly, her pulse quickening. "The nursery," she whispered.

Callum straightened from the hearth. "What nursery?"

"The one Seraphina spoke of. The one they locked away."

She didn't wait for him to answer. The diary still lay open on the table, but whatever truths it held could wait. Something was calling her, and she had the sudden, unshakable certainty that if she followed it now, she'd find the next piece of the puzzle—one that might not wait for her twice.

Vivienne's steps echoed down the corridor, each one pulling her deeper into the oldest bones of the house. The west wing had always felt different—narrower hallways, lower ceilings, the faint scent of limewash clinging to the walls. These were the first rooms ever built, she remembered from the diary, finished while the rest of Ashcroft Hall was still a skeleton of timber and scaffolding.

They passed faded portraits whose faces had blurred beneath a film of age. The floorboards here groaned more heavily, as if reluctant to bear the weight of the living.

At the far end, tucked into the corner where the corridor bent sharply, stood the door. Its paint had once been a cheerful white, now cracked and yellowed like brittle parchment. The brass knob was dulled to a dark green patina.

Vivienne hesitated, her fingers hovering over it. "This would have been one of the first rooms completed," she murmured. "If the twins were born here… they would have slept in this room."

Callum glanced at her, his voice low. "And after they were gone?"

"They sealed it," she replied, though the words felt like someone else's memory on her tongue.

Vivienne reached for the knob, but it would not turn. The metal was icy beneath her fingers, as though it had been steeped in winter. She tightened her grip and tried again—nothing.

Frowning, she pulled the heavy master key from her pocket and slid it into the lock. The metal clicked into place, but when she turned it, the mechanism refused to yield.

"It's like it's fused shut," she muttered, trying again, harder this time. Still nothing.

Callum stepped closer, taking the key from her and testing it himself. "It's not the lock," he said quietly. "It's the door. Something's holding it from the other side."

Vivienne's gaze swept over the doorframe. In the dim light, she noticed something crusted along the seam where the door met the jamb—wax, brittle and yellowed with age, poured in a thin line from top to bottom. A seal.

"Someone didn't just shut this room," she said softly. "They meant for it to stay closed."

Her pulse quickened. She took the master key back. With slow, deliberate strokes, she scraped the wax away, each curl falling to the floor like a relic. The air beyond the door seemed to press forward, waiting.

Callum braced himself, shoulder to the wood. "On three," he said.

The first shove rattled the hinges. The second splintered the dried paint. On the third, the door gave way with a wrenching shriek, the sound echoing down the west wing as if the house itself cried out.

What came from the gap was not just stale air—it was a cold that slid over their skin, carrying the faintest trace of lavender and something older, sharper… like the breath of an unmarked grave.

Light spilled in through a single high window, revealing furniture swaddled in yellowed sheets: two cradles, a small dresser, a rocking chair that faced the wall.

Something shifted—so slight she might have missed it—on the cradle's edge. A porcelain doll, its painted eyes catching the light, seemed to be watching her.

Vivienne crossed the room slowly, the floor whispering underfoot. She reached for the doll, and as she lifted it, she felt the weight was wrong. Vivienne's fingers brushed past the doll's porcelain cheek to the hidden seam along its back. The latch gave with a tiny click, and inside, tightly rolled and bound with faded ribbon, was a slip of parchment.

She eased it free, the paper brittle yet warm as if it had been waiting for her touch.

"It's not just a toy…" she whispered, her voice carrying in the hushed nursery. "…it's a message."

Carefully, she unrolled the scroll. The ink had faded to a smoky brown, the hand elegant but urgent. She read aloud:

*When innocence is veiled, truth hides in shadow.*
*Seek not the obvious, for wisdom lies where the heart once played.*
*The choice will not be yours alone—*
*but the righteous path will reveal itself in the listening.*

The words seemed to breathe in the stillness, as though the nursery itself was holding them.

Vivienne's gaze drifted to a tarnished brass plaque fixed high on the nursery's wall, the letters etched deep enough to survive time's wear.

THE FORGOTTEN NURSERY
— Consecrated in 1938 —
Dedicated to Ophelia Ashcroft
Bearer of the Word of Wisdom
Where laughter lingers in the silence,
And innocence guards the truth unseen.

A chill curled up her spine as she stepped back, the porcelain doll still in her hands. The firelight from the hallway lantern flickered across the plaque, making the last line shimmer faintly, as though the metal itself breathed. She exchanged a glance with Callum and Adele—none of them spoke. Words felt too heavy here.

They left quietly, closing the nursery door behind them. The west wing seemed darker than before, the air thick with something unspoken, as if the house itself had listened in.

Back in the parlor, the warmth of the fire drew them closer. Vivienne set the doll carefully on a side table, beside the diary wrapped in its faded veil. The room's hush was broken only by the pop and hiss of the logs until Callum strolled in a few minutes later, a silver tray in hand. He set it down on the low table—cheese, bread, and a decanter of deep amber liquid—his way of breaking the spell without saying so.

# Chapter 58

The fire's glow danced lazily on the parlor walls, but it did nothing to quiet Vivienne's mind. Sleep would not come—not after what she'd uncovered.

Nine Resonant Objects. Each hidden, each whispering fragments of a truth buried for centuries. And now... she had them all.

Her gaze shifted to the mantel, where several of the objects rested side by side—the comb, the doll, the ornate hand mirror—silent witnesses to a puzzle finally complete.

Her thoughts snagged on the names.

Genevieve.

Isolde.

Ophelia.

Evadne.

Anastasia.

Viviette.

Isadora.

Cordelia.

Seraphina.

She had seen them before—not just on room plaques, but carved into cold stone deep beneath Ashcroft Hollow. That day in the underground chamber, the narrow corridor had opened into the circular vault hewn from the bedrock itself. Nine columns had stood sentinel around the perimeter, each etched with a woman's name… the same nine names she'd been walking past for weeks without seeing the connection.

Her pulse quickened. Those names weren't random. They weren't merely memorials. They were markers—each tied to a Resonant Object, each object meant to be found.

Vivienne looked at Callum, who was still lounging in the armchair, eyes half-closed but watching her closely.

"They weren't just women of the family," she said slowly. "They were chosen. Guardians, maybe. Each one kept a piece of something… and now they're all here."

Callum leaned forward, resting his elbows on his knees. "And when all nine pieces come together?"

She glanced toward the diary still lying open on the side table. "That's what I intend to find out."

She reached for it, fingers brushing over the worn leather cover—knowing that somewhere between its inked pages and those carved names lay the key to Ashcroft Hollow's deepest secret.

Vivienne thumbed through the fragile pages, the scent of old paper rising like a faint ghost from the past. Her eyes skimmed over passages of household accounts, garden plans, and polite correspondence, her mind barely registering the mundane details. She was searching for something… anything… that might explain the names, the objects, the hidden chamber in the rock.

Halfway through, her gaze caught on an entry dated *October 14th, 1813*—its ink darker, the script tighter, as if the writer's hand had been guided by urgency.

*There are moments when the air itself bends to one's will, when sound carries farther than it ought, and whispers travel to ears they were never meant for. Today, as the mist clung low to the orchard, I found I could still the wind with nothing more than a thought. The leaves froze mid-rustle, the world holding its breath for me. I did not tell Thaddeus. I fear even he would not understand… yet the power grows. Each day, it grows.*

Vivienne stilled. The words were not a fanciful turn of phrase—they were a confession.

She read on, feeling the rhythm of Seraphina's pen quicken:

*It began when I held the ornate hand mirror my mother left me. The world grew sharper—sounds more distant yet more clear, like bells rung in the fog. At first, I thought it a blessing… but blessings carry their own shadows. Sometimes I hear voices when no one is near. Sometimes I know things I should not. I fear what this makes me, yet I cannot turn away from it. It is mine. It is me.*

Vivienne's fingers tightened around the diary's spine. A gift. A power. And if Seraphina had one… perhaps the other women did too.

She looked toward the mantel, where the Resonant Objects seemed to gleam faintly in the firelight, as though listening.

Vivienne turned the page. The next entry was dated only weeks later, and the handwriting had shifted again—firmer now, as though Seraphina had embraced what she once feared.

*It came to me through my mother's mirror—the one with the gilded frame and the roses etched in silver. When my fingers brushed its surface, the glass rippled as though it were water, and then… I saw. Not my own reflection, but the memory of a girl I once knew, kneeling in the rain, burying something she swore she'd never speak of. I had not thought of her in years, yet there she was before me, as real as the fire in my hearth.*

*I have tried it again and again. Each time, the mirror reveals a truth someone has kept locked in their heart—a moment never told, never written, never confessed. I cannot choose the memory; it chooses me. And though it feels a trespass, I cannot deny the pull. The Word of Knowledge, the priest called it when I asked in careful half-truths. But I do not think even he understood the cost.*

Vivienne's pulse quickened. She thought of the chamber carved into the rock, the nine names etched into its columns. Genevieve. Isolde. Ophelia. Evadne. Anastasia. Viviette. Isadora. Cordelia. Seraphina.

Nine women. Nine gifts. Nine Resonant Objects.

The ornate mirror she had placed on the mantel seemed to catch the flicker of the fire in a way no other object did—holding the light, bending it, almost breathing with it.

She closed the diary slowly, her mind heavy with the knowledge.

The firelight glinted faintly on the fractured glass of the ornate hand mirror. Vivienne rose, the diary still in her hand, and crossed the parlor.

She hesitated before touching it—her reflection was broken into jagged shards, each piece catching her eyes at a slightly different angle, as though they belonged to many versions of her at once.

The moment her fingertips brushed the cool silver frame, the air shifted. The crack running through the glass gave a delicate ping, like the faintest note from a crystal goblet.

She stepped back, startled, as the fracture began to knit itself together—slow, deliberate, and soundless now, the edges of each splinter sliding into perfect alignment. Within seconds, the glass was whole, clear, and impossibly smooth.

The flames in the hearth dimmed, their orange light replaced by a strange silvery glow that seemed to emanate from within the mirror itself. Her reflection wavered and then vanished entirely.

In its place: a scene she could not possibly know.

A woman—Seraphina—stood in a candlelit chamber, the mirror cradled in her hands, her eyes fixed not on the glass but on someone beyond Vivienne's sight. And then the scene changed again: a boy hiding a folded letter beneath a floorboard, his hands trembling; an older man sitting alone in the chapel, weeping into his palms.

The images bled into one another, flashes of moments ripped from lives long past, none of which had ever been spoken aloud.

Vivienne's breath caught. The mirror was showing her what it had once shown Seraphina—the unspoken truths, the memories locked in silence.

And yet… she felt it wasn't done.

The silver light pulsed once, faint but insistent, like the heartbeat of something alive.

# Chapter 59

The embers in the hearth had burned to ash, the silver light of the mirror gone as though it had never been. At some point, sleep had claimed her—though it was not a restful sleep.

Vivienne drifted through dreams stitched together from fragments she'd seen: Seraphina's solemn eyes, the boy with the letter, the chapel shadows, the laughter of unseen children. Nine objects shimmered around her in the dream, circling like planets around a sun she couldn't quite make out.

When morning light finally broke through the parlor curtains, she woke with a jolt, heart pounding.

For a moment she sat in the quiet, the dream still clinging to her like mist. And then the realization struck—sharp, electric.

She had them. All nine of the Resonant Objects.

The hair comb from the Bridal Suite that had Evadne's name on the plaque. The porcelain doll from the Forgotten Nursery. The cracked (now whole) hand mirror from the Mirror Room with Seraphina's name on that plaque. The others, each in their careful wrappings, all gathered.

But what now?

She went up stairs and dressed quickly, her mind buzzing. The diary, the columns in the cavern, the matching names—all of it pointed to something bigger, something she was meant to see.

In the dining room, Dominic was already pacing with a mug of coffee in hand. Callum sat at the far end of the table, flipping through a worn leather-bound atlas. Adele was near the window, sketchbook open, half-listening to the others.

Vivienne stepped in, the air shifting with her urgency.

"I've figured it out," she said. "Or at least, part of it. I have all nine of the Resonant Objects."

Three heads turned toward her.

Dominic set down his mug. "All nine? You're certain?"

She nodded, pulling the list from her coat pocket, tapping each name with her finger. "Every one. And I think the women whose names are on those columns—they're the same ones tied to the objects. Genevieve, Isolde, Ophelia, Evadne, Anastasia, Viviette, Isadora, Cordelia, and Seraphina. Each one connected to a word, a gift, a… power."

Adele's eyes narrowed in thought. "So now what? What do they do?"

"That," Vivienne said, exhaling, "Is the part I don't know yet. But I think—no, I know— they're meant to be used together."

Callum leaned forward, forearms on the table. "Then, we'd better be ready for whatever comes with it."

Before anyone could respond, a low vibration shuddered through the floorboards—so faint Vivienne wondered if she'd imagined it. But then the chandelier above the table trembled, crystal drops clicking together like distant chimes.

Callum looked up sharply. "That wasn't wind."

In the silence that followed, a muffled thud echoed from somewhere deep within the west wing, followed by the slow, deliberate creak of a door swinging open.

"We locked everything last night," Dominic said, already moving toward the hall.

"No," Vivienne whispered, her mind racing. "Not everything."

They followed the sound through the narrow corridor. The air grew colder with each step, the scent of old wood and something metallic seeping in. At the far end, where the corridor bent toward the west wing, a strip of pale light glowed under a door—one Vivienne knew for certain had been shut for decades.

She reached for the handle but stopped. The metal was warm—unnervingly so, as though someone had just let go.

Dominic stepped forward, but Vivienne held up a hand. "Wait." She pressed her ear to the door. Nothing—no footsteps, no rustle—only the faint ticking of something mechanical.

Callum crouched and peered at the thin line of light spilling under the door. "That's not candlelight. Looks like it's moving."

Adele leaned closer. "Almost… flickering?"

Vivienne's breath caught. She twisted the handle again, and this time it turned with a reluctant groan. The hinges creaked as the door swung inward to reveal a small, dust-laden room. Everything inside was covered in white sheets, except for the far corner where an old wooden rocking horse stood—its eyes glassy, its head tilted toward them.

Beside it, a toy lantern swung gently, casting that strange moving light. But the light wasn't coming from a flame—it pulsed in time with a faint hum, like the resonance of a tuning fork.

Vivienne stepped forward and lifted the lantern. Inside, instead of a wick, there was a tiny compartment. She opened it to reveal a folded scrap of parchment, brittle with age.

Unfolding it, she read aloud:

"Nine voices bound, nine truths entwined. Seek the place where stone remembers and the living cannot tread."

Callum frowned. "That… sounds like the crypt."

Vivienne met his eyes. "Not just any crypt. The one carved into the rock under the hall— the place with the columns."

Dominic's voice was low. "Looks like you've just been handed your next step."

# Chapter 60

The morning air was damp with mist, curling in from the hills and wrapping Ashcroft Hollow in a ghostly shroud. Vivienne was halfway down the staircase when the heavy brass knocker echoed through the hall.

She opened the door—and froze. "Jessie?"

Her friend stood there grinning, a satchel slung across her shoulder, cheeks flushed from the chill. "Surprise! I was in the area for… well, work," she said, brushing past Vivienne without waiting for an invitation. "I just couldn't resist finally seeing this place you've been buried in."

Vivienne blinked. Jessie never "just happened" to be in this part of the country— it was miles from anywhere connected to her job. "How… thoughtful," Vivienne said, shutting the door behind her.

Jessie's gaze roamed the entry hall, lingering a little too long on the carved banister, the oil portraits, the shadowed corners where the light didn't quite reach. "Wow. It's even better than the stories."

"The stories?" Vivienne asked sharply.

Jessie's smile didn't waver. "Oh, you know. Old houses, creaky floors, secret histories… I love this kind of thing." She set her satchel on a side table with a casual air that somehow felt like she was staking a claim.

Vivienne tried to shake off the unease creeping up her spine. "Well, it's… not exactly a tourist stop. I'm working on something here. A… restoration."

Jessie's eyes sparkled. "Even better. I can help. I've been dying for a break from my routine, and this is exactly the change of pace I need."

Before Vivienne could object, Jessie launched into a story about "bad timing" with her apartment repairs—water damage, mold, and a landlord "on vacation until next month." It was all very convenient. Too convenient.

"Just a few days," Jessie promised, squeezing Vivienne's hand. "I'll stay out of your way. You won't even know I'm here."

Vivienne forced a smile, but her thoughts churned. She couldn't very well throw Jessie out—not without looking paranoid—but she couldn't have her poking around either. Not now, when she'd just unlocked all nine objects and was close to discovering their purpose.

From the corner of her eye, Vivienne noticed Jessie glancing toward the west wing—the sealed corridor. Her pulse quickened.

"Guest room's upstairs," Vivienne said quickly, steering her toward the opposite side of the house. "You'll be more comfortable there."

Jessie let herself be led, but not before Vivienne caught the flicker of a smile that didn't reach her eyes.

—

The warm scent of baking bread drifted through the corridor as Vivienne led Jessie toward the kitchen. The steady clink of crockery and the low hum of Adele's voice—singing something soft and old—spilled into the hallway.

When they stepped inside, Adele was at the long wooden counter, sleeves rolled up, flour dusting her forearms. She glanced up, ready with a smile—until she saw Jessie.

"Oh! Jessie," Adele said, setting down the rolling pin. "Well, isn't this a surprise."

Jessie beamed. "Adele! It's been ages. Boston, right? For Viv's birthday. You made that incredible lemon tart."

Adele wiped her hands on her apron. "That's right." Her tone was warm, but her eyes flicked briefly to Vivienne. "Though I wasn't expecting to see you... here."

Vivienne caught the faint emphasis on here and wished she could pull Adele aside for a private word.

"Yeah, total coincidence," Jessie said lightly, helping herself to a chair at the scrubbed oak table. "I had some unexpected time off, figured I'd finally see this place for myself. Viv's been keeping it all to herself for far too long."

"Mmh," Adele murmured, returning to her dough. "Well, Callum and Dominic are out with the horses. They'll be back before lunch. You'll get to meet them too."

Jessie's gaze shifted toward the window, where the mist rolled low across the paddock. "I'd like that."

Vivienne set Jessie's satchel down by the door. "I'll show her to her room in a bit," she said, a little too quickly.

Adele's hands kept working the dough, but Vivienne saw it—the slight tightening of her jaw, the flicker of a look that said, *We'll talk later.*

Jessie leaned back in her chair, surveying the kitchen with idle curiosity. "So, this is the famous Ashcroft Hollow kitchen. It's… cozy."

"Cozy," Adele repeated, the corner of her mouth twitching. "Yes. For now."

Vivienne forced a smile, already dreading the conversation Adele would want to have once Jessie was out of earshot.

# Chapter 61

The back door banged open, letting in a gust of cool air and the faint scent of hay. Callum strode in first, tugging off his gloves, Dominic a step behind, his boots leaving faint smudges on the worn flagstone floor.

"We've been talking," Callum began, brushing straw from his sleeve, "And I think the way those objects—" He stopped dead mid-sentence, his eyes landing on Jessie at the table. "Uh… who's this?"

Vivienne set down her mug, her voice deliberately casual. "Callum, this is Jessie—my friend from Boston."

Jessie's smile curved slow, assessing. "Well… you're just as cute as she said."

Callum blinked, a faint flush creeping up his neck. "Uh… thanks?" He shot Vivienne a sideways glance, but she ignored it.

Dominic stepped in, the door swinging shut behind him. His gaze swept the room once before settling on Jessie, sharp and unreadable.

"And this," Vivienne continued, "Is Dominic. My biological father."

Jessie had just taken a sip of coffee. The words hit her mid-swallow, and she sputtered, coughing as dark liquid sprayed onto her napkin.

"Your—?" she started, wiping at her mouth quickly, her eyes flicking to Dominic with something that looked almost like... recognition.

Dominic's expression didn't change, but there was a weight to the way he regarded her, as if measuring the exact depth of her surprise.

"You weren't expecting me?" he asked lightly, though the undertone was anything but casual.

Jessie recovered her composure with a quick, practiced laugh. "I just... didn't know. That's all. Vivienne has never mentioned you."

"Mm." Dominic moved past her to hang his coat, his gaze lingering just a fraction too long. "Well. Now you do."

The silence that followed was thick enough to cut, broken only by Adele setting a basket of bread on the table.

Dominic slid into the chair opposite Jessie, his movements unhurried, deliberate. "It's been a long time since I've seen eyes like yours," he said, tearing a piece of bread.

Jessie froze for just a beat—too quick for anyone but Vivienne to catch—before smiling in a way that didn't quite reach those eyes. ""I'm… not sure what that's supposed to mean."

Callum frowned, glancing between them. "Okay… anyone else feeling like I missed a chapter?"

Adele busied herself at the stove, but Vivienne didn't miss the faint crease between her brows. She knew Adele well enough to recognize when her mom was filing away a detail for later.

"Maybe," Dominic said smoothly, "We'll all be caught up soon enough." He looked to Vivienne. "You going to tell us why Jessie's here?"

Jessie jumped in before Vivienne could answer. "Spur-of-the-moment road trip. I just… needed a change of scenery." Her tone was light, but there was an undercurrent to it—like a note played just off-key. "And when you told me that you'd inherited Ashcroft Hollow…" She trailed off, sipping her coffee.

Vivienne forced a polite smile. "Well, here she is."

Callum leaned back, watching Jessie as though trying to decide whether she was trouble or just odd. Dominic's gaze, however, was sharper—assessing in a way Vivienne didn't like.

Lunch carried on with small talk, but the easy warmth of the kitchen felt distant now, replaced with something brittle. Jessie laughed at Callum's stories, asked Adele for seconds, but Vivienne's mind was already elsewhere.

Because if Dominic knew something about Jessie's past—and Jessie knew more about Ashcroft Hollow than she was admitting—then Vivienne had a problem.

And problems here had a way of turning into curses.

# Chapter 62

Jessie set her coffee cup down and turned to Vivienne with an eager brightness. "Why don't you show me around the place? I've only seen bits and pieces so far."

Vivienne hesitated—something in Jessie's tone made it sound less like a question than a claim—but she forced a smile. "Sure. There's plenty to see."

The two women disappeared down the hall, their voices fading into the stairwell.

Dominic waited until the sound of their footsteps were gone before leaning toward Adele and Callum, his voice low.

"Those eyes," he murmured. "I've seen them before."

Adele frowned. "What are you talking about?"

"In a portrait," Dominic said. "Up in the west gallery. Malrick Vexmoor's portrait."

Callum's brows rose. "You think she's—"

"I don't think. I know," Dominic cut in.

Without another word, the three left the kitchen and climbed the narrow back stairs. The west gallery was dim, its long row of portraits half-swallowed by shadows. Dominic stopped in front of one—Malrick's—a tall, dark-eyed figure rendered in oil with a gaze that seemed to follow them.

"Tell me you don't see it," Dominic said.

Adele stared. "It's… uncanny."

Callum gave a low whistle. "Exactly the same eyes."

Later, when Jessie and Vivienne returned to the parlor, the air felt heavier somehow. Dominic, still standing near the mantel, asked casually—too casually—"What's your last name, Jessie?"

She glanced between them. "Vexmoor. Why?"

The silence that followed was thick enough to taste.

Callum shifted uncomfortably, Adele's expression tightened, and Vivienne's smile faltered just enough for Jessie to notice. Jessie's gaze swept the room, a flicker of something—amusement? satisfaction?— glinting in her eyes.

"Well," she said lightly, "That was awkward."

Jessie leaned back in her chair, the corners of her mouth twitching as if she were suppressing a smile. "You'd think I'd just confessed to a murder with the way you're all looking at me."

"No one's saying that," Vivienne replied quickly, though her voice had an edge.

Dominic's gaze stayed fixed on Jessie, measuring her. "The Vexmoor family has… history with Ashcroft Hollow."

Jessie tilted her head, her expression innocently curious. "Oh? You'll have to tell me all about it."

"Some of it isn't exactly pleasant," Adele said, her words careful but cool.

Jessie's eyes glinted. "That's the best kind of history."

Vivienne stood, forcing the moment to end. "Come on, Jessie. I'll show you the upstairs study—you can see some of the restoration work."

They left the room, Jessie's boots clicking softly against the wood floor, her laughter trailing faintly behind.

# Chapter 63

When Vivienne closed the parlor doors again a few minutes later, the old latch caught with a dull click.

"You're back fast," Callum remarked, brows raised.

"I just remembered something I needed to check with you," she said quickly, moving deeper into the room before Jessie's echoing voice could catch up with her.

Callum exhaled, gaze dark. "She's enjoying this. Every second of it."

Dominic's jaw tightened as he gave a sharp nod. "And she's not here just to visit Vivienne."

Vivienne crossed her arms, steadying herself. "There's no way Jessie can be from the same Vexmoors you're talking about. I've known her for years—birthdays, work trips, late-night calls. Never once has she said anything strange. Not about family. Not about Ashcroft Hollow. Nothing."

Dominic didn't answer right away. He leaned against the mantle, watching her closely. "People hide things, Vivienne. Sometimes for years."

Callum shook his head slightly. "Her eyes, though. You can't fake that shade. I've only seen it once before—in Malrick's portrait."

Adele's voice was softer, but no less wary. "It's possible she doesn't even know the whole truth about her own family."

Vivienne bristled. "Or maybe she's just… Jessie. My friend. Who happened to show up at a bad time."

"Or a very convenient one," Dominic said, his tone unreadable.

From the other side of the parlor doors, the old floorboard just beyond the rug creaked. It was faint—barely more than the sigh of the house settling—but Jessie froze where she stood in the hallway. She had come back, meaning to ask Vivienne about an upstairs corridor she'd glimpsed earlier, but the sound of her own name—low, tense—had stopped her.

She leaned ever so slightly toward the seam between the double doors.

"…very convenient one," Dominic's voice was saying, each word slow, deliberate.

Convenient? Her?

Inside, Vivienne's voice rose, sharp with defense. "She's my friend. And until I see proof otherwise, I'm not treating her like a suspect in whatever game this house is playing."

Jessie's lips curved into the faintest smile. Oh, if only they knew.

She eased back before the latch rattled or a shadow betrayed her. By the time Vivienne opened the door a minute later, Jessie was standing a few paces away, pretending to study an old side table as if it were the most fascinating thing in the house.

"Find anything interesting?" Vivienne asked.

Jessie turned, her expression all innocence. "Just… wondering what else this place is hiding."

Vivienne forced a polite smile, though something in Jessie's tone snagged at the edge of her thoughts. "It's got plenty of corners we haven't explored yet," she said carefully.

Jessie's eyes brightened—not the way they usually did when she found something charming or beautiful, but with a glimmer Vivienne couldn't quite name. "Then maybe you could show me a few? I saw a hallway upstairs earlier, past the landing, with these strange carved panels. I thought it might lead somewhere interesting."

Before Vivienne could answer, Adele's voice carried from the parlor. "Vivienne, could you come here a moment?"

Vivienne glanced at Jessie. "Give me five minutes, and then we'll go take a look."

"Of course." Jessie's smile was warm, almost eager.

She watched Vivienne disappear through the parlor doors, then turned toward the grand staircase. Her hand lingered on the banister, the wood smooth from generations of touch. The hallway she'd mentioned did lead somewhere interesting—she'd made sure of it earlier.

She climbed the steps in silence, her footsteps swallowed by the thick runner. At the far end of the hall, just past the carved panels, an old door stood slightly ajar. Beyond it, the air was cooler, tinged with the scent of dust and something faintly metallic.

Jessie stepped inside, letting the shadows close around her.

If this house had treasures… she was going to find them before Vivienne ever knew they were gone.

# Chapter 64

That night, Jessie excused herself from the parlor earlier than the others, claiming the day's travel had caught up to her. Vivienne offered to walk her to her room, but Jessie waved her off with a quick smile.

She closed the heavy oak door behind her, sliding the bolt until it clicked. The room's single lamp cast a pale, amber glow over the four-poster bed and faded damask curtains. From her travel case, Jessie drew out a leather-bound book so old the spine had begun to crumble.

The cover was unmarked, but she didn't need a title. She knew every inch of it—the journal of Althea Vexmoor, the woman who had been Malrick's chosen confidante before his death. The one he had trusted with his darkest work. Passed from mother to daughter, generation after generation, until it reached Jessie.

She sat cross-legged on the bed, fingers tracing the brittle edges of the pages. A faint scent of ash and myrrh clung to the paper, as though it had soaked in decades of candlelit rituals.

Jessie turned to one of her favorite passages, written in a looping, slanted hand:

*December 14th, 1948*

*Malrick says the walls will remember us. Tonight, the mirrors hummed again, their glass rippling like water as the circle chanted. The Ashcroft woman sleeps two floors away, unaware her fate has already been sewn. Malrick took a lock of her hair and set it in the black salt. The air thickened—sweet, then bitter. He says the house will breathe for us now.*

Jessie's lips curved slightly. She turned the page.

*February 2nd, 1949*

*The oak in the chapel yard whispered to him today. I heard it—low, grinding words in a tongue older than the stones. Malrick pressed his palm to its bark and blood ran from the cracks. He said the tree would hide what must never be found until the right bloodline came to claim it. The roots will choke any unworthy hand.*

Another page, this one smudged with something dark:

*October 31st, 1950*

*We completed the Ninth Binding. The objects are*

*awake now. He says they will answer only to the chosen—one for each Gift. But gifts can be stolen, given, traded. All it takes is the right… persuasion. And if persuasion fails, there are older ways.*

Jessie's fingers tightened on the paper. Her pulse quickened—not in fear, but in anticipation.

She closed the journal gently, as if not to wake something sleeping inside.

Outside, the hallway groaned under a weight that wasn't footsteps. The lamp flickered. Somewhere, faintly, a mirror hummed.

Jessie smiled in the dark.

# Chapter 65

The morning light spilled weakly through the parlor windows, catching in the dust like golden threads. Vivienne stepped inside, her eyes instantly darting to the table where the nine Resonant Objects had been laid out the night before.

The table was bare.

"Callum," she called toward the open doorway.

He appeared from the hallway, rubbing his hands with a towel. "What's wrong?"

She gestured to the empty surface. "What happened to all the objects? Did you move them?"

He shook his head. "Haven't touched them. Thought you took them."

Her unease deepened. "Where are my parents?"

They were in the study, going over a thick folder of old estate papers when she entered.

"Mom, Dad," she began without preamble, "The objects—where are they?"

Dominic set the papers aside. "Safe," he said simply.

"Safe where?"

"Hidden," he replied, "Where Jessie can't find them."

Vivienne hesitated. "Maybe we should just... include her. Let her help."

Dominic and Adele spoke at the exact same moment, their voices cutting sharp through the room.

"No."

The firmness in their tone made her blink.

Adele softened hers only slightly. "There are things you don't know about her yet, Vivienne. Until you do, she can't be part of this."

Vivienne wanted to argue, but something in her father's eyes stopped her. A wall had gone up there—one she didn't think she could break through.

That night, long after everyone had gone to bed, sleep finally claimed her.

She was standing in the great hall, yet it wasn't quite the same—shadows bent unnaturally, and the air shimmered with a dull, silver light. One by one, the nine Resonant Objects appeared before her, each resting on its own column of carved stone. The mirror gleamed, its once-cracked surface now flawless. The porcelain doll's painted eyes seemed to follow her. The comb, the diary, the veil, each radiated a subtle pulse, like the beat of a distant heart.

They were waiting.

When she reached out, the scene shifted— columns stretched high above her, carved from rock that dripped with centuries of damp. This wasn't the hall upstairs. It was the crypt, carved deep into the stone beneath Ashcroft Hall. She could feel it in her bones.

Footsteps echoed, though she couldn't see who made them. Somewhere beyond the columns, water dripped in a slow, steady rhythm.

Vivienne's gaze fell on one column in particular—its surface etched with spiraling script she didn't recognize. As she drew closer, the objects seemed to lean toward her, silently urging her forward.

A shadow passed behind her.

She turned—and found Dominic standing there, his face lit by the faint glow of the mirror he held.

"Not just any crypt," she heard herself say, the words forming without thought. "The one carved into the rock under the hall—the place with the columns."

Dominic's voice was low, certain. "Looks like you've just been handed your next step."

She woke with a start, her heart hammering. The echo of his voice still lingered in her mind, as if it had been more than just a dream.

# Chapter 66

Vivienne found Dominic in the library, a half-empty cup of coffee steaming beside a stack of ledgers. She closed the door behind her before crossing the room.

"I need to tell you about my dream," she began, perching on the edge of the leather chair across from him.

He looked up, attentive but wary.

"It wasn't just a dream—it was… the objects, all of them, gathered on stone columns in the crypt. And then it replayed— word for word—the moment from the other day. My own voice saying, *Not just any crypt. The one carved into the rock under the hall—the place with the columns.*"

Dominic's gaze sharpened as she continued, "And you were there. You said, *Looks like you've just been handed your next step.*' It felt… real. Like you were actually there."

He was silent for a moment, then leaned back slowly. "And you think this crypt is where the objects need to be?"

"I know it is," she said. "But I can't go down there with Jessie hanging around. I need her… distracted."

From the doorway, Callum's voice came lightly, though his eyes told her he'd heard more. "I could take her riding this morning."

Vivienne turned in surprise.

He stepped in, leaning a shoulder against the doorframe. "We can make it sound like a casual thing—no suspicion. I'll say you've got to go see Maggie about something important. That should buy you a few hours."

Dominic considered, then gave a small nod. "Make sure she believes it. And Vivienne…" He held her gaze. "You've been down there before, but that doesn't mean it will be the same now. Places like that… they shift. Sometimes what waits for you isn't what you left behind."

A chill rippled down her spine at his words. "All the more reason I have to go back," she said quietly.

Dominic's expression hardened with resolve. "Then I'm coming with you," he said, his voice leaving no room for argument. "And I'll bring the objects. All of them."

Before Vivienne could respond, footsteps sounded in the hallway. Adele appeared in the doorway, wiping her hands on a linen towel. "Good," she said briskly, her eyes moving from Dominic to Vivienne. "Because you're not going down there without me, either."

Vivienne blinked. "Both of you?"

Adele crossed the room, her tone steady but laced with something darker. "If the crypt has changed, you'll need more than just the objects to get through whatever's guarding it now. And with a Vexmoor sniffing around, we can't afford to take chances."

———

Callum leaned casually against the doorframe. "You ever ridden before?"

Jessie's eyes lit with a challenge. "Not since I was a kid, but I'll give it a try."

"Good. I'll saddle two of the calmer ones. Meet me at the stables in fifteen," he said, disappearing down the hall.

Jessie smiled sweetly, then slipped away toward her guest room. The moment the door shut behind her, the mask of pleasant curiosity melted from her face. She crossed to the small travel trunk at the foot of her bed, lifting the false bottom to reveal the leather-bound journal—its cover darkened with age, the edges curling like withered leaves.

She sat on the edge of the bed, fingers tracing the faint embossing: Vexmoor. The pages crackled as she opened to a section marked with a strip of faded black ribbon. The spidery handwriting belonged to a lady long dead—Malrick's confidant, the last one to serve him before his death.

Her lips moved silently over the words, a chant carried from another century. The air seemed to thicken, shadows along the walls stretching unnaturally toward her. A low vibration rattled the glass on the nightstand, though the rest of the house remained still.

She sprinkled a pinch of black salt from a small pouch, letting it fall into the journal's spine. The ink shimmered, as though the letters themselves were waking.

Her voice dropped to a whisper, the final line curling with intent:

"Stone, remember not the seal but the shadow—

Let the key grow cold and the lock forget its shape."

From far beneath the house, deep in the rock under Ashcroft Hollow, something answered.

The crypt's columns, once carved in perfect alignment, shuddered. Fine cracks laced across the stone floor, and the air inside thickened with a metallic tang, as though the earth itself had drawn a slow, dangerous breath.

Jessie closed the journal with a satisfied snap, tucking it back under the false bottom of her trunk. Her expression smoothed again into casual charm as she reached for her riding boots.

No one needed to know what she had just done. Not yet.

# Chapter 67

Vivienne was halfway down the corridor toward the library when the world seemed to shift under her feet.

It wasn't enough to make her stumble—just a strange, tilting sensation, as if the floor had risen and dropped again in the space of a breath.

She stopped, hand braced against the wall.

A faint, metallic hum brushed her ears, so low she couldn't tell if it came from outside or somewhere deep within the house itself. Then, like a whisper through glass, she thought she heard her own name.

She shook her head, blaming the restless night. But when she stepped away from the wall, a sharp ache bloomed behind her eyes— brief, but sharp enough to make her catch her breath.

In her mind's eye, the crypt flashed: the ring of columns, the cold stone, the dais at its center. Only this time, it wasn't as she remembered. The torches were out. The columns… wrong somehow, their shapes distorted, closing her in. And in the shadows between them, something moved.

She blinked hard, and the vision was gone.

Callum's voice carried faintly from the stables, Jessie's laughter following close behind. The sound made Vivienne's stomach tighten, though she couldn't have said why.

She tried to shake it off, telling herself it was just the weight of what lay ahead—finding the crypt, unlocking its secrets. But even as she headed for the library, the thought lingered like a burr under her skin:

Something had changed down there. And whatever it was, it was waiting for her.

—

The stone steps to the crypt were colder than Vivienne remembered, each one seeping a chill into her bones. Their lantern light barely dented the dark, pooling in weak circles as they descended into the vast chamber beneath Ashcroft Hall.

The columns stood as they always had— nine in a perfect ring, each carved with the names she'd now committed to memory. Yet something about them seemed… duller. The air lacked its usual hum, as if the place itself were holding its breath.

Dominic set the satchel down in the center of the room. One by one, he withdrew the objects: the comb and veil, the pressed herb book, the porcelain doll and scroll, the hand mirror, the crystal singing bell, the multilingual rosary, the jet pendant, the brass oil lamp, and the silver hourglass locket —they looked strange here—too fragile against the looming stone.

"Well," Dominic muttered, "Where do we start?"

They tried arranging the objects at the base of their corresponding columns, matching each artifact to the name carved in the stone. Nothing.

Adele suggested placing them in the center, forming a circle of their own. Again, nothing.

Vivienne hesitated, then picked up the hand mirror. She held it toward the columns, wondering if it might reveal some hidden mark or inscription. The glass rippled faintly, but the image it returned was wrong— columns leaning inwards, their carved names melting into something unreadable. She jerked it away, unsettled.

"Maybe they have to be used," Dominic said, taking the comb and running it through the air as though over an invisible head. Adele hummed an old hymn near the bell. Vivienne opened the herb book, reading aloud one of entries. The echoes faded almost instantly, swallowed by the stone.

Nothing worked.

The longer they stayed, the heavier the air felt. A faint draft slithered through the crypt, carrying a whisper too low to make out. Vivienne rubbed her arms against the sudden chill, unaware that it carried the same cadence as the one Jessie had spoken hours before.

Dominic broke the silence. "It's as if something's resisting us."

Adele's voice was tight. "Or someone."

They packed the objects away, none of them admitting the uneasy truth—they had no idea what they were doing, and whatever this place had been waiting for, it was no longer entirely theirs to control.

# Chapter 68

Vivienne was waiting in the courtyard when the thud of hooves announced their return. Jessie swung down from the saddle with surprising grace, cheeks flushed, hair wind-tossed beneath her riding helmet. Callum led the horse toward the stable, throwing Vivienne a look that was part question, part warning.

Jessie brushed a few stray hairs from her face and crossed over.

"God, Viv, that was incredible," she said, her voice still carrying the thrill of the ride. "Haven't done that in years. Callum's got a real knack for keeping things… interesting."

Vivienne smiled faintly. "Glad you enjoyed yourself."

Jessie tilted her head. "And you? Find what you were looking for in town?"

Vivienne met her gaze. "Something like that."

Jessie's smile didn't quite reach her eyes. "Mysterious as ever."

"Maggie didn't have what I needed, but said she would order it in," Vivienne replied, her tone light but edged.

For a moment, they stood in the quiet of the courtyard, each measuring the other, both acutely aware of the unspoken—Vivienne thinking of the crypt, Jessie thinking of the journal tucked away upstairs.

Callum re-emerged from the stable, wiping his hands. "Either of you ladies want some tea?

Jessie laughed and looped her arm through Vivienne's. "Tea sounds perfect. Lead the way, Viv."

Vivienne led her, but every step back toward the house felt like walking a fine, fraying tightrope—both of them smiling, both of them hiding more than they were saying.

They settled in the small sitting room off the kitchen, A tea tray between them. Jessie curled into the armchair like she had a hundred times before in Vivienne's Boston apartment, legs tucked beneath her, fingers wrapped around a steaming cup.

"So," Jessie said, voice low and warm, "How are you, really? I mean… all this." She gestured vaguely toward the window, where the gables of Ashcroft Hollow rose dark against the afternoon sky. "The house, your dad suddenly being in the picture—this is a lot, Viv."

Vivienne shrugged, though the weight in her chest made the gesture feel hollow. "It's been… a lot to take in, yeah."

Jessie leaned forward, her eyes wide with concern. "And your grandmother? You mentioned before there were… secrets. What did you find out? Anything interesting?"

Vivienne hesitated. She didn't know much—too much of what she'd learned was tangled up in the strange events of the last few weeks. But Jessie's tone was so familiar, so normal, that for a heartbeat she almost forgot the unease prickling at the edges of her thoughts.

"To be honest… she seemed complicated," Vivienne said finally. "Kind I guess, but… there's more to her story than I realized."

Jessie nodded sympathetically, taking a slow sip of tea before setting her cup down. "Families are always more complicated than they look. And the Ashcrofts? I bet there's more than one skeleton in these closets."

There was a slight pause before she added, almost casually, "What about Malrick? You've mentioned his name once or twice when we were talking about the portraits. Was he some sort of… black sheep or something?”

Vivienne's eyes narrowed slightly. “Black sheep?”

Jessie smiled—soft, disarming. “Just curious. You know me, I love a good old family scandal. Especially when we have the same last name.”

Vivienne tried to smile back, but the air between them felt just a little too heavy now, the shadows in the corners just a little too deep.

Vivienne hesitated, every instinct telling her to change the subject, but Jessie's expectant look was hard to sidestep.

“Fine,” Vivienne said at last, setting her teacup aside. “If you really want to see him, come on.”

They took the narrow back stairs, their footsteps echoing faintly. The west gallery opened before them, a long corridor lined with heavy frames and dim pools of light from the tall windows. Dust hung in the air, swirling like pale smoke with every step.

Vivienne slowed near the far end, stopping before a towering portrait. Malrick Vexmoor's painted eyes glinted with something unreadable—dark irises that seemed almost alive in the shadows. His posture was regal, his hand resting on a silver-topped cane, but it was his gaze that unnerved Vivienne most.

Jessie stepped closer, tilting her head, studying the details. Her voice was soft but edged with something like satisfaction. "Huh… look at that."

Vivienne frowned. "What?"

Jessie glanced at her, a small smile tugging at her lips. "The eyes. Don't you think they look like mine? Same shape, same color—kind of eerie, actually." She let the words hang for a moment before adding, "Do you think… there's any chance we could be related?"

Vivienne's pulse skipped. "Why would you even think that?"

Jessie shrugged, still staring at the portrait. "I don't know. Just a feeling. Maybe it's the house getting to me. Or maybe," she said with a slow, deliberate smile, "Family resemblances run deeper than we realize."

Her reflection shimmered faintly in the glass covering the portrait—so much so that for a flicker of a second, Vivienne could swear it was Malrick himself standing there beside her friend.

# Chapter 69

They turned from Malrick's portrait, their footsteps hushed on the creaking floorboards. Jessie's words still hung in the air—maybe we're related—as Vivienne traced the faint outlines of another frame further down the row. The gilt edges caught what little light seeped through the high windows.

"I don't know much about my great-grandparents," Viv said quietly, almost to herself. "I wish I did."

The silence that followed seemed to deepen, pressing in around them. Almost as if in answer, the portrait of Isolde gave a low, protesting creak.

Both women froze. The sound had come from the portrait of a pale woman in lace, her painted eyes shadowed with sorrow: Isolde, Malrick's wife. Slowly, as though moved by an unseen hand, the massive frame shifted forward on its side hinges. The scent of dust and something older—something metallic, almost coppery—spilled out.

Jessie flinched. "Did you see that?" Her voice cracked, higher than she meant it to be.

Vivienne swallowed hard, then stepped forward. "Help me."

Together, they opened the portrait like a book. Behind it stretched a cramped chamber lined with shelves—dusty glass jars, tattered lace bundles, and, at the center, a carved chest with clawed feet. Resting on top was a leather-bound diary, its cover mottled and dark with age.

Vivienne reached for it, fingers trembling.

"Viv," Jessie hissed, panic curling sharp in her tone. "Don't. Some things—some things shouldn't be touched."

Vivienne hesitated, the weight of the air thick, watching. She could almost feel Isolde's eyes on her through the canvas, waiting.

When her fingers brushed the diary, the chamber seemed to breathe—shadows shifting, a faint rustle like skirts dragging across stone.

Vivienne turned, studying her. "Why do you sound like you *know* that?"

Jessie's throat worked. Her eyes darted to the jars filled with black sediment, to the faint symbols scratched into the walls. "Because…" She stopped, breath quickening. "Because I've read about this kind of thing. Malrick wasn't… he wasn't just dabbling. He bound things. People. Souls. If that's her diary—" Jessie cut herself short, realizing too late the slip.

Vivienne's gaze narrowed. "How do you know that about him?"

Jessie froze. She had been so careful until now, pretending to be the old Boston friend—the girl who drank wine on rooftops and shared secrets under blankets. But here, in the reek of the hidden chamber, her mask cracked.

"I—I overheard things," Jessie stammered, backing toward the doorframe. Her voice dropped to a ragged whisper. "I wanted to believe it was all just stories. I've… I've done little things, Viv. Circles, chants, the kind of magic you laugh off in candlelight. But this—" Her eyes swept the chamber, terror glistening in them. "This isn't games. This is real. And it's hungry."

The silence that followed seemed to breathe, thick and alive. Somewhere in the darkness beyond the shelves, wood creaked as if something shifted on its own.

Vivienne clutched the diary tighter. "Then maybe," she said, her voice low and defiant, "It's time I finally know the truth."

A sudden voice from the hallway snapped the air.

"Viv? You in there?"

The girls froze.

The beam of a flashlight swept across the cracked plaster and into the chamber as Callum's head poked through the doorway. His brow furrowed. "What the hell is this place?" He stepped in, brushing cobwebs from his shoulder.

Vivienne held the book tighter to her chest, her face pale in the flashlight's glow. She hesitated, then looked at Jessie. "She just told me... she knew something about my great-grandparents."

Callum blinked, looking between them. "Wait—what?"

Jessie shifted uneasily, her dark-painted nails picking at the sleeve of her sweater. "I didn't mean—" She swallowed hard. "It's just... I've heard things. About Isolde and Malrick. My parents used to whisper that they were... caught up in rituals. That's all."

Vivienne's stomach knotted, the words chilling her more than the draft that seeped through the chamber's stone walls. "Rituals," she echoed, her voice barely audible.

Callum's gaze dropped to the object clutched against Viv's chest. "And what are you holding?"

Vivienne looked down at the leather-bound diary, its edges cracked and brittle, the faint imprint of a sigil pressed into the cover. She swallowed, her pulse quickening. "It was hidden here behind the portrait. It's hers, I think."

The silence that followed seemed to throb, broken only by the faint creak of the house settling. Somewhere above, a door banged shut on its own.

# Chapter 70

The three of them moved through the chamber slowly, the flickering candlelight making the shadows twitch along the walls. Vivienne brushed her fingers over the old stone, still clutching the leather-bound book against her chest. Callum examined the strange carvings etched into the archway while Jessie hung back, her shoulders drawn in as though the walls themselves pressed too close.

"There's nothing else here," Callum muttered after a while, running a hand through his hair. "Just dust, bones of a house that doesn't want to give away its secrets."

Jessie's eyes darted everywhere but the book Vivienne carried. "It's enough," she said quickly. "We shouldn't stay longer. I don't like it in here."

Vivienne exhaled and nodded. The unease in Jessie's voice only mirrored the tightness building in her own chest. "Let's go back to the kitchen. We need to tell them."

They slipped out of the chamber, the secret door closing behind them with a groan that echoed too long. By the time they reached the kitchen, the warm glow of the hearth felt almost unnatural, too safe against what they had just seen. Adele stood by the stove, stirring a pot, while Dominic was at the table, polishing an old hunting knife.

Adele's face lit with relief at the sight of them. "There you are. We were beginning to worry. Where have you guys been?"

"Viewing Malrick's portrait," Vivienne answered, her voice steady though her hands still trembled slightly. She placed the book on the table, the leather creaking as it settled. "We found… a hidden chamber behind Isolde's portrait. And Jessie told me something—something she should've said sooner."

Dominic's eyes narrowed, his hand stilling on the knife. "What kind of chamber?"

"Stone walls, carvings, symbols. It felt… wrong," Callum cut in, shooting Jessie a look. "And Viv found that." He gestured to the book.

Vivienne glanced at Jessie before continuing, her words deliberate. "Jessie admitted she knew something about the house. That she's heard things."

The air thickened in the kitchen, the only sound the slow bubbling of Adele's pot. Dominic leaned back in his chair, his gaze fixed on Jessie. "Is that true?"

Jessie's lips parted, then closed again. She shifted from one foot to the other. "I didn't mean—"

"Answer me," Dominic snapped, his voice sharp enough to cut the silence.

Jessie flinched. Her bravado, the one she usually wore like armor, seemed to falter. "I've… I've practiced things, okay? Magic. But I never thought it was real. Not like this." Her eyes flicked toward the book on the table, then away quickly. "The shadows—I thought it was in my head. I thought if I ignored it, it would stop."

Adele moved closer, her expression unreadable. "Why didn't you tell us sooner?"

"Because I didn't want to believe it," Jessie whispered, her voice breaking. "Because if I said it out loud, it would mean it was real. And I wasn't ready for that."

Dominic leaned forward, his elbows on the table, eyes boring into her. "Well, Jessie, it's real. And now you're going to tell us everything. Every ritual, every word you've spoken, every shadow you've seen. No more secrets."

Jessie's throat worked as she swallowed, her hands twisting together. For once, the girl who played at being fearless looked very much like a child cornered in the dark.

Jessie's face went pale under the warm kitchen light, her dark eyeliner smudging faintly as she rubbed her wrist anxiously. Everyone was staring at her—Dominic's sharp gaze, Adele's searching eyes, Callum's unreadable expression, and Vivienne's expectant one. The silence stretched long until Jessie finally broke, her voice low but hurried, as if the words had been trapped for too long.

"Fine," she muttered, her bravado crumbling. "I'll tell you. I know more than I let on." She swallowed, her throat bobbing nervously. "My grandmother… she used to talk about this house. Said it was older than the town itself. Said the women here—your women," she glanced at Viv and Adele, "Were tied to something deeper. Not just family history, but bloodlines, rituals… things people stopped talking about centuries ago."

She twisted the black ring on her finger, a nervous tic. "I always thought it was just stories. Scary bedtime stuff meant to keep me intrigued in the old ways. I played at witchcraft, sure—candles, herbs, protection spells. But I've never… never felt anything like what's in that chamber. That place isn't for play. It's real. Too real."

Dominic leaned forward on his elbows, his tone clipped. "And you've been keeping this from us? From Vivienne?"

Jessie winced. "I didn't think it mattered. I thought it was all smoke and mirrors. But when Viv found that room—when she touched that book—I felt it. Like the walls were watching us. Like the house knew."

Adele's lips pressed thin, her eyes darting to Viv's hands where the leather-bound book still rested. "What else did your grandmother say?"

Jessie hesitated, then whispered, "That the house chooses who can open its secrets. That once it lets you in… you can't walk away."

The air thickened. Viv's grip on the book tightened, her heart pounding at Jessie's words.

Callum finally spoke, his voice steady but edged with unease. "So Viv's been chosen? By what—this house? By whatever's inside it?"

Jessie nodded, shame flickering in her eyes. "I think so. And I think I dragged her in deeper by not warning her sooner."

Vivienne's pulse quickened as Jessie's words lingered in the air. She stared at her friend— her cousin—unable to process it all at once.

"How are you related to Malrick?…" Viv's voice cracked, anger lacing her tone.

Jessie nodded slowly, guilt clouding her face. "My grandmother… was Althea's daughter and Malrick's sister?"

"Which makes us… related." Viv's breath caught, fury flaring in her chest. "All this time? We've been side by side, working late nights, laughing, fighting like sisters, and you never once thought to mention that we actually were family? How long have you known?"

Jessie flinched but held her gaze. "I've known since before I started at the company with you."

Viv's eyes widened in shock, then narrowed. "Since before?" Her hands trembled as she gestured wildly, unable to contain the betrayal coursing through her veins. "You knew when we met, Jessie! You knew for years—every single moment we've shared—you knew, and you said nothing?"

"I didn't know how!" Jessie's voice broke, a raw mix of desperation and shame. "What was I supposed to say? 'Oh, by the way, I'm your long-lost cousin from a cursed bloodline?' You would've hated me before I had the chance to prove I wasn't like them."

Viv shook her head, her curls whipping across her face as she backed away. "You don't get it! Do you have any idea what it's like to feel completely alone in this mess, only to find out the person I trusted most—the one person I leaned on—was lying to me the entire time?"

Jessie's eyes filled with tears, but she didn't move closer. She stood frozen, letting Viv's words pierce her. "I didn't tell you because I was terrified. Terrified you'd push me away. And now… maybe I was right."

Viv turned sharply, her throat tight. She wanted to scream, to run, to slam the heavy oak door behind her. But the part of her that still loved Jessie, still remembered every shared laugh and secret, kept her rooted in place, trembling with the weight of betrayal.

The kitchen felt colder now, the echoes of their bloodlines twisting between them like a curse that had been waiting centuries to surface.

# Chapter 71

The tension between Vivienne and Jessie thickened, silence stretching until it nearly snapped. Vivienne's knuckles whitened as she gripped the diary, her anger still simmering. Suddenly, a low hum pulsed beneath her fingertips. The leather cover grew warm, vibrating against her palms.

With a startled gasp, Vivienne flinched—the book wrenched itself free, as though alive, and landed with a heavy thud on the table. It flew open, pages flipping in a rush before halting on one marked in deep, ink-stained scrawl.

The room held its breath.

Dominic stepped forward, his voice low and reverent as he read aloud:

*"The chamber of nine pillars stirred tonight. The walls whispered with voices not of this world, soft and solemn, echoing truths only silence can hold. I lit the brass oil lamp, not with flame but with prayer. The*

*scent of frankincense filled the chamber, and in the stillness, faith itself became the fire. Light bloomed from the lamp, steady and pure—proof that when prayers are genuine, selfless, and unshaken, the unseen answers. My gift is faith, and it must be wielded not for power, but for surrender. In silence, faith becomes unbreakable. In surrender, it becomes eternal."*

Dominic lifted his eyes from the page, his voice hushed. "Isolde Ashcroft… she's writing about the gift of faith. The lamp was more than a relic—it was a vessel."

Vivienne stared at the glowing words, her anger dissolving into awe and unease. Jessie's lips parted, as if she wanted to speak, but thought better of it.

The faint trace of frankincense drifted through the room, though no lamp was lit. The walls themselves seemed to hum in response, a whisper too low to decipher but filled with a weight that pressed into each of their chests.

Vivienne whispered, "Faith and silence…"

The diary pulsed again, as if acknowledging her.

Dominic's voice grew steadier as he continued, the chamber's atmosphere thickening with every word:

*"The walls whispered back to me as though alive, their murmurs twining with the prayers that left my lips. In silence, I felt His presence. Not through sight,*

*nor sound, but through stillness. I lit the brass lamp— yet no flame caught. Instead, a soft glow pulsed from within, born not of oil or wick, but of faith itself. When prayers are genuine and selfless, the light endures without fire."*

His eyes flicked up, meeting the others'. The faintest shimmer lingered across the diary's pages, as though the words themselves were etched in light.

Jessie whispered, "She's describing the Chamber of the Nine Pillars…"

Viv's voice, tight with awe and unease, cut in: "And the gift of faith—she actually saw it manifest."

Dominic turned back to the entry, finishing aloud:

*"To walk in faith is to walk without proof. To believe without demand. The lamp shines only when the heart carries no shadow of selfish intent. This is the gift I was given—faith not as blindness, but as light in the dark."*

The room fell utterly silent.

Then, without warning, the brass lamp— appeared—flickering to life. Not with fire, but with the same soft, unearthly glow Isolde had described.

The scent of frankincense drifted through the air, though none had been burned.

Vivienne clutched the edge of the table, eyes wide. "She's here… Isolde… she's *showing* us."

Jessie's breath caught, her fear from moments ago paling beneath a new, bone-deep tremor. She turned to Vivienne, whispering hoarsely, "If this is her… then everything… all of it… was true."

Dominic slowly closed the diary, but the lamp's glow remained, casting their shadows long across the chamber walls.

The silence stretched. Not empty, but alive. Whispering.

Jessie leaned forward, her eyes glinting strangely in the firelight.
"You found them, didn't you? The Resonant Objects. Do you have all nine?"

Vivienne opened her mouth, but Dominic's voice cut through, sharp as steel.
"Before we answer anything—why don't you tell us what you know?"

The silence pressed heavy. Adele's gaze sharpened. Callum shifted, his hand brushing against the armrest as though grounding himself.

Jessie tilted her head, lips curving in something that wasn't quite a smile. "Fine," she said softly. "But don't pretend you don't already know."

She began to recite, her voice calm, practiced—like a litany she had known since childhood:

The Mirror Room. Seraphina Vexley, bearer of the Word of Knowledge. The ornate hand mirror shows the past no one dares speak aloud.

The Healing Conservatory. Cordelia Ashcroft, gifts of healing. The pressed herb book glows warm, leading to remedies that mend body and soul.

The Music Room. Isaldora Ashcroft, the gift of tongues. The crystal singing bell, a voice for forgotten languages.

The Blue Library. Viviette Ashcroft, interpretation of tongues. A multilingual rosary to read what time itself forgot.

The Glass Atrium. Anastasia Ashcroft, discerning of spirits. The jet pendant, burning in the presence of lies or malevolence.

The Bridal Suite. Evadne Ashcroft, worker of miracles. An ash-dusted comb that defies ruin, even fire.

The East Chapel. Isolde Ashcroft, bearer of faith. The brass oil lamp, lit only by prayers pure of intent.

The Moon Room. Genevieve Ashcroft, prophetess. The silver hourglass locket, keeper of visions and warnings not her own.

The Forgotten Nursery. Ophelia Ashcroft, wisdom of innocence. The porcelain doll with a hidden scroll that speaks in riddles of truth.

Her gaze returned to Vivienne, unwavering. "Nine women. Nine gifts. Nine anchors binding this place. Don't insult me by pretending you haven't found them."

The diary on the table thrummed once, as though stirred by her words, before falling silent again.

Dominic didn't flinch, though his knuckles whitened against the edge of the table. "You know too much," he said slowly, evenly. "And yet not enough."

Vivienne felt her throat tighten. Jessie's knowledge was too exact, too precise—yet something in her tone rang like a warning.

# Chapter 72

Viv's jaw tightened as she stared at Jessie, the weight of betrayal sitting heavy in her chest. Before she could say more, the diary in her grip began to hum—low at first, then with a violent vibration that shocked her fingers.

"Viv!" Jessie gasped as the book's pages fluttered with a life of its own until it stilled on another single passage.

Dominic, his voice steady but wary as he read aloud:

*"In the chamber of nine pillars, by the glow of brass oil, faith becomes sight. The walls themselves whisper when prayers are selfless, when silence is chosen over demand. Frankincense drifts as offering, unseen flames spark in truth's presence. Faith, pure and unfeigned, lights the dark without fire. This is the key to awaken the unseen—the binding of house and soul."*

The room seemed to darken at the words, and the faint scent of frankincense filled the air, though no incense burned. Jessie's eyes widened. Viv's breath caught.

Dominic closed the diary with deliberate force and looked straight at Jessie. "You cast a spell on this house. Didn't you?"

Jessie swallowed hard. "I… I wanted to protect it. To hold the silence, the faith of our bloodline. I never meant—"

"Remove it," Dominic ordered, his tone leaving no room for argument.

Her hands trembled, but her chin lifted in defiance. "I will. But only if you show me the chamber. The one with the nine columns."

The silence stretched until Dominic's jaw relaxed with a reluctant nod. "Very well. But not now." He glanced around the tense circle, eyes settling on Jessie, then back to Viv. "We meet at midnight. Rest while you can."

The air felt charged, alive with both dread and promise, as the diary pulsed faintly one last time before falling still on the table.

—

Midnight came dressed in frost.

They gathered in the long corridor where the old stones bled into bedrock and the air changed—colder, older, as if steps here crossed not just distance but years. Dominic led with a lantern; Callum carried the satchel with the Objects; Adele held Isolde's diary to her chest like scripture. Jessie trailed, her boots soundless, her expression politely blank and hard to read.

At the end of the passage, the chamber opened—circular and low, its ceiling black with mineral sheen. Nine stone columns ringed the room, each carved with a woman's name. The basin in the center was dry tonight, a bowl-shaped absence waiting for a meaning.

Dominic set the lantern on the floor. "Read."

Adele opened Isolde's diary to a page that had started vibrating earlier, as if it recognized the hour. Ink ached across the paper, dense and neat:

*In the Chamber Beneath the House, each Gift must face its witness.*

*Align the Objects with their columns, each to the name it was given.*

*Lamp to Faith — Isolde Ashcroft (East Chapel).*

*Mirror to Knowledge — Seraphina Vexley (Mirror Room).*

*Hourglass to Prophecy — Genevieve Ashcroft (Moon Room).*

*Herbs to Healing — Cordelia Ashcroft (Healing Conservatory).*

*Bell to Tongues — Isaldora Ashcroft (Music Room).*

*Rosary to Interpretation — Viviette Ashcroft (Blue Library).*

*Jet to Discernment — Anastasia Ashcroft (Glass Atrium).*

*Comb to Miracles — Evadne Ashcroft (Bridal Suite).*

*Doll to Wisdom — Ophelia Ashcroft (Forgotten Nursery).*

*Ring no more than once. Speak nothing you do not mean.*

*When the House breathes at the Third Hour, let the one who is chosen remain.*

The last line seemed newer than the rest, like it had been added after everything else.

Viv's pulse quickened. "We start there."

They did. One by one, Dominic withdrew the Objects from the satchel, the shapes catching and swallowing the lantern-light: the ash-dusted comb wrapped with the bridal veil; the pressed herb book; the porcelain doll with its hidden scroll; the small ornate hand mirror; the crystal singing bell; the multilingual rosary; the jet pendant; the brass oil lamp; the silver hourglass locket that had once stirred like a living thing against Viv's skin.

They moved clockwise around the chamber.

Viv placed the hand mirror before *Seraphina.* A ghost of her own face rippled across its cracked surface and settled.

Adele set the lamp beneath *Isolde.* Without flame, it glimmered—once—then steadied into a quiet glow.

Callum knelt by *Genevieve* and laid the hourglass locket at the base of her name. For a breath, the silver sand flowed upward.

Dominic propped the herb book under *Cordelia* and turned it to a page that warmed under his fingertips.

They went on: the bell beneath *Isaldora*; the rosary beneath *Viviette*; the jet pendant hung upon *Anastasia's* cut-stone; the bridal comb and veil draped across *Evadne*; the doll, carefully, beneath *Ophelia*.

When everything was set, the chamber felt full—like a lung at the end of a long inhale.

"Now what?" Callum asked.

Adele ran her finger under the next lines.

*Kneel at the circle.*
*One voice to vow, eight to witness.*
*Ask only what you can bear to carry. Give only what you will not take back.*

They formed a rough ring, the basin at their center. Viv knelt because it felt inevitable. The others remained standing behind their chosen columns, shadows thrown tall, faces outlined in lantern-gold.

Viv drew breath. The vow formed without effort.

"I ask to see what is hidden if seeing it will heal. I give what I can—fear, pride, the need to be right—so the House will remember with mercy."

Silence. Stone. A faint perfume of frankincense from nowhere.

They waited.

Minutes slid into an hour. Then two. The lamp guttered and revived with no wick. The bell thrummed once in a register they could feel in their bones more than hear. The jet pendant warmed, cooled, warmed again—as if judging the heartbeats in the room.

Nothing else.

Jessie shifted. "It's not working."

Dominic frowned. "We follow the text." He turned the page; the script blurred, lines overlaying like double exposure, a paragraph bleeding through the paper that hadn't been there:

*If the circle is too crowded, the House withdraws. It answers one anchor. Not many.*

Callum rubbed his palm over his jaw. "So… we're in the way."

Adele met Viv's eyes. Something like understanding moved between them. "We can give you space," she said softly. "But not the whole night."

Viv nodded once. "Stay close. Just outside the door."

They tried again. This time, they dimmed the lantern. They spoke no words. Viv focused on each Object, touching only with her eyes: mirror, lamp, hourglass, herbs, bell, beads, jet, comb, doll. She held them in mind like points of a constellation.

Still—nothing.

Hours wore down. The silence became sticky, heavy with disappointment. Dominic's eyes had that faraway look that said he was arguing with history. Adele paced once, twice, then forced herself still. Callum leaned against *Anastasia's* column, watching Viv in the low light, ready to move the second she needed anything and too smart to speak.

Finally, Dominic exhaled, a thread of sound. "We're wringing water from stone. Let's pick this up tomorrow."

"No," Viv said, but her voice held no heat. She was exhausted. Empty. Discouraged.

Adele's palm skimmed her shoulder. "Five minutes," she murmured. "Sit, breathe." To the others: "Give them space."

Dominic hesitated, then nodded, ushering Adele and Callum toward the arched entry. "We'll be right outside the corridor. Whisper if you need us."

Footsteps retreated. The chamber returned to its own pulse.

Jessie slid down beside Viv without asking, their backs touching—bone to bone through wool and fatigue. The closeness should have annoyed her; instead, it grounded her.

"I'm not the enemy," Jessie whispered.

"I haven't decided yet," Viv said, too tired to temper it.

A small pause. "Fair."

They sat in the hush, backs aligned, breaths eventually syncing. The lamp's glow wavered and steadied. Somewhere, far above, the house shifted—timber settling or memory sighing.

Viv thought of the plaques. The nine-sectioned circle, the segments that had darkened when she found an Object. She pictured the circle here, beneath the floor. She pictured it whole.

Time thinned.

A current went through Jessie—subtle, almost a shiver. She pushed to her feet in a smooth, practiced motion that didn't match her earlier weariness. "I'm going to get some air," she said lightly. "Don't wait up."

"Jessie—" Viv started, but the other woman was already backing toward the arch. For a breath, her pupils seemed too wide. Then she was gone.

Vivienne was alone in the ring of women.

The lamp brightened a fraction.

Her gaze slid to the hourglass—still, silent, silver grains poised like a held breath.

The house inhaled.

Above, the ancient tower clock began to turn its teeth.

One chime.

Two.

Moments passed the third strike—3:03— the chamber woke.

Light bled from stone like sap from a wound. Faint at first—lines outlining the carved names—then branching, webbing, connecting column to basin, basin to floor, floor to the nine Objects. The circle she had imagined drew itself in living fire, all nine segments filling in with a slow, inevitable glow.

Viv couldn't move. The light wasn't bright; it was deep, the kind you feel pressing under your ribs.

The hourglass locket tilted, and the sand flowed upward in a silver thread that didn't spill but stitched itself into the air—over the basin, where it hovered like spun moonlight.

The bell rung a single, pure note. The sound fractured into a dozen languages she didn't recognize—then understood, all at once, as if the meanings perched on her tongue like birds.

The rosary lifted, one bead rising, then another, until a circle formed above the basin, the gap in it closing with a soft click that sent a tremor through her spine. Words bloomed across the walls where there had only been mineral sheen—scripts she couldn't name, praying the same thought in a hundred voices: *Do not fear the remembering.*

Heat poured from the herb book, not scorching but clean, the warmth of a healed fever. Viv felt tears prick for no reason she could name—only that something broken in her was knitting without scar.

The jet pendant flared white-hot, then cooled past warmth into a steady, living heat—the kind you associate with a hand you trust. The shadows in the corners flattened and fled.

The doll's porcelain eyes caught light and held it. The scroll inside unfurled of its own accord, the tiny riddles rearranging like falling leaves until they resolved into a single line that wasn't a riddle at all: *Choose kindness when power would be easier.*

The comb pulled the veil through its ash-dusted teeth. Each pass plucked gray from white, until the lace shone like water. The smell of smoke lifted from the cloth and dispersed—gone.

The mirror healed.

The crack in its face drew shut like a stitched wound, and the surface flashed, reflecting not her, not exactly, but a pattern—nine faces overlaid on hers: Seraphina's steady gaze, Cordelia's gentle mouth, Isaldora's listening tilt of head, Viviette's considering brow, Anastasia's cold discernment, Evadne's wild grief, Ophelia's clear child-light, Isolde's unshakable faith, Genevieve's storm-lit eyes.

They looked at her. Not as ghosts; as witnesses.

A filament of brightness rose from the basin and threaded into Viv's sternum, not piercing, not injuring, but aligning—like a compass finally finding north. She arched, breath torn from her in a sound that wasn't pain.

"Okay," she whispered to no one and everyone. "Okay. I hear you."

Something answered.

*Then take us all.*

It didn't come as words. It came as capacity. Her mind made room and then more room; her body learned the feeling of holding. Knowledge slid into her hands like weight she had always been strong enough to bear:

—The way to lay a palm on fever and draw it down without taking it into yourself.

—The way to separate true vision from fear's echo.

—The way to speak a language you'd never

learned and be heard in the marrow.
—The way to read the unreadable.
—The way to call a miracle only when every other road would harm.
—The way to hold faith like a lantern and not as a blade.
—The way to know a lie even when it wears your favorite face.
—The way to gather knowledge without turning people into pages.
—The way to choose wisdom, even when the answer costs you your pride.

Vivienne's hair stirred in a wind that didn't exist. The veil brushed her cheek. She felt nine pulses align with her own. The lamp burned steady without flame. The hourglass sand hung motionless in the air, turning slowly like a planet.

When the clock finished breathing the third hour, the light didn't disappear. It settled into her. The Objects eased back to stillness on the stone. The columns dimmed to a soft ember.

And the basin—empty all night—held water. Dark, clear, reflecting her face and nine others, all at once, then only hers, newly bright at the edges—as if lit from within.

Footsteps skidded in the corridor. Dominic reached the arch first, then Adele, then Callum, faces pale and eyes wide at the soft glow still threading the room.

"Viv?" Adele whispered.

Viv turned. She was shaking and laughing quietly and trying not to cry. "I think—" She swallowed. "I think it worked. Or I finally did."

"What happened?" Dominic asked, voice hoarse.

Viv looked at the Objects without touching them, and they answered in her mind like the names of old friends. "I… I know how to use them. Not tricks. Not rituals. Why they were made. When to refuse them."

Callum took a step toward her and stopped, checking her with his eyes. "Are you hurt?"

Viv shook her head, breath hitching. "No. I'm… full."

They stared at the water in the basin, then back at her.

"How?" Adele asked. "What changed?"

Viv glanced toward the archway where Jessie had vanished a minute before the hour. The pendant hung warm at her throat, not warning, but aware.

"It needed one anchor," she murmured, hearing Isolde's line inside her like a promise. "And the right hour. The House breathes at the third hour. It always has."

Adele squeezed Viv's hand until it almost hurt. "You scared me."

Viv's smile trembled. "Me too."

From the passage, a small clatter—like someone misstepping and catching herself. Jessie hovered in the shadow just beyond the threshold, eyes wide, expression fixed on the basin. The smell of something bitter—smoke without fire—trailed after her like a wrong note.

"You left," Viv said, not a question.

Jessie lifted her chin. "You didn't need me."

Viv didn't answer. The jet pendant warmed, then cooled. In her chest, nine rhythms steadied.

She looked down at the basin again. Something glinted at the bottom—etched not in the water, but in the stone beneath it. A sigil she had never seen before. Not Malrick's thorned knot. Older. The same seal from the deed, but completed—no broken lines, no missing arcs.

"Another seal?" Dominic whispered, his voice tight with disbelief. "I thought there were only three."

Vivienne's fingertips grazed the surface. The reflection rippled outward like disturbed breath, and words rose in silver frost across the water:

*Three opened. One remains beneath what is buried alive.*

The letters bled away as quickly as they had appeared.

Callum's frown was sharp. "Buried… alive?"

Adele's expression shifted—the kind of shift that happens when memory finally drags its furniture into the right rooms. "It must be the cellar under the west wing," she whispered. "The one my grandmother always forbade. I don't think because she thought it was dangerous… but because it was grieving."

Vivienne glanced at the objects laid out around her. Each seemed to be watching, waiting.

"Grieving," she said, her voice steadier than her pulse.

The lamp flared once, though no wick burned.
The bell thrummed low, almost like a warning. And above them, the House drew in another long, rattling breath.

# Chapter 73

Vivienne hadn't seen Jessie since the night before. Her door was closed when the others gathered for breakfast, and by midmorning, her suitcase was gone from her room. No note. No explanation.

"Did she say anything to you?" Adele asked, her brow tight.
Vivienne shook her head. "Not a word."

Curiosity tugged at her until she found herself back at Jessie's room. The door creaked open under her hand. The air inside felt wrong—stagnant, but charged, as if the walls themselves had been listening.

The bed was neatly made, but the rug near the window bulged slightly. Vivienne knelt, pulling it back. A loose floorboard revealed itself—freshly pried, the edges raw. Beneath, a hollow space.

Her breath caught.

Inside lay a small, leather-bound journal, its cover scorched as if it had survived a fire. Around it, chalk markings stained the wood— sigils etched in a hand both hurried and practiced. A faint scent of iron and smoke still lingered.

Dominic entered quietly behind her, his face darkening as he crouched to look. "She left this behind… on purpose. Not carelessness. A message."

Vivienne lifted the journal. It hummed faintly, a low vibration against her palms, before falling still again. The sigils under the floor glimmered once, faintly red, then dulled to ash.

"So, before she left," Callum said from the doorway, voice low. "She did a spell or something… I can feel it."

Vivienne shivered. The Hollow seemed to exhale around them, the boards creaking as though answering.

"She'll be back," Dominic murmured. "Mark me, Vivienne. She isn't finished."

Vivienne slipped the journal into her coat. The wood under her hand was warm, as if something had passed through it only moments before.

She straightened, her chest tight. Jessie's absence was no relief. It was a shadow stretching further than before.

They had barely stepped into the corridor when Callum's voice stopped her. "Vivienne—wait. Can I speak with you?"

Something in his tone—quiet, almost conspiratorial—made her pulse quicken. She turned, searching his face. "Of course. What is it?"

He hesitated, as if weighing whether the words should ever leave his mouth. "I need to know."

Her brows knit. "Know what?"

"How you feel about me." His voice was low, steady, but edged with vulnerability.

Vivienne blinked, startled. "I thought that was obvious."

He stepped closer, the faintest shadow of a smile pulling at his mouth. "It isn't. Not to me. Vivienne, I'm in love with you—and I need to hear if you feel the same."

The air between them seemed to still, heavy with the house's watchful silence.

She stared at him, her breath caught.

"We've already established we're not bound by blood," he added, almost fierce. "If that's what's holding you back, it doesn't have to."

For a long heartbeat, she only studied him—the lines of his face, the quiet strength that had kept her anchored when everything else threatened to unravel.

And then, without another word, she reached up, caught his face between her hands, and kissed him.

Her lips brushed his, and for a heartbeat it was just them—no legacy, no secrets, no weight of the Ashcroft name. Just warmth and breath and the impossible relief of choosing, finally, something that was wholly theirs.

But then the Hollow stirred.

The sconces along the corridor flickered, flaring and guttering in the same breath. The air pressed close, thick with a heat that wasn't theirs. Above, a floorboard groaned as though someone—or something—shifted its weight just out of sight.

Vivienne broke the kiss, breathless, her hand still resting against his cheek. "Did you feel that?"

Callum's eyes stayed on hers, steady but shadowed. "I think the whole house felt it."

The corridor seemed to exhale, the draft curling around their ankles like fingers. Not quite welcoming. Not quite condemning. Watching. Waiting.

Vivienne swallowed hard, pulse still racing. For all her certainty a moment ago, she suddenly felt like the Hollow itself had marked their union—not as blessing, not as curse, but as a reckoning yet to come.

# Chapter 74

Vivienne and Callum stepped into the kitchen, hand in hand, the faint smell of coffee and woodsmoke still lingering. Adele sat at the table, her hands wrapped around a mug. Dominic stood at the counter, pouring a second cup.

"Dominic," Vivienne said, her voice tentative.

He turned, eyebrows lifting slightly. "Dad," he corrected gently as he passed her the mug. A crooked smile tugged at his mouth. "What's on your mind, little star?"

The pet name caught in her chest. She swallowed, fumbling. "Dad... where did you go?"

He blinked, pausing mid-motion. "What do you mean? I just fed the horses."

"No," Vivienne said, tightening her grip on the mug. Her pulse was loud in her ears. "Not now. I mean, for all those years. Why didn't you want me?"

The kitchen fell still. Even Adele froze, her breath caught. Dominic lowered his cup slowly onto the counter, then turned to face her fully. His eyes locked on hers—steady, unflinching, filled with something she couldn't name.

"My little star," he said again, softer this time. "I never left."

Adele and Vivienne spoke at once, their voices overlapping. "What do you mean?"

Dominic's gaze didn't waver. "I never left the Hollow."

Confusion rippled through them both. Adele shook her head. "But—you vanished. No letters. No calls. No trace."

"Because I was here," he said, his voice low, almost reverent. "Not alive in the way you think, not gone either. The Hollow… it keeps what it wants. It bound me here—between stone and shadow. I could watch, but not touch. Guard, but not hold. Until now."

Adele's eyes filled with tears, her hand trembling against her mug. "All those years… I thought you abandoned us."

Dominic's expression broke with sorrow. "I tried, Adele. God knows I tried. But the house doesn't release what it claims. And it claimed me."

The silence that followed was thick, almost suffocating, as if the Hollow itself leaned in to listen.

Vivienne's fingers tightened around Callum's, grounding herself against the weight of her father's words, against the enormity of what lingered between them all. The fire cracked once in the hearth, and the shadows seemed to shift closer along the walls.

Adele broke first, her voice trembling. "What do you mean, you never left?"

Dominic's gaze lifted, steady, unfaltering. "I mean the Hollow kept me. Bound me. Every man it could not erase, it buried. I was not gone, Vivienne… only unseen."

The words sent a chill across her skin, and for a moment she thought she heard the faint, childlike laughter that haunted the nursery echo through the beams above. Her pulse quickened. So many secrets. So many lies stitched into the bones of this house.

She swallowed hard. "Then what happens now?"

No one answered. Not at first. The question seemed to drift upward, absorbed into the beams, into the stone, into the listening silence of the house itself.

Then the brass lamp in the corner flared without flame, just a heartbeat of light, before going still again. The Hollow exhaled a long, low breath—timbers groaning, glass rattling—like something ancient had stirred.

Vivienne's chest ached, but she stood taller, her voice quiet yet resolute. "We don't run. Not anymore. We face it."

Adele reached for Dominic's hand. Callum's grip tightened around hers. For the first time, they all stood together, not as fractured pieces but as one.

Above them, unseen in the dark rafters, the house listened. It remembered. And somewhere deep within its walls, something shifted, waiting for the day it would rise again.

# *Acknowledgments*

The Hollow does not stand alone, and neither did I in writing this book.

To those who lent me their voices when the silence grew too heavy, who reminded me to return to the world outside its walls — thank you. You kept the lantern lit.

To the ones who shared their stories, their shadows, their fragments of history — you are written here, between every line.

To the unseen, whose whispers became inspiration, whose echoes guided the shape of this tale — I heard you.

And to you, reader: by opening these pages, you became part of the house. The Hollow remembers you now. It always will.

With thanks that will not fade, even in the dark, **Constance Santego**

# The Author

**Constance Santego** writes gothic tales where bloodlines whisper, houses remember, and love refuses to die. Drawn to places where silence is heavier than sound—crumbling manors, hidden crypts, diaries that burn with unfinished words—her novels blur the line between ghost story and romance, mystery and fate.

She's lived in an old castle tucked deep in the mist-drenched woods of British Columbia, where candlelight competes with the dark and every stair seems to creak in recognition. When not writing, she collects forgotten artifacts, studies ancestral superstitions, and wanders ruins that others have long abandoned—yet never truly left.